NICOLE PUTTER

A Shattering Glimpse

First edition

ISBN: 978-1-990989-68-1

This book was professionally typeset on Reedsy.
Find out more at reedsy.com

I

Dreams

1

Claire

Thursday, 2 June 2022, 11 pm

Damn, Oscar Wilde and Eleanor Roosevelt and anyone else who has ever romanticized the notion of dreams. "The future belongs to those who can find the beauty in their dreams." *Yeah, right*, thought Claire Baxter. Mrs. Larson may as well have put a target on her back the day she recited that quote in class. That is if her dreams could be considered beautiful. They felt more like an unwanted cargo that Claire had to convey through life without a map or destination. Although, she had to admit, some of them were beautiful. From her seat on the floor, she looked up at the unfinished sketch peeking from her sketchbook.

She pulled it out, grabbed a pencil, and started adding shadows to the dark hair waving in the wind. Claire knew the outlines of her phantom's face; the deep-set eyes and the dimples around his mouth better than the test material she had studied for the past three days.

"Who are you and why won't you leave me alone?" she demanded from nothing but charcoal lines etched into paper. Grinding her teeth, she tore the sheet in half. Then in four. Then eight, and watched as it coasted to the ground. As the last shred dropped to the floor, she crawled into bed, wishing she could wake up to find her life had only been a series of bad dreams.

* * *

Friday, 3 June 2022, 7 am

A painfully shrill scream snatched Claire from sleep. For a moment, all connection between her brain and limbs was severed. Panting, she stared at the ceiling as she realized that her own lungs were the cause of the noise. Yet, she couldn't pinpoint the cause of her agitation. Could it only be the exam that had her stomach in knots?

"This thing, called love. I just, can't handle it," groaned her mother's ringtone. Still a little disconcerted and in no mood for Mom, she fumbled for the phone on her nightstand.

"Hello," she croaked, her voice hoarse from screaming.

"Morning, Clairy, are you still asleep?" Molly chirped, her usual bubbly self.

Claire wiped a hand over her husky eyes and stretched the arm not holding the phone. "Ugh. No, Mom."

"Honey, it's already seven. Don't your classes start at eight?" Of course, there was a little judgment in her mother's tone. "I'm calling because I haven't received the info about your graduation or summer plans yet."

"Mom," griped Claire, pretending to throw the phone. "I emailed it to you two nights ago. Check your Gmail."

"Yes, that's right, you said you would email it. Oh, technology."

Claire rolled her eyes. How else would she have sent it? By pigeon? "Okay, Mom, check your email and let me know. I have to go. Love you. Bye."

"Love you too, honey. Oh, how're Leanne and Brent?" she carried on, in no hurry to hang up.

"They're good. Bye, Mom, talk to you soon." She had no sooner ended the call than the fleeting nightmare returned, as tangible as the test she would take in an hour. Her hands started to shake, causing her phone to drop to the floor. Sweat striped the back of her neck. Her phantom was in danger. As she raked her trembling fingers through her blonde curls, she experienced a sense of déjà vu from her 14-year-old self.

30 March 2014

Claire woke in a pool of cold sweat. That was a first. She had always been able to predict the future of those with whom she came into physical contact. Never before had she seen someone without touching them, let alone not knowing them at all. Her visions were subjective. If she warned the receiver of her touch, it could change, though she would never tell. Only her parents and best friend, Brent Lee, knew about her unique gift. They called it a gift, but Claire often considered it a damn curse.

The man from her vivid dream was tall, not buff, but rather lean and toned. He was at the beach with his friends: Tanned with dark, ruffled hair and deep, brown eyes above a sharp jawline. A deep scar puckered his left cheekbone.

Attempting to impress some girl, he meandered deeper and deeper into the ocean. Later, he was laboring for breath as the wild rollers clutched at him and the desperate torrent sucked him further and further from the shore. It was a battle of arms, legs, and waves. He coughed and gasped, splashed, and jolted, doing everything in his power to stay alive until a coastguard came to his rescue. Once they reached the safety of the beach, she learned his name as everyone bustled around to ensure he was okay. He was alive and smiling and called Byron.

That night Claire had met Special Agent Black of the FBI for the first time. He had been the centerpiece of her dreams for the next eight years. Okay, perhaps centerpiece was overdoing it, but he did feature often. Not every night, but at least once a month. Maybe less. Definitely less. The dreams changed. Sometimes they reflected significant instances in his life, like graduation and his sister's wedding. Other times, she merely saw his face. No sound, just him. She knew a lot about the man of her dreams. Nope, the man from her dreams. Now she even knew how he would die. If he even existed.

I can't let this happen. She squeezed her eyes shut and flopped back down on to her black-and-white mess of a bed. *I must warn him.*

She marched through their shoebox apartment toward Leanne's room. The purple-patterned linen was still untouched. Clothes littered the bed and shoes were strewn all over the floor – proof of the countless outfits Leanne had tried on before her night out. It was clearly a good one since she hadn't yet returned home.

Head hanging low, Claire went back to her own room to check her phone and found three unread messages.

> **Leanne:** Hey hun, won't be home tonight. Don't worry. Good luck with your final tomorrow. Luv ya!

> **Brent:** Hey Clairy, good luck with your final. I know you'll do well. We're already celebrating on your behalf.

His text was accompanied by a photo of her three best and only friends toasting their freedom. Brent's face squared even more when smiling, while his perfectly gelled hair remained, well, perfect. He was only half-Chinese, although he had inherited all of his father's oriental features. His blue-eyed rocker boyfriend, Ted Barnes, dabbed above Leanne's head, where her pearly whites glistened from her beaming lips.

In First Grade, Brent had stood behind her in a bake sale line and had told her that girls smelt funny. She had giggled and responded similarly about boys. And that was it. To this day, they were inseparable. Freshman year of college, she had met Leanne, her dorm roommate. As is the case with every person, Claire had danced extensive circles around her. Everyone had always been a threat; trying to learn or expose her secret, but this girl had refused to accept the sidelines. After careful consideration and shared tragedy, she became an acquaintance and later a friend.

She scrolled down to the last text.

> **Mom:** Clairy, you haven't texted me the details of

your graduation ceremony. Daddy and I want to make plans for the summer.

No Mom, YOU probably want to make plans for the summer, Daddy will just follow along. She discarded the phone and headed for the shower. Washing required an energy that the dream had selfishly leeched from her body. She hadn't the faintest idea how she would get through her Computer Apps final. Despite her countless hours of studying, more important thoughts occupied her mind.

Once clean, Claire pulled on a pair of black skinny jeans, a Nirvana T-shirt, and sneakers. She applied the bare minimum make-up to emphasize her high cheekbones and disguise the length of her face. Preparing herself in the dresser mirror, she mustered all the motivation she could find to take that test. After a quick-fix of the bed, she slung her backpack over her shoulder and hauled herself to the University of Oregon campus.

* * *

Friday, 3 June 2022, 2 pm

The final was barely over before she had to start her shift behind Arista's counter. The bohemian coffee shop was conveniently located near the University of Oregon's School of Design. Low lighting and dark, stone walls created a cozy ambiance, along with the distinctive smell of fresh brew. Chocolate-colored booths on both sides nestled below pictures of smiling faces and cappuccinos. Some natural light filtered through the glass doors at the front, where her friends arrived, pale and lifeless. No doubt an after-effect of the alcohol they had consumed the previous night.

"So, how'd it go?" Brent slouched, approaching her.

Claire shrugged. "Long."

"Don't worry, hun. It's over now." Leanne joined them at the counter. Her long, dark hair was wrapped in a messy bun. Even without make-up, she was the clichéd version of Latina-gorgeous. Sure, she had to run every day to maintain her figure, unlike Claire, who was naturally tall and slim without effort, but Leanne's beauty was magazine-flawless. Without Photoshop. Fricking unfair.

"Yeah, I guess. Listen, I've got a break in 10 minutes, I need to talk to you guys about something important." The dream was still stationary in her mind. "Can I get you the usual?"

Brent and Leanne nodded.

"I'll have a double espresso," Ted said, rubbing his temples between strands of blonde hair, attempting to soothe his hangover. Where he would usually tower over the other two, his slumped posture now brought him down to their level. He was by far the worst-off.

"Coming right up." She spun to the espresso machine to prepare their order.

The moment Claire's break started, she slipped into the booth beside Leanne. Her roommate now knew about her superpower, too. One night during sophomore year, after one too many glasses of sweet wine, she had dragged the secret out of Claire. Being a great friend, Leanne had appointed herself fierce protector of the clandestine information. Claire had never told Ted, though, but she couldn't wait any longer. "I dreamt of him again last night."

"What's new?" Brent chuckled.

"No, this time was different." Claire's chin dropped to her

chest. "I saw him dying."

Brent and Leanne's eyes widened. Ted frowned.

"I'm going to find him. I always knew there was a reason that I kept seeing him, and I think this is it. I have to warn him." She kept her voice low to prevent the other customers from overhearing. Question marks appeared in their eyes. Yes, it was a potent bomb to drop out of the blue.

"How did he die?" Leanne asked.

"Wait," Ted interrupted. "Can someone please explain to me what's going on here?"

"Clairy," Brent ignored his boyfriend, "you don't even know if he's real."

"He is real," Claire argued.

"Honey," Leanne pulled her into a side hug, "it might seem real to you, but that's only because he's been such a big part of your life for so long. Maybe you want it to be real."

"Have you ever found him on Facebook or Instagram?" Brent asked.

"Can someone please explain to me what the hell is going on here?" Ted threw his arms in the air.

"Sshhh... Keep your voice down." Leanne glared at him.

"Claire can predict the future," Brent whispered. "When she touches you, that is. Not more than a day or two. Since she was 14, she has been dreaming about Byron Black. Her theory is that they are all visions of his future, but she has no idea who he is, or if he's real."

"What?" Ted exclaimed, followed by a loud yelp. "What was that for?" He glowered at Leanne who gestured with her hand to lower his volume. Leaning closer, he continued, "Sorry. So, you wanna tell me if you've seen into my future?"

"Well, not really, I have a few times. I saw you and Brent

kissing before it happened." Claire winked. "Have you never noticed how I avoid touching people?"

Ted nodded. "Yeah, I always thought you were a germophobe. Now it all makes sense... Why you're not good with people I mean, other than us... Why you shy away from big crowds and parties.... Hell, I would do that, too, if I saw the future every time I touched someone."

"It doesn't happen every time," she clarified. "I don't befriend people because I don't want anyone to know about my gift." She turned to face Brent. "Anyway, to answer your earlier question: No, I've never found him on social media. He's an FBI agent. I doubt he wants to be visible anywhere, but... " She pursed her lips. "I think I've found his sister."

"Claire," the manager called, gesticulating to his watch. "Break's over."

"Okay, I have to go, but I'll see you guys tonight. I'll come to your place." She excused herself and returned to the counter.

Time dragged by at the speed of a tortoise with a limp as Claire worked her shift. On any other day, she enjoyed her job, since she loved cooking and experimenting. Technically, she wasn't a cook, only a barista, but she knew exactly which drink complimented which pastry, and she often assisted in the kitchen.

Every five minutes she checked the minute arm on the wall clock behind her, which didn't seem to move at all. And it didn't quite help that the place was a ghost town, given most students had already gone home for the summer. At a nearby table, a professor was reading a newspaper, sipping his coffee. While she restacked the cups, her eyes scanned the cover:

President Cahill's Opinion on Ballistic Missiles

The headline spurred an urge to grab it from his hands. It was too related to her dream to ignore. She neatened her apron, slowly squashed the impulse, and decided to search for it online after her shift.

How Close Is a Cure for Cancer?

Space and Time Travel: Literary Devices or Reality? (Tech Genius Edward Tomb explores)

When 7 pm finally came, she ripped off her apron and called the manager to cash up. It took 10 minutes too long before Claire grabbed her bag and fled. Her legs trailed behind her mind on the way to Brent's apartment. Luckily Green Gables was only a 15-minute walk from the University of Oregon campus.

Night was taking over, the sun but a line of pink, deep in the distance. The moon was barely visible.

"It's Claire, right?" A voice said.

When she looked up, Tanner or Tucker or something was standing in front of her. "Yes, hi. Sorry, can't remember your name."

"It's Travis. Travis Ross. We had Calc together."

She half-laughed. "Yeah, no, I remember."

"So, what're you up to? I'm kinda bored. Wanna maybe go for a drink?"

Claire stepped back. He wanted to get closer than was

12

allowed. "Sorry, I'm into girls," she lied to discourage him.

"Really? Huh. Well, you know, I didn't mean as a date."

"Uhm, I'm actually on my way to friend's place and I'm late. So, if you'll excuse me..." She tried to walk around him.

He touched her elbow and gently felt her back. "Want some comp... "

Claire sat on her bed, her back propped up on a pillow against the wall. Deep in concentration, she sketched the interior of a new hair salon. Her phone pinged. She grabbed it from the nightstand and saw a PM on Messenger. Claire barely received any of those. She had acquaintances on Facebook and Instagram, none of them friendly enough to send her personal messages.

When she opened the app, it was from Lucy Bates, a girl with whom she shared a few classes, but no more than a few words.

Lucy: *Please watch its important*

Claire cringed when texts held no punctuation. It was as if people had become savages of digitalism. Below the text was a link. She was usually careful about unsolicited links, although this one appealed to her curiosity. So, she clicked on it. The YouTube app opened, buffering, testing her patience.

The video started with a photo of Travis Ross, another unspoken-to classmate. He was handsome in every sense of the word: Dark, tousled hair, a dimpled smile, forest-like eyes that could be mistaken for crystal balls of the future, if you dared to lose yourself in them.

The photo cut to a video of Lucy. "Travis Ross is totally hot, right? And charming, and such a gentleman at first, but he's a rapist... "

"Claire! Claire!" Travis weaved his arms around her shoulders. "Are you all right? You just blanked out there."

"Sorry, it could be all the stress from finals."

"Hey, it's okay." He pulled her into his chest. "Come on, let's get you home."

Claire felt her fear hormones awaken. She could smell his inviting deodorant. He was touching her, holding her. No one was allowed up close and personal – her friends knew their boundaries. Travis was confining her to a broken elevator. *Rapist.* Her breath was frayed, making it hard to focus. He guided her forward down the path. She desperately needed out. She stopped and turned towards him.

"You sure you're okay?" he asked with a genuine hint of concern.

Claire smiled but didn't answer. She stared into those eyes, something she had never done before. They looked hopeful. Excited. Then she kneed him in the groin with every inch of power she possessed. Travis folded forward and she ran. Given her bony frame, it had to have hurt. She stretched her long legs further than they usually allowed. Her footfalls were loud and frantic, as were his behind her.

Travis was fit, he would soon catch up to her. Claire heard the space narrowing and she prayed silently. Brent's building became bigger than a mere dot in the distance. She trained her eyes on the goal, ignoring the threat behind her until she heard a thumping noise that sounded like he had tripped. Still, she didn't look back and kept sprinting until she reached the door. For a moment she couldn't remember the code, but apparently her fingers had their own memory.

Inside, she slouched to the floor in fearful puffs. She allowed herself a moment to catch her breath before attempting the stairs. The door was open when she reached Brent's apartment. Claire passed the small cherrywood kitchen on her way in and grabbed an apple from the fruit bowl on the counter.

"Hey," she greeted, falling into one of the empty seats on the black double-seater couch.

"Hey Claire, up for some Minecraft?" Ted asked, placing a disk into the PlayStation.

She looked up at the small flatscreen against the wall. "Not tonight, Teddy Bear." Leanne had awarded him the nickname when they had first met. "I need your help."

Unimpressed, Brent sighed next to her. "Is this about the dream again?"

"You already know she won't let it go." Leanne emerged from the bedroom. Her disheveled hair suggested she'd been taking a nap.

"Clairy," Brent had adopted the nickname from her parents. "Can we talk for a sec?"

"Sure." Claire followed him through the glass sliding door on to the balcony, already knowing what he was about to say.

"Listen, I know you might believe that he exists, and maybe a part of me does, too. But one, you don't know where to find him, and two, you can only see two days into the future, tops. That means it'll happen tomorrow and there's nothing you can do about it."

"I understand your concerns, but one, if I find his sister, I find him. And two, I've seen no one that I haven't touched,

15

apart from him, so why should the two-day rule apply?" Claire's hands disappeared into her jean pockets. A nervous habit. "Brent, I appreciate you trying to look out for me, but I just know in my heart that this is the right thing to do."

He shook his head, not having any of it. "Well, I don't. I think you have a wonderful life. You're graduating, we have that summer trip to Bend planned, you have two loving parents who miss you back home in Portland, and you have us."

Ah, the graduation trip to Bend they had been planning and saving for since freshman year. It wasn't that far from Eugene and apparently spectacular. Brent didn't have to tell her what she would be giving up. All of her life she had questioned her purpose, and now she had found the answer.

"I know that, but this gift I have, it means something."

"What?" Brent wiped a hand over his face in frustration. "So you can venture, woman-alone, into the unknown, to find someone who may or may not exist? It's crazy!"

Claire turned to look at the view, leaning back while holding on to the railing. She knew how foolish it sounded, yet nothing had ever made more sense to her. A small voice whispered: *You're out of your mind,* but her heart was already on the road.

"Sometimes you just have to trust your instincts. Sometimes you have to be spontaneous."

Brent brushed her off. "Whatever, Claire, spontaneity makes you cringe. Whenever I suggest something new and adventurous, apart from a recipe, you run for the hills."

She clenched her jaw. "Says the one who won't even hold his boyfriend's hand in public."

"That's not fair. You know I'm scared of people's reactions. Besides, what does that have to do with anything?"

She wasn't quite sure how to answer the question. "I don't know," she admitted. "Look, you know why I avoid the 'new and adventurous', as you call it because of my abilities. But my gift is the reason I'm planning this quest. I have to embrace it. I can't run from it anymore. And neither should you. You should be proud of who you are."

Brent scoffed. "You're not comparing apples with apples here. Becoming proud of being gay is hardly the same as becoming more spontaneous by going on a suicide mission."

Hesitantly, Claire took his hand in both of hers. No visions. "It's clear we won't be seeing eye-to-eye on this. I'm doing it with or without your help, but without, it'll take longer."

He pulled her in for a hug. "I wish you weren't so damn stubborn. I'll agree, only if I come with you. What do you need me to do?"

Claire smiled. There was no way she would ever allow him to relinquish his own life and accompany her on a potentially disastrous mission. "Sure, I guess you can come." It was only a little white lie. She would disappear before dawn and hope for his forgiveness. "I need your help to locate his sister."

Brent cocked one skeptical brow: "Thought you said you had found her on Facebook?"

"Yeah, I think it's her. There were lots of Erica Klein's to filter through. Facebook doesn't show your location if your profile's not public. Not hers, anyway."

"Okay, so what's your plan? Come on." Brent pulled her back inside.

Biting her lip, she asked: "Can you maybe use your computer-genius mind and find her location somehow?"

"You want me to hack her Facebook account?"

Claire pouted. "Please? It's for a good cause."

"It's a criminal offense," he argued.

"Whose Facebook account are we hacking?" Ted asked, his attention still on the game.

"Erica Klein?" Leanne guessed.

"Yup, that's the one," Claire agreed.

"So that's the sister of the guy you've been dreamin' about?"

"Uh-huh."

"Well, if Brent won't do it, I'll help you. I don't know much about this gift you got, but it seems like the right thing to do."

"Really, Teddy Bear?" Claire crossed the room and threw her arms around him from behind. A huge gesture, given her touch-phobia. "Thank you."

"I never said I wouldn't do it," Brent spoke up. "Besides, Ted doesn't have my skills."

"Gee, thanks," Ted said, mock-offended.

Claire couldn't care less about how they got the information, as long as they did. Sure, she would miss her friends. but she couldn't miss the opportunity to save lives. Byron's life wasn't the only one in danger. Other people would die, too, in a blast that could crush concrete like it was paper.

As her friends retreated to the bedroom, she searched for the article she had earlier spotted in the *New York Times*. Although she didn't know that much about nuclear weapons, apart from what she had learned in history, the crux of the matter was that they could destroy major cities in seconds. In the feature, the president stated that it was of vital importance for the US to keep nuclear arms deployed, and at the same time improve their early detection systems to defend against incoming attacks. He considered it a peace-keeping mechanism. Claire shook her head. *Sorry, Sir, all of your efforts will fail.*

2

Claire

Claire had been pacing around Brent's apartment all morning. Trying to keep busy, she had made blueberry pancakes for breakfast, which everyone had devoured as if a week-long fast had ended even Leanne, who was never keen for too many carbs. Claire wanted to ask for an update on the guys' progress every half-hour, but that would end with her butt on the other side of the apartment door. Time was ticking by and she couldn't help worry about Brent's two-day comment.

If he was right, hundreds or thousands of people could die soon. Families would be torn apart, cities destroyed and economies shaken. War. Her overactive mind kept checking the news, and every time, there were the same old stories. Instead, she decided to read. At least that would keep her mind occupied for a while.

She stepped into the bedroom. "I'm just here for a book," she said, heading for the shelf.

"Claire, we've tried everything we can think of. Erica's not taking the bait," Brent spoke up.

"What do you mean?"

"See, first we tried the honest way and sent her a friend request, but she didn't accept. Then I tried to connect with her via one of her friends, but none of them are visible. We have no mutual friends we can use, either." He sighed like it was a hopeless case, but Claire knew that he was secretly ecstatic. "Facebook has iron-clad security. We can't penetrate it unless we use phishing or spoofing. And to do that, we need an email address."

Ted spoke next, "We've even sent login requests to all the Erica Klein email addresses we could find. None of them's the one we're looking for."

"What else can we do?" asked Claire.

"Maybe this is a sign that you're not meant to go in search of this woman." Brent persisted.

"No, I'm not giving up." Claire shook her head vigorously. "There has to be another way."

She noticed how Brent's jaw squared even more in a clench. "Can you remember anything about the visions? Places? Street names? Anything at all?"

"No, not really." Her visions of Byron weren't all that detailed, almost as if they were some riddle that offered an invitation to be solved. "I know they're from New York, and I saw them on vacation once."

Claire rubbed at her temples, trying to recall any information that could be useful. Nothing. The only thing Erica's Facebook profile revealed was the college from which she had graduated. "What about college? Can you hack a college's alumni database?"

Brent frowned. "We don't have to hack it. We can just call the college and ask for it."

"Do they just hand that information out to the public?" Claire pulled a doubtful face. Personal information was supposed to be confidential.

"I don't know." Brent shrugged. "But it's worth a try. We can pretend to be a school trying to recruit her and just ask whether they would supply us with her email address."

"I guess it's worth a try." Claire moved closer. She stood behind Brent, bent down, and placed a hand on his chair to steady herself. She touched his shoulder by accident.

"Woo-hoo!" Brent yelled as his feet touched the ground. "That was a-ma-zing."

"Yeah!" Ted agreed. "If it wasn't so damn expensive, I'd do it again."

Both of them turned to watch Leanne coming down the zip line with an ear-piercing yelp.

"Seems like someone's scared of heights?" Ted said, pointing to the woman in the air.

"I wonder what Claire would look like up there?"

"Yeah, too bad she ditched us for her boyfriend," Ted yelled as if trying to say: I hope you heard me and feel ashamed.

Claire didn't move. She tried to act oblivious to the dream. The Bend trip wasn't until a few weeks from now, which meant she could see further than a couple of days. Ted's last sentence suggested she had to be in the vicinity except she felt separated from it. Blinking, she shoved it away.

Although a road trip with her three best friends would have been incredible, this mission was something she couldn't abandon. Acting as if nothing had happened, she asked, "So, are you gonna call them, or should I?"

"You can call. Here's the number." He pointed to the spot on the screen.

Claire dialed and a woman answered on the third ring. "Pennington College, good afternoon."

"Good day, my name is Eve Lauren." She thought on her toes. "I'm calling from Bayport Elementary School and I'm trying to get hold of an alumnus. Could you perhaps assist me?"

"I'm sorry, ma'am, we can give you a confirmation of the alumnus or alumna's graduation, but for any other information, we would have to seek permission from the student. Would you like me to send your contact details to the person of interest?"

Since she had nothing to lose, she pushed her luck. "Yes, please. Can I give you my number?"

The woman took down all the details before hanging up.

"Really, Claire, Eve Lauren?" Brent mocked her. "Like that didn't come from Yves Saint Laurent. I'm surprised you even know designer brands."

"I made it up in the moment." She stuck her tongue out. "I might not wear it, but my roommate does."

* * *

Tuesday, 7 June 2022, 3 pm

Days had passed with no news of any blasts and no progress with Erica, but her nightmare was too overpowering to denounce as fantasy. Claire lay on her bed, her eyes boring into the roof. Every single approach Brent and Ted had taken had led to yet another security barrier. Erica hadn't returned her call either. She wasn't even completely sure whether she had found the correct person since her profile picture was of her husband and two girls. However, all the visible particulars matched. Could it be a coincidence?

The thoughts in her head spun on a loop, as she recollected every souvenir of the Blacks her mind had to offer. Something disturbed her as a movie of the ghosts replayed through her thoughts, yet she couldn't put her finger on it.

She thought long and hard. Then longer and harder. There had to be something. When she closed her eyes again, she nodded off. This time, the dream was more photo-like than lifelike, as some of the visions of him were. They emerged often after she had thought of him or sketched him, almost as if summoned. This time, though, the FBI agent wasn't the subject, it was his sister. She was standing in front of a school surrounded by a group of kids. Etched into the wall above them was a sign: "Williamsville Elementary".

She opened her eyes, smirking like a cat toying with its prey. Without hesitation, she searched for the school and found it in Williamsville, New York. Claire packed at graveyard volume, so as not to alert Leanne. Only the basics: Clothes and toiletries. She couldn't deny being terrified; she had no idea what to expect. Her dream version of Erica was a kind and wholesome person, but Claire was a complete stranger to the woman. Fortunately, those fears had to wait.

The trip to Williamsville would take three or four days. After meticulous planning, she booked a motel in Brigham City, Utah, for the first night the least creepy, least expensive one she could find online.

"What you up to, hun?" Leanne peeked in the door.

"Oh, you know, looking for ways to locate Erica," Claire lied, slowly shutting the laptop. Leanne was probably sick of the subject already.

"What are we having for dinner?"

"Maybe we should just get pizza?"

At that, her roommate's face showed concern since Claire was no fan of take-out. She walked straight over and placed a hand on Claire's forehead. "Are you ill? Giving up the opportunity to cook?"

She giggled, removing her friend's hand. "No, I'm just struggling to find this woman."

"Honey," Leanne sat down next to her on the bed, "this is becoming an obsession for you. You can't go on like this."

"It's important, L. A lot of people could die."

"A lot of people?" Leanne's brows rose in puzzlement. "You never told me how he died?"

Claire closed her eyes and shook her head, not wanting to relive the memory. "There was this major bomb explosion. It seemed far off. I can't explain exactly... an umbrella of smoke puffing from the source... Then... " She rubbed her temples, willing the image away or recalling it, she wasn't sure. "I saw Byron in a building that shook with earthquake ferocity. A large beam tore off and pierced straight through his heart."

"Were you there?"

"I'm not sure. It was all muddled."

"Oh." Leanne looked around the room as empathy settled in her eyes. "I didn't know, but at the end of the day it's him you're really trying to save, right?"

Claire lifted her gaze from the bed, shocked at the accusation. "No, you're wrong. It's about more than just me or him. A bomb will explode and possibly kill an entire building or block, and I can stop it."

"I'm not trying to offend you. I want to enlighten you. You're infatuated with the man. How old is he?"

"About 30."

"What college did he attend?"

"Columbia."

"What sport did he play?"

"Basketball."

Leanne's mouth stretched into a wicked grin. "See, you answered each of my questions without hesitation."

"That doesn't mean anything." Claire tossed a pillow at her.

"Claire, look, I'm worried about you. You need to realize that there is a whole other life around you."

"Fine." She slumped forward. "I'll let it go," she agreed only for Leanne to backpedal. In the morning, when her friend woke, Claire would be consigned to the long road.

3

Claire

Wednesday, 8 June 2022, 4.30 am

With Leanne being a wake-at-the-drop-of-needle type, Claire couldn't risk setting an alarm. Their walls were practically translucent. Instead, she set a reminder on vibrate and placed it on the pillow next to her ear. The previous night she had feared it wouldn't work, but it did. Or perhaps she had been awakened by the anxiety stewing within her.

I need coffee or a morning-person brain! She sighed, pulling herself to her feet. Listlessly, she grabbed her sparse luggage and tiptoed to the front door, carefully unlocked it, and turned the knob. Her throbbing heart was loud in her ears. She knew even the teeniest tiniest sound would wake her roommate.

She barely touched the steps on her way down. In the car, Claire let out a sigh of relief and started the engine. Just when she thought she was in the clear, the car's headlights revealed an angry-looking Latina. Leanne shrugged as if to say, "What the hell are you doing?"

Almost as if programmed, robot style, Claire jerked the car into reverse and slammed on the gas. She sped out of the parking lot without casting another glance in her friend's direction. The speedometer kept climbing, but she didn't give a damn. Leanne was determined enough to follow her. She had to widen the gap.

When the traffic light turned red, she screeched to a stop. As she counted the seconds until it turned green, a feeling of nausea clambered up her throat. Nerves. *Calm down,* she coaxed herself and wiped the sweat from her forehead. Before long she was on the I-105, heading east, and the phone didn't stop ringing. Brent, Leanne, Ted, and later even her mother called. She ignored all of them.

After an hour, when the first of the sun's tentacles wrapped around the horizon, her father called. He was the one person who she could drizzle with honey. "Hello, Daddy?"

"Clairy, what are you doing?"

There was no point in fabricating a story. Her father would see through it and Brent would have told them, anyway. "I saw people dying in a bomb explosion, I have to warn... someone."

"You know how many times your mother and I have begged you to keep your gift quiet. If the wrong people hear about this, you will be in trouble... " He started preaching, but she cut him off.

"I've heard the speech many times. I can trust this person, promise." Not that she had ever met him, but deep down, she knew.

"Let me guess. A hunch? Who is this person, Claire?"

"Daddy, you have to trust me, I'm doing the right thing." Her father had never been able to resist her innocent, little-girl charm.

"Claire," his voice broke, stifling tears, she assumed. "I don't like this one bit. I want an update every day. If not, I'm

27

calling the police. And Honey, be careful. If you need anything, whatsoever, you call me... It's hard... knowing you're all grown up."

"'kay, Dad, I promise, I'll be fine."

"Sweetheart, I love you." Now that was something her father did not say often. He didn't have to say it. She always knew.

"I love you too, Dad." She ended the call.

Claire slightly pushed the speed limit, listening to old-school rock on high volume. Driving through Bend, she found herself on a guilt trip because of the actual trip she had now abandoned. *This is more important. Lives to save.*

Ha-ha. Her inner voice of reason taunted. *Who do you think you are? James Bond? Captain Marvel?*

Nope, just a regular girl going to seek the help of a somewhat superhero, she argued with herself and turned Metallica louder to drown out her own mocking. *That won't help. I'm still here.*

Shut up!

Claire thumped the brake as the car in front of her jolted to a sudden halt. The car shrieked in protest at the abrupt force, as rubber melted against tar. The slight push-and-pull motion forced her head back into the seat. At least the internal conversation had dampened her vigorous speed. For a moment she just sat there, frozen. Her eyes blinked, unfocused. The bang was so fleeting that she wasn't even sure it had actually occurred, until a knock on the window. She switched on her hazard lights, opened the window, and looked up.

"Hi, are you okay?" The concerned words came from an older woman, perhaps her mother's age. "I'm so sorry about that, some animal jumped into the road."

"I... Yes." Her lip quivered. She didn't have time for this. Hesitantly, Claire opened the door. She knew the procedure, but swapping insurance details was the last thing for which she had the focus. While the woman apologized profusely, Claire inspected the damage. Her silver Ford Fiesta had minor scuffs, but the little blue Chevy's back fender was blemished with scrapes and craters.

Her eyes darted between the cars as she assessed their damage. It wasn't quite her fault, and her current quest was a great deal more important than car repairs. "Ma'am, I'm in a real big hurry, would you mind if we forgot this happened?"

"But, the dent... We have to report it."

"Thank you very much, I hope you have a lovely day." She kept smiling as she backed into the car and drove off. Did she just take part in a hit and run? Would that lead to a license suspension, or worse, jail? Surely the woman had taken down her license plate number. *One thing at a time, Claire.* She would have to cross that bridge when she got to it. Forget fish, right now, she had sharks that needed frying.

It was already dark when the GPS alerted her: "You have arrived at your destination." Blue neon flashed the name 'Skyline Motel, Brigham City'.

The musty smell of dust hit her as the door creaked open. Creepy. Maroon-and-pink bedsheets covered the cheap, wooden furniture, and the walls were bland with old-fashioned art. *Just for one night,* she told herself, falling onto the bed. It wasn't just one night, though. She would have to stay over another night on her journey and sleep at a motel in Williamsville while searching for Erica. All she wanted was to close her eyes, but first, she had work to do.

The easy part was figuring out where to stop for another

night. The hard part was finding Erica. All she knew was the school's name, which didn't help her much. Most schools would be closing soon for the holidays.

This is harder than I thought. There was no way she could just walk up to the front door and say, "Hi, I'm Claire, I've been dreaming about your brother for the last couple of years and I think he's going to die." Nope, that would earn her a door in the face. Besides, she had to find her before she could befriend her. Claire scribbled and mind-mapped every option she could think of. Somewhere in the midst of her plotting, she fell asleep at her laptop. The dream started with coffee dribbling over Erica's dress, yet pivoted into something completely different...

* * *

Friday, 10 June 2022

Claire developed a bizarre relationship with the road: The trees mocked her as she whizzed past, the cars giggled, and the heaving trucks gossiped. Sweet ballads pouring through the speakers were her only companions. She drove for over 15 hours that day until her Ford finally came to a stop in front of a McDonald's in Williamsville. The physical ache of hunger was an unusual experience. She had to eat.

The drive-through, temporarily closed, sent her wandering inside. Exhaustion was slowly erasing her from existence and the smell of burnt meat and day-old oil made her want to hurl violently. Nonetheless, she stood in the queue and ordered a Big-Mac.

Five minutes passed before the attendant called her number. She collected her order and turned around. Her eyes met the person approaching the door. Blinking, she turned her face away, dropping her bag in the process. A lack of sleep was toying with her mind.

"Are you all right?" A bald man to her left asked. "Miss, you don't look so good. Come here, sit down." He steered her towards a table.

"Thank you," she managed.

"Are you okay?"

She wasn't. "Yes, I'm fine." Claire succeeded in wringing out a small smile.

Her attention turned to the food. She ate away half of the hunger, deposited the contents back into the bag, and rushed to the parking lot. A torrid flash of pain surged through her when someone grabbed her by the arm. It took Claire a second too long to realize what was happening. Her assailant had her in a painful vice. She tried to wriggle herself free from the grip, but the more she squirmed, the deeper his fingers dug into her skin. He was too deft and too strong; an unfair opponent for her feeble arms.

4

Byron

Monday, 6 June 2022, 3 pm

Byron walked down the pristine carpeted halls to Mr. Hoff's personal assistant, as if summoned to the principal's office for bad behavior. He searched through the lobbies of his mind, trying to figure out what the boss could possibly want now.

"He asked to see me." Byron motioned towards the large, wooden double doors across from her desk.

"He's just busy on a call. You can take a seat and I'll let him know you're here." Smiling, his PA picked up the phone's earpiece.

He nodded and sat down in one of the brown, suede leather chairs.

"Would you like something to drink?" the PA asked.

"No, thanks. I'm good.".

After 20 minutes of waiting, he regretted declining the drink. Having nothing else to do, he responded to some emails, then twirled his phone between his fingers as he dreamt up strategies to succeed with the mission at hand.

"He's ready for you," the PA called.

Finally, he thought, plodding towards the CEO's office.

"Ah, Bob, please have a seat." Mr. Hoff motioned to the chair across from his desk.

"Thank you." He did as instructed. "You wanted to see me, Sir?"

"Yes, I'm concerned about the numbers." He stood with his back to Byron, staring out the windows.

"I don't understand. All of the hotels are fully booked for the entire summer."

Hoff cricked his neck. "Are you that narrow-minded? All of Florida is fully booked for the summer. That's three months. What about the three months after that?"

Byron narrowed his eyes, not quite understanding the task before him. "We're already at 70% occupancy and it's still three months away."

His boss swiveled back to the desk. "Do you know why I hired you, Mr. Schroeder?"

Realizing it was a rhetorical question, Byron didn't respond.

"Not because you graduated from business school with honors or because of your previous experience. In fact, not because of your resumé at all. I hired you because you convinced me that you have a way of turning my vision into reality. And my vision is to run at 100% occupancy all year round."

Asshole, he thought. "I'll get right on it, Sir, but we may need to lower our rates and offer some promotions."

The balding man's blue eyes daggered him from across the table. "One hundred percent occupancy at the current rates. Do promotions if you have to, but keep it as low-budget as possible. You can't do it, you might as well clear out your desk right now."

Byron nodded. After the recent knock to the industry, it was once again booming, but Hoff's expectations often stretched the rubber band to the limit. "You have nothing to worry about, Sir. I'll make it happen."

"Nothing further." Hoff waved him out.

He rolled his eyes at the PA on his way back to his own office. *I'll just have to find a solution, no two ways about it.*

* * *

Monday, 6 June 2022, 8 pm

Byron's suit jacket flew to the couch as he entered his apartment. He slammed his fists on the kitchen island, grabbed a bottle of scotch from the cupboard, and poured himself a glassful.

Loosening his tie, he glared at the luxury Miami apartment. For the past two weeks, he had lived as an alien in this place. It was cold and spacious: Beige walls, with coffee-colored, modern furniture to match the dark-wood interior. A 65-inch flat-screen decked the wall, along with a few abstract artworks. It was a far cry from his cozy brownstone in New York City. The wide, glass sliding doors led him to the veranda, where he sat down to enjoy his drink.

It would be another late night, trying to come up with marketing strategies to fulfill the boss's wishes. Since Byron had an MBA and experience in business management, the Bureau had chosen him for this mission. After quite a few tip-offs about Jonathon Hoff, the FBI had started to investigate. When the initial investigation proved no foul play, Byron was the perfect candidate to infiltrate the corporation and get close enough to uncover his secrets. He kept auditioning for a starring character in Hoff's good books but was never awarded the role.

A knock on the door lured him from his thoughts and back inside to open. Taylor Penn sported a long cardigan, hat, and summer scarf as a disguise.

"Hi, come on in," he offered. They should not be seen together. To the rest of the world, they had to be two strangers working for the same company: Himself as the operations manager and his partner, Taylor Penn, as Hoff's PA. Though, his duties far exceeded his title.

"Hey." She stepped inside, discarding the unnecessary accessories. She was a good-looking woman: Tall, with long, dark hair, jade eyes, and sharp features. Five-foot-seven of tanned skin and toned muscles.

"You want a drink?" He returned to the kitchen. "I have beer and scotch."

"Scotch, I need it after a day with that slimeball." She placed her bag on the counter.

"Please, tell me you've got something? I can't wait to get out of this place. I've been checking the books. So far, nothing's stood out. The auditors haven't picked up on anything either," he said, sounding slightly defeated, even to his own ears.

"That only means he's hiding it well. I listen in on all of his calls and meetings. Everything seems above board, but he has no respect for women. Every time I go in there, I have to fight the urge to knock him out."

Byron chuckled. "You and me both. We can work on this later. Let's have a drink first."

She took a swig of her scotch. "I love my job, but Hoff, he gets to me."

"I get it, he has that effect. Typical asshole dictator."

"At least you don't work directly for him. Try being his PA." The resentment graveled through her words while her unoccupied hand spasmed into a claw, indicating how she would strangle him.

"Yeah, I think I could pull off those sexy dresses and high heels," he mocked, trying to lighten her mood.

"Probably. You do look good in everything. Just know that carrying a gun holster underneath that is far from comfortable."

Byron hoped she wouldn't take the conversation any further down that path. She had been subtly hinting for the past few weeks, but he couldn't jeopardize their partnership, nor was able to engage in any relationship. His twin sister had been born with traits such as affection and devotion, but all he'd got was skepticism. Relationships were built on trust, and he didn't trust anyone apart from Erica. Not even Taylor Penn.

Early-in-life cynicism combined with the carbon molecules of his body. Their mother abandoned them at nine, leaving them in the care of their alcoholic, narcissistic father, who had had time for nothing but his work. 'Trust no one, and no one can betray you', became Byron's life motto.

Day by day, Douglas Black had beaten the life out of him. No matter how many A's he'd get on his report card, or how many baskets he'd made, the man had always found a reason to chastise him. Sometimes he could still feel the belt ripping into his flesh, and the sound of the slaps swelling through the room. Jonathon Hoff couldn't scare him. Nothing could. He had always found a way to better the risible reason for his punishment. Until the next.

Changing the subject, he said, "I've started watching cooking shows. Thought I'd learn a new craft."

Taylor snorted, almost spewing the liquid from her nose. "You? Cook?"

"Yeah, why not?"

"You don't even know how to fry an egg."

"I know, my sister took real good care of me, but I'm a fast learner and we need to cut down on take-out." *Like that would ever happen.*

"How is she, by the way?"

"I should probably call. Haven't spoken to her in a while." Looking down at his glass, he rubbed his finger along the edge. "I miss them."

"Does she know?" Taylor asked. "About the mission, I mean."

He shook his head. "No, I tell her as little as possible. She's happy. She has a good life and a great family. No need to include her in my turmoil."

"You guys are lucky to have each other." He sensed some melancholy in her voice.

He jumped up. "Okay, enough chatting. Let's order and get started. The usual?"

"Thanks." She nodded.

5

Byron

Tuesday, 7 June 2022, 4:30 am

Byron awoke before his alarm sounded. He was usually an early riser, but something prickled his sixth sense. Dread lurched in his stomach. Obviously, there was something wrong. The hotels had to be fully booked for the next couple of months or he would be fired. Not an option.

Feeling frazzled, he yanked on some exercise wear and hurried down the stairs to the building's gym. He passed all the equipment and headed straight for the boxing bag to relieve some tension. Each punch he threw was another entry on his to-do list.

Analyze low season guests. A loud thud erupted as his fist connected with the latex.

What extras do they buy? The air bubbled from his lungs with an exhale.

How many guests per booking? "Uh!" He banged it again.

The frequency of his punches increased.

Develop a social media competition. Four nights. Five days. Bed and breakfast. Left, left, right.

Spa treatment. Promote weddings. Promote other events. Breathe.

Get 100% occupancy. He slammed the bag through the air, gasping as it whirled back to him.

That was one part of his job; the other was to expose Hoff's corruption.

Analyze his patterns. His knuckles bumped against his opponent with raging force.

Find out more about him. "Huh!" he yelled as the other arm pushed forward.

Scrutinize each ledger entry. Byron's narrowed airways produced heavy pants.

After a thorough workout, his sense of disquiet had not yet dissipated. Once he was back in his apartment, he called Erica to assure himself they weren't the cause for his concern. Little Cassie should have woken her by now. It rang for a while before his sister answered.

"Hey, stranger, I was starting to think you've disappeared." Her voice brought a sense of relief he didn't know he needed.

"Hey, Sis, you know how it goes, life gets in the way. Sorry to bother you so early, I just wanted to check in on you and the girls."

"Yes, Byron, we're fine, like always." He heard the rolling of Erica's eyes. "Listen, school's almost out and we're thinking of taking a summer trip, if Dan can get off work. Maybe you want to join us?" Her tone was hopeful, almost pleading. She already knew his answer.

"Erica," he sighed, wishing he could go with them. "You know I won't be able to go."

"I know, I know. Just thought I'd take a chance. Ellie keeps asking when you're coming to visit. I think she's mad at you.

Says you don't love us anymore."

His mind's eye revealed a picture of the three-year-old pouting. "I'm sorry. I'll try to come through for a weekend soon. How's Cassie?"

"She's great. Just started walking and is throwing tantrums. It's adorable. You should come see for yourself. We miss you."

Erica's arrows of guilt hit the bullseye right in the middle of his heart. "I miss you guys, too. I'll come soon. Promise."

It was quiet for a moment. Perhaps she didn't believe him, but he would always scrape together some time for them. Always. "Sis, you still there?"

"Yeah, I'm here. By," she paused. "How about this weekend?"

His plate was too full, without even a tiny gap for a helping of family time. But, the shoemaker's elves produced shoes while everyone slept. Perhaps he could, too. "I'll think about it."

"That just means 'no'," she whispered, crestfallen.

He didn't respond since she was likely right. Elaboration would merely fuel her disillusion.

"So, how are you?" she continued, knowing better than to dwell on the subject.

"I'm all right," Byron said, trying to convince himself more than her.

"You're lying. I know when you're lying. I know you can't say much about your new job and all, but I worry about you." Again, her voice constricted with frustration.

It wasn't a complete lie. He was fine, except for some inexplicable feelings with which he had awoken, two demanding, dangerous jobs, and a partner who might have more than platonic feelings for him.

"I miss your cooking, that's all." He checked the time on his watch. "Listen, Sis, gotta run, but I'll talk to you soon."

"Okay, talk soon then. Bye"

6

Claire

The hand dragged Claire to a secluded corner behind the building and pushed her into the wall. Her head thumped against the bricks with a stabbing knock, causing her vision to blur. Pain rang through her ears and fear butterfly-stroked through her veins. One arm held her in place while the other obstructed her breathing.

Claire had read books and watched shows about people getting kidnapped. No empathy she felt for those victims could begin to describe the terror that shook and spasmed within her body. The arms were too strong, and her fear too wild to accomplish any sort of escape. Her mind frailly grasped for any sort of self-defense knowledge it held.

She looked up. The obnoxious banging in her head and claustrophobia slipped right out the window when she looked into the eyes of the man she had been wanting to meet for so long. Claire even welcomed the salty smell of his sweat and the evident moisture stains on his T-shirt.

"Who are you?" Byron whispered.

"My name," she croaked, "is Claire Baxter."

"Who the hell are you?" he demanded, his voice still low and raspy.

"You're... hurting... me."

The grip on her neck loosened no more than an inch.

"I'll... I'll do whatever you say, just please, let go, you're hurting me." Tears stung her eyes, and she felt bruises forming where he was pinning her down. "I'm no one. Please, you have to believe me."

"Nice try, blondie, I know all about acting. Pretending to be all sweet and fragile I don't buy it. You recognized me when I entered the McDonalds, then immediately hid your face."

Her pocket vibrated.

A snarl slid over his face. "Let's see if you're telling the truth."

He grabbed the phone. *Brent or Leanne. Please let it be Brent or Leanne.*

"Claire's phone?" Byron answered politely.

She strained her ears, trying to overhear the conversation, but battled to make out what the person said.

"She's busy right now. Who is this?" Byron asked.

"Is this Byron?" She heard Leanne's voice. *Thank heavens.*

"No, my name's Bob," he lied.

Again, she couldn't hear Leanne's response.

"Here she is now," he said with a warning glare before switching on the speakerphone.

"Hi, L." Claire heard the strain in her own voice.

"Claire, you don't answer your phone for three days and then some random dude does. Where are you? Are you okay?"

"Yeah, actually we walked into the same McDonalds by chance," she explained, trying to make Byron understand

43

the situation.

"So, it is him?" Claire couldn't distinguish whether her friend's tone held shock or concern.

"It's him. I'm fine. I'll be in touch. Promise."

"I can't belie... " Byron ended the call.

"I think you and I should go for a drive." He pulled her towards the parking lot with no less force than before. Claire couldn't deny the dread forcing up from her lungs. Byron Black was nowhere near the man she had expected. The phantom who had infiltrated each vacant corner of her mind was an imposter.

7

Byron

In a sphygmomanometer grip, he steered the girl towards the White Nissan he had rented. He opened the passenger door and gave her a slight shove. She got in without protest. There was something peculiar about her, he knew it from the moment they locked eyes in the McDonalds. It was not just because she had almost fainted, there was something oddly familiar about her. It could all be a performance, but she appeared harmless. Her muscles weren't even toned, which one would expect from a trained spy. Even so, he retrieved the handcuffs from his backpack, secured her wrists, and buckled her seatbelt.

"So, what's your deal? Who do you work for?" he asked as soon as the wheels touched the road.

"No one," she stated nonchalantly. "I'm about to graduate from college."

"Yeah, what'd you study?"

"Architecture."

He scoffed. She was clearly not an inventive liar. "Then

what do you want with me?"

"If I tell you, you won't believe me."

"Try me."

She remained quiet for a moment, seeming to prepare her answer while his fingers tapped impatiently on the steering wheel.

"This case you're working... I can help you solve it," she finally said.

"What are you talking about?" He hid his identity. Nobody knew about the case, except for himself, Penn, and the Bureau.

She slumped her shoulders, biting her lip, her hands in her lap. *What is up with this girl?*

"I think you may be looking in the wrong place," she said, looking up.

"So are you, apparently."

"Cut the crap, Byron." Her composure vanished. "I know you. Since I can remember I've been getting future visions of people I touch." The girl took a deep breath, seemingly in preparation. "Except for you, I've been seeing you in my dreams for the past eight years. Don't ask me why, I don't know."

Inwardly, he chuckled. He hadn't expected that farfetched a lie. Definitely imaginative.

"I know what you're thinking," she continued, "I'm lying, right? No such thing exists, but I can prove it. I know your partner's name is Taylor. Your sister is Erica. She's married to Daniel Klein and they have two beautiful blonde girls. This case you're working on has something to do with Hoff and hotels."

Mixed emotions swirled through him at once: Doubt, fear, trust, happiness, and fury. But it wasn't possible. No one could predict the future. That only happened in comic books and fairytales. "Looks like someone's seen *Ghost* one too many times."

"What?" She frowned.

"The movie, where that Oda Mae Brown woman tries to convince Demi Moore that her boyfriend's ghost is real. Is that what you're trying to achieve here?"

"I've never seen it." Claire turned to face him. "Pull over."

"You're not in a position to make demands here." His voice betrayed him, not quite instilling the authority he had hoped for.

"Just do it." She wasn't afraid. She didn't care that he had her in handcuffs or that she had been caught.

Without thinking, he took a right at the next street, the one he knew led to the abandoned baseball grounds. His mind yelled: *Call it in*! Instead, he gave her the benefit of the doubt. Never before in his life had he taken such a leap of faith, but a minuscule inner voice told him to yield to her.

"Now what?" He pulled the car into the empty lot, making sure that all of the doors were locked. Before giving her a chance to speak, he checked her phone. Instagram, Gmail, Twitter, even her Google, and Maps search history. It all rang true a college student. The last email was from her mother. Something about her graduation ceremony. But a good spy would ensure their backstory was intact.

"You read body language, right? That's how you knew I recognized you. Read me now. Ask me anything."

The girl is smart, using my own tactics against me.

"I have a better idea. How about you tell me what you're doing here? Give me your hand." She did. Lesions had formed on her milky skin under the chaffing metal bands.

47

Her arms were so bony and fragile, he feared he would break them with a too hard a push of his thumb. "Go on," he encouraged, removing the cuffs as a ruse to measure her pulse and perspiration for hints of a lie.

"Everything I told you before is the truth. I came here looking for Erica. I had no idea I would find you." She shook her head and closed her eyes. "I saw you dying... in a bomb blast." Her voice was barely audible.

All of the hair on his body rose and his throat closed up, prompting him to take a puff of his asthma pump. He felt sick. When someone tells you that you'll die in a bomb explosion after revealing facts no one should know, it's hard to ignore.

She didn't wait for a response. "You shouldn't smoke when you have asthma. Well, you shouldn't smoke, period."

"I don't smoke." *One every once in a while isn't smoking.* "And my asthma is intermittent."

Claire raised a brow. "Hiding it doesn't make it any less true. By the way, I see this is a rental car. Are you no longer afraid of flying?"

What the hell? How does she know all of these things? Byron didn't answer the question. He refused to let her know she was right.

"When will this supposed bomb blast happen?"

"That's the one thing I don't know. With everybody else, I can see two days ahead, tops, and only when I touch them. With you, it's different."

"If you can see my future, how come you didn't see me coming?" he asked, scowling.

"Because I don't see everything. It's not in sequence, either. In your case, I've seen mostly big moments in your life."

Is this girl for real? They sat in silence for a while, both staring

48

into the vibrant night sky. There was no sound, save for the low hum of the air conditioner.

"I guess now you're gonna tell me werewolves and vampires exist, too," he said as he glimpsed at the moon.

She smiled, and for the first time he noticed her beauty. "I guess it's possible."

"It's surreal, I'll tell you that." She could be a spy for Hoff or his father. She could be anyone. "Where are you staying?"

"I've booked a motel."

"No, you're coming with me." Under his roof, he could keep a close eye on her until he figured out what else to do. Like the old saying goes: Keep your friends close... She could be a threat or a con artist. He didn't like the idea of her in his sister's house, but he would just have to keep her under his thumb all weekend.

Claire's eyes grew wide and wary at the instruction.

"I thought you knew Erica?" he challenged.

"What will you tell her? I... uh... I don't like people knowing about my secret."

"Pretend to be my girlfriend." He meant it as a demand, but it sounded more like a plea.

Claire snorted. "Why? Won't she be suspicious if you suddenly show up with a girlfriend?"

She had a point. The girlfriend thing wasn't for him. One-night stands once in a while, which he wasn't proud of, but no commitments. "You got any better ideas?"

"Just tell her I'm a friend?"

"And why would I invite a friend to her house for a whole weekend?"

Wild-eyed, she looked down at her feet, whispered, "I'm not good with strangers."

49

"Could've fooled me."

"You... You're not a stranger. Not to me."

Byron's patience with this intruder was starting to wear thin. "You came here to help me, right? We have a lot of stuff to work out. The case, the bomb you mentioned... we can only do that if we work together." He pretended to believe her, but in truth, he needed to study her, to uncover her agenda.

She didn't respond and he couldn't help but glower. "Is there something else going on here?"

"No, even befriending Erica scared me, but I was desperate to find you. That bomb could kill thousands. Not just you."

"Can you tell me more about it? Where did you see it?"

"I don't know where." She hugged herself as goosebumps started to assault her skin. "It resembled Hiroshima. I even googled it to make sure."

"No, you must be mistaken those are nukes." For a mere second, he turned numb, but there was no way. "America has early warning systems in place to counter any nuclear attacks."

"I'm not mistaken. It was in the far-off distance, like in my mind's eye or something, but you were a victim of the impact."

Byron almost couldn't believe the bullshit she was trying to feed him. Still, he decided to play along. "Claire, then you need to tell the FBI or Homeland Securi... "

"No," she shouted. "I'll help you only you no one else can know. I'll become a lab rat, a pawn."

"You'll become dead if you don't speak up." *Hypothetically,* he wanted to add.

"I'll send you emails from an unknown address."

"They'll trace the source."

"Please, understand," her face softened, "not everyone in the FBI is as good as you. This gift could be dangerous in the wrong hands."

Her imploring words touched him. She was either truly scared or a pathological liar, although every word so far had held no trace of untruth: No blinks or change in speech patterns or body language. All the bombs she had dropped so far had overwhelmed him and his mind was swimming. Now he had more than just two demanding and dangerous jobs; as a bonus, he'd received a girl to babysit. Before he could respond, his phone rang.

"Hi," he answered. "Sorry, I got held up. We're on our way."

"We? Who's we?" Erica asked.

He took a deep breath. Erica was the one person who had always seen through his deceit. "It was supposed to be a surprise. I'm bringing my girlfriend."

"What?" she screeched. "You're telling me this now? You have a girlfriend? You have feelings? Oh shit, am I on speaker? Please tell me I'm not on speaker."

"You're not on speaker, but you were so loud I think she might have heard you."

"I will kill you, Byron Black."

Nope, apparently I'm dying in a bomb explosion. "She's cool, Sis, you'll like her, stop stressing. See you just now. Bye." He ended the call while Claire glared at him.

"What else do you want me to do? It's only for two days. Just keep your distance."

"That'll be rude."

"As much as you can, obviously." He started the engine.

"What about my car?"

51

"We'll leave it at the motel."

She nodded, yet her face exposed the dread she felt. But, right now, she was the asset, and he was the handler. It hadn't even been an hour and this blonde had turned his entire life on its head. Only time would tell whether she was a psychic or an actress. Either way, she had to remain under his protection. *If she does one little thing to show me that my trust is misplaced, I'll call Trevor.*

8

Claire

Euphoria and fear took turns flowing through Claire's body. She had found him. Her mission was accomplished before it had even started. The preliminary part of it at least. She had won him over with little difficulty, and the task was a lot easier than expected. Of course, she had manipulated the situation. She had hit him where it hurts (I saw you dying) and conveyed both strength ("Pull over. Just do it") and vulnerability ("I'm not good with strangers).

Frankly, his admittal that he didn't fully trust her was bull. The guy hung on her every word. Claire gave herself a figurative pat on the back for being able to win over the most suspicious person she had ever met. Sitting next to him felt bizarre quite literally, a dream come true. Everything else in her life seemed trivial in comparison. In all honesty, she had thought this day would never come.

"We need a back story," he muttered.

"Huh?"

"For our 'relationship'. Usually, I would need much more

53

time to create a believable lie, especially for my sister. But time is a luxury we don't have right now."

"Oh. We met at a bar and it was love at first sight?" She scrunched her nose.

"You believe in that crap?"

"Hell no, but Erica might."

Byron chuckled. She noticed the joy on his face every time his sister's name was mentioned. "Yeah, probably."

"Which bar? According to your phone, you're from Oregon, so that'll be where we met."

Odd, if they could pretend to have met in Oregon, Erica clearly didn't know where he found himself in the world. She wouldn't have been much help anyway. "There's this bar close to campus called Shameless. We could use that?" Claire suggested.

"You hang out there much?"

"Nope, my friends do. Told you, I don't do well with strangers."

He eyed her with an intense, uncomfortable gaze. "Touch me."

Claire almost jumped out of her seat at the request. "What?"

"See if you get a vision. Focus your energy, I'm curious."

"Oh," she breathed and placed a hand on his shoulder. Drowning out her surroundings, she directed her mind. Her touch and energy remained on him for several minutes.

"Nope, nothing."

He nodded. "Tell me some things about yourself."

"I'm 22. Middle name, Valerie. Birthday, 22 March. My parents are Molly and Kurt and I have three best friends: Leanne, Brent, and Ted. That's me in a nutshell. Oh, and I love classic rock and cooking."

"That's a mouthful. Got it. Anything you wanna know about me?"

"Nah," she winked, "I think I've got it covered." Claire spoke too soon. There were some important particulars missing from her file. "Okay, maybe your age and birthday."

"Excuse me?" he spluttered. "That's the most basic info."

"Well, most of my dreams were soundless. I can make an educated guess, though."

They discussed the rest of the details about their sham relationship all the way to the McDonald's parking lot. Claire pulled the lever to open the door when he grabbed her by the arm. "Nice try, Blondie." He cuffed her to the steering wheel, then pulled the car keys from her bag. "You don't really think I'm that stupid, do ya? I'll pay a random teenager to drive it."

He didn't trust her completely. *Ugh.* An urge to kick the dash of his rental car started to build. She watched through the window as he jogged to an outside table surrounded by a group of teens. After a short conversation, two of them followed Byron. Before long, they were back on the road. At least he had removed the cuffs. When they reached the motel, she took care of the formalities while he lurked behind her, gesticulating to his watch.

They dropped the two who had driven her car back at the parking lot on their way to the Klein's. Claire's heart rate increased with each mile they progressed. *Just hide the visions.* But it wasn't that easy. Leanne had said that they resembled silent epileptic fits. Her parents and the doctors had considered the same diagnosis before she was old enough to explain what she had seen.

"Okay. You ready?" He pulled into the driveway. "If they ask questions I can't answer, take the lead. Don't be afraid, they're great."

Byron opened the car door, taking her hand in his to help her out. Claire's heart leapt into her throat when the front door swung open. Erica was the spitting image of the woman in her dreams: Short, dark hair framed her pixie-like face. Her hazel eyes were radiant as she caught sight of her brother. Erica and Dan were an odd couple: She was petite, while her husband was tall and brawny. Dan was older than the image she held in her mind. His blondish hair receded and he had a few light wrinkles around his grey eyes.

"Erica, Dan, this is Claire." From the small of her back, she felt him nudge her forward.

Erica hugged both of them, but Dan just offered his hand. Fortunately, no visions. Yet.

"Nice to meet both of you," Claire said. "I've heard so much."

"I, unfortunately, can't say the same." Erica glared at Byron. "Please, come in and make yourself at home. Byron has never introduced us to a girl before. In fact, I'm sure he's never had a real one."

"I know." Claire smiled. "He told me."

"So, you must have done something right to overcome that hurdle," Erica said, returning the smile.

"Well, look at her, Sis, couldn't let her slip through my fingers."

Claire tried to remain calm, but he had just explicitly called her beautiful. *It's just an act,* she reminded herself. *It meant nothing.*

"You guys must be tired. Would you like something to drink?" Dan asked as they sat down in the living room.

The room felt homey, the smell an uncanny mix of cinnamon, oil paint, and fabric softener. It was cluttered: Toys, paint, and books were stacked on the table and in other openings. Claire liked the proof of a lively family. Bright walls, decorated with Erica and Ellie's art. Photos she had dreamt of encircled artsy furniture.

"Do you have beer?" Byron asked Dan.

"Sure, what about you, Claire?"

"Thanks." Claire nodded.

"So, how long have you been together?" Erica asked as soon as Dan left for the kitchen.

"Two months," Byron answered. "Erica, please don't scare her away with all of your questions."

"Fine." She pulled a face. "Claire, would you like to go shopping in the morning, then we can have some girl-talk without this one sticking his nose in. I don't bite, I promise."

Claire didn't do shopping. Only when she had no other choice. She did most of it online or through Leanne. She felt Byron tense up next to her, not sure whether it was because of her own anxiety or the idea of her leaving the house with his sister. Probably both.

"She doesn't like malls, Sis. She gets claustrophobic. Rather do your girl talk here while preparing breakfast? Claire likes to cook."

"Oh really, then you must be a perfect fit. This one," Erica pointed to Byron, "is spoilt rotten. You know, I used to do everything for him until the day I moved in with Dan. Even then, I invited him over for dinner, just to make sure he ate."

Claire laughed and looked up at him, noticing the flush on his cheeks. Erica was exactly as she had imagined. They had their drink and made some small talk before Byron called bedtime. Erica showed them to the spare bedroom. Claire hadn't thought that far ahead. They would have to share a room.

"I'll sleep on the floor," Byron offered.

"Don't be ridiculous. We're both adults here, we can sleep in the same bed for two nights. Besides, I think it might help my visions."

His face was intense, but he agreed before retrieving their luggage from the car. Once they were settled in, he started pacing the room, deep in thought. Claire itched to know what he was thinking.

"This thing, can you explain..."

Her phone rang. She removed it from her pocket and glanced at the screen. "It's my dad. He threatened to call the cops if I don't check in." Byron nodded and she answered, "Hey, Dad."

"Claire," Kurt fumed. "I told you to call me."

"Sorry, I lost track of time." That was the truth, with everything that had been going on, calling her parents was the last thing on her mind.

"That's no excuse. You promised. Your mother and I are sick with worry."

"Sorry." She clenched her teeth. "It won't happen again."

"Are you all right?"

"I'm good. How are you?"

"Disappointed, I was supposed to watch you graduate today. Now I might never have that experience." *There's always grad school, if I live that long.*

Avoiding the subject and out of true concern, she asked, "How's Mom?"

"Worried sick, as I told you."

"Dad, I'm safe. I'm with good people, you needn't worry."

"One day when you have kids of your own, you'll realize a

parent never stops worrying. Be safe, sweetheart."

Claire had never considered marriage or kids; her condition had always hindered her from relationships. "I will, bye, Dad." She put the phone away and turned back to Byron. "You were saying?"

"It doesn't matter." He waved her off. "Moving on to the case. You said I was looking in the wrong place?"

"Can we perhaps work on this tomorrow?" She bit her lip, not sure whether she was allowed to ask. "Sorry, I've been driving 15 hours for three days straight. I really need some sleep."

"Oh yeah, sorry." He half-smiled. "I forget not everyone's a workaholic like me." His demeanor had undergone a 180-degree flip from when he'd thrown her against a wall. "You mind pointing me in the right direction?"

"In the dream I heard you telling your partner that you overlooked the boutique hotels."

The half-smile morphed into shock, almost as if struck by an epiphany. "If you turn out to be right about this, you might become my new best friend."

Lips pursed, she nodded, knowing a little more than she let on.

"Well, the bathroom is across the hall if you wanna shower or change, or whatever."

"Thanks." She grabbed her backpack to take a much-needed hot shower in a clean and decent bathroom.

* * *

Saturday, 11 June 2022, 9 am
When a sliver of sunlight sneaked through the leafy, green

curtains, Claire woke to an empty bedroom. The other half of the bed was still untouched. He must have slept on the floor, or not slept at all. Nature's call lured her to the bathroom. She peeked out the door, and with no one nearby, crept across the hall.

Footsteps neared, and the door to the bedroom screeched open.

"Claire," Byron called.

She didn't want to answer, but if she kept quiet, he might assume she had left. "In here," she said. After an attempt at making herself decent, she returned to find him waiting, a tray with coffee and biscuits on the nightstand.

"Morning."

"Morning, I made you coffee. I had to pretend I knew how you take it, so I added sugar and milk. You strike me as a latté girl," he whispered.

"Thank you."

"My sister is waiting for you in the kitchen."

"I'll be right down."

She drank her coffee, got dressed, and made her way downstairs. Erica was scrubbing a bottle and humming some kid's song as Claire stepped into the kitchen.

"Morning."

"Good morning." Erica sent a bright beam her way. "Did you sleep well?"

"Very well, thank you." Claire looked around at all the ingredients standing ready to be used. "So, what can I do?"

Erica wiped her hands on a dishcloth, then handed Claire a tray of eggs. "French toast?"

She agreed and used a butter knife to crack an egg over the unused bowl on the counter.

"Claile." A blonde little girl came running in and hugged her leg. "You up! I'm Ellie."

"Uncle By, push me again," Ellie shouted from the swing.

"What do you say?" Erica gave her a stern look.

"Peez, Uncle By?"

"That's better."

"I'm coming." He settled Cassie on his hip and made for the swings. The one-year-old giggled every time he pretended the swing would hit them, then 'blew' it away.

Claire absorbed the scene in front of her. "He's great with them," she told Erica.

"Yes, he is. Are you in love with him?"

"I... uh... we haven't been together that long."

"That's as good an answer as any. I see the way you look at him. I can tell."

Claire blinked.

"Are you all right?" Erica asked.

"Sit down, here's some water." Byron pulled out a chair and handed her a glass. "She has epilepsy," he lied on her behalf, "but, she'll be okay."

"Thanks." Claire drank her water while everyone faffed around.

"Should we call 911?" Erica asked, worry lines etched on her face.

"No!" Claire and Byron blared in unison. Erica didn't look convinced.

Byron brought her back to the bedroom, keeping both arms

around her shoulders to steady her. Not that it was necessary. He made sure she was comfortable on the bed before he asked, "What did you see?"

"We were at the park," Claire started and explained the events of her glimpse in detail. His head shook a couple of times, but his eyes remained fixated, analyzing her. She couldn't get a read on his observations, only his reservations. It was hard for a realist to grasp a situation that belonged only between a hardcover or on a Hollywood set.

After the incident, everyone treated her like an invalid (except for Ellie), even though she was fully willing and capable. Becoming the subject of sympathetic looks and whispers was awful, but Claire acted unfazed. It stemmed from concern, after all. Dan's stares were the worst. His eyes were lasers trying to penetrate the thick skin she had always used as a cover.

Despite the small incident, the day went off without a hitch. Ellie had indeed begged Byron to take them to the park and except for the placement of equipment, the actions mirrored her preview. She enjoyed it. Maybe a little too much.

9

Byron

Byron noticed Claire itching to help Erica with the cooking and cleaning, but the Kleins would have none of it. Lazy and indolent didn't seem to exist in this girl's world. He observed her like an experiment, trying to figure out whether she was truthful or not. If the vision that morning was an act, damn, the girl deserved a Golden Globe. And the way she sidestepped touching was more evident than he knew she wanted to express.

As tradition had it, he read the girls a bedtime story. Claire sat on the edge of Ellie's bed, intently listening to his terrible voice-overs. She giggled at his meager impersonation of Papa Bear and snorted when his raspy voice dropped an octave for Goldilocks. Byron couldn't deny the purity that radiated from her. Something he didn't experience much in his line of work.

Just when he thought it time to get some work done, Erica brought out the board games. "Since Claire is our guest, I'll let her choose which one we play," his sister ordered. There was no room for argument in her tone.

Being polite, Claire scanned the selection. "Hmm... What about good, old-fashioned Uno?"

"As long as I don't have to sit next to Erica." Byron knew his sister's cheating tendencies all too well.

"In that case," Claire smirked, "it's exactly where you'll sit. Your sister made me the boss."

"Oh, you've just poked the bear." He stared her down in challenge. He wouldn't go down easily. And what a match it was. They made it their mission to bring each other down with plus-fours, turn-skipping, and cheating accusations. Time flew by the time he had set aside for the case but observing the girl he knew nothing about was far more intriguing than his job.

Their competition wore on and Dan swept the floor with them, since his concentration was on the actual game. For once, losing didn't bother Byron. He had fun a word that had seldom existed in his vocabulary.

Byron had to admit, he could no longer ignore what Claire had told him. Would he die in a nuclear explosion? Was that even possible with the current technology that existed? After the game, they headed upstairs.

"Tell me more about these visions."

"I've already told you everything. You're just in denial. All my visions so far have come true, except if I've deliberately changed them." Her face turned serious, her eyes drilling into his. "Unless we do something, you will die."

Her gravity sent a chill down his spine. "Any ideas?"

"Well, you said an email won't work."

"No, it can't be electronic at all. They have ways to trace anything."

"Then only a letter?" She bit her bottom lip.

"Yeah, that's what I was thinking, too, as old-school as it might seem. You'll have to use cut-out letters, though."

"Can I type it on my laptop first?"

"Yes, but don't save it. At all."

Claire opened her laptop. "Who should I address it to?"

"To no one, short and sweet. But you'll hypothetically slip it under my door."

"Why not just send it to the FBI's contact center directly?" Her brows knit in confusion.

"I need to be a part of the investigation to help them and to protect you. They'll be looking for you, I'm certain."

Byron wasn't sure whether there would even be an investigation, or if there was any truth to her claims at all. If she sent the letter, the FBI would have to inform their counterparts, the CIA, and the Pentagon. At least that would lead to tightened security.

She stiffened, wordlessly turning to her laptop to type the letter. A few keys clinked. "Done."

Byron sat next to her on the bed, his eyes skimming over the words.

```
My employer or an accomplice will attack with
nuclear weapons. I do not know the cause, time, or
destination. I overheard conversations that led me
to this inference. This letter is not a hoax and
should be taken seriously. Thousands of lives are
at stake.
```

"This is a lot of words that don't say much, Claire."

Her eyes blinked in slow motion. "I don't have much information."

"They won't act on something so bare."

She stared at the screen and sighed with the frustration of a CEO voted out of his own company.

"Never mind," he continued, "we'll figure it out on the cut-out letter version. Come on." He waved for her to follow him. Byron checked the halls to ensure no one was around before he led Claire downstairs. In the kitchen, he gingerly opened all the cabinets to check for old newspapers, while Claire went in search of Erica's art supplies.

When he couldn't find anything, he joined her in the small space his sister used as a studio. Byron found her holding a few magazines and whispered, "Newspaper letters work best 'cause of their uniformity."

"Works best for what?" Dan's voice said behind him.

Claire looked up in horror. A few beats followed before she spoke: "For my project. Byron's helping me."

"Yes," he said, turning around. No other words came to mind.

The grey in Dan's eyebrows shot to the top of his head. "If you don't mind me asking, what project could require uniform newspaper letters?"

For some reason, Byron grabbed her hand and squeezed it for reassurance.

"It's for my upcoming internship," Claire explained.

Finally, an idea crossed his mind. "She has to design a lobby out of recyclable materials, and she wants to put the company's name against one wall."

"I see," Dan said, though his dubiety slithered through his words.

"Do you have some newspapers we can use?" Claire asked in a voice that reminded him of caramelized sugar.

"Uh, yes, of course." Dan opened the linen closet next to the steps, reached for the top rack, and pulled out a few crumpled pieces of print. He handed them to her and returned to the stairs without acknowledging her thanks.

"You've got some manipulation skills," Byron noted back in the bedroom. It worried him. She could be manipulating a little hole into his life and he would be a fool to trust her.

She didn't comment. "So, you don't think the FBI will be suspicious?"

"Oh, they'll be suspicious, all right, but it's the best we can do for now. The more dreams you have, the more we can help."

"Does this mean that you believe me?"

"Do I have a choice? If you're lying, then I have to arrest you." He assessed her face for any tell-tale signs of fear. None. So far everything had pointed to the truth. As he had thought before, only time would tell.

* * *

Sunday, 12 June 2022, 11 am

After an amazing weekend with the Klein's as usual the time came to head back to Miami. With reluctance they parted before returning to the motel for Claire's car.

"I believe you," Byron reiterated, opening her car door. "I do, it's just... Never mind. Claire, you take one wrong turn, I'm calling my superiors, and they'll come at you like a swarm of bees."

"I won't. You can trust me. Thanks for the weekend, by the way. It was great."

67

It was perfect, aside from the vision and Dan's skepticism. Erica didn't seem to doubt their lie for a second. A few times, Byron had almost believed it himself, as if they were one big happy family. Right on cue, his life's motto came to mind. Claire could only be an ally, assisting him with important cases. Nothing more, nothing less.

"Just follow me to the airport. Stay close."

She nodded, sliding into the driver's seat. As they drove, Byron kept glancing in his rearview mirror to check for her car behind him. She was always there. Perhaps he secretly wanted her to take off and become someone else's concern. Perhaps he wanted everything she had told him to be a lie. He wasn't ready to die, but deep inside he knew that she was telling him the truth.

Driving instead of flying back was the one thing for which he was grateful, except Hoff would be furious with him for taking a day's leave. In his email, he had explained that it was a family emergency, but he knew the 'boss' didn't care about anything other than his hotel group.

It didn't take all that long to drop his rental back at the airport, after which he took the wheel. They didn't talk much, a hushed tension between them. The airconditioning on high prevented him from experiencing the change in climate until they made a necessary stop. But the smells provided an easy differentiation between states. The distinct fishy scent of the Ohio River announced that they were nearing Pittsburg. When the trees faded into grim buildings and the skunky odor of weed touched his nostrils, he knew they had reached DC.

That night, they slept at a hotel in Charlotte. Without a companion, Byron would've driven through the night. Sleep may have been a priority on Maslow's hierarchy of needs, but not on his own.

"This is much nicer than the crummy motels I stayed at," Claire remarked as they entered the room.

It was a standard room with wreathed, brownish walls, soft white linen, a television, and a coffee station. At least they had two separate beds. His back ached from sleeping on the floor.

"Mm-hm," was all he said.

His new ally had probably noticed his attitude change since she occupied herself with her phone and a book. Stephen King. He wasn't much of a fiction reader himself, but King's books were usually not for the faint of heart.

"Listen," he looked up from his laptop, "when we get home tomorrow, you'll have to stay out of sight. Taylor, I mean Penn... she won't be as understanding as I've been."

Without lifting her eyes from the book, she said, "I know."

"Good." He continued examining Hoff's hotel numbers. They had gone up because of the Facebook and Google promotions but were still only at 80%.

"Have you got any insight into boosting a hotel's occupation rate?"

"I do."

"You wanna tell me?"

"No."

"Are you being childish?"

"Maybe."

He sighed, clenching his jaw to keep from saying something he might regret. "Why?"

"Because you're treating me like one."

That explained a lot. She expected a push-and-pull relationship. She was only 22, barely a woman, straight out of college, still innocent and naïve. She had never lived in the real world to find out that life isn't a fairytale. He truly felt like a babysitter. He wasn't in the mood to argue with the girl. Instead, he focused on the marketing strategies he had mastered.

Monday, 13 June 2022, 4 am

Byron peered over to Claire's bed. Blonde hair splayed out over the pillow. The whole room smelt like her, sweet and vanilla-y. He wanted to wake her but imagined her being a hungry lioness in the mornings. Indeed, a task one shouldn't attempt without gloves. Major corporations were a breeze, a thrill even, but this skinny girl scared him. *That makes complete sense.* He wiped the sleep from his eyes and let out a soft guffaw at the ridiculousness of the entire situation.

Postponing the lion-wrangling for a while longer, he hopped into the shower, letting the hot water seep into his taut muscles. Claire was still fast asleep when he approached. It almost felt like a sin to disturb her peace. Byron had always envied people able to cross over into the veil of deep unconsciousness.

"Claire," he said, first trying to wake her without a touch. Not even a glimpse of a movement. "Claire!" he called again, louder this time. "Get up, we have to go."

"Mmm," she mumbled without opening her eyes. "Byron, please?"

"What?"

"Please... I... you... no!"

He realized she was talking in her sleep, dreaming about him.

"Claire, wake up."

He sat down and jiggled her shoulder.

Finally, her eyes fluttered open. On instinct, he moved away, curious what the dream was about. He made a mental note to ask about it later. For now, he was in a hurry to get going.

"Morning, if you wanna shower, you'd better make it quick," he said over his shoulder.

"You mind if I have some coffee first?" she retorted.

"Get ready. I'll make the coffee."

"Is this how things will be from now on?"

He had never asked to be in this situation. He wasn't used to anyone cramping his style. "We're forced to work together. I don't like this any more than you do, but we don't have a choice."

"We have a choice. What happened to: 'I'll be your new best friend?'"

"Friend was the wrong word. Now get ready, or I'm leaving without you."

Sulking, she made her way into the bathroom and muttered, "I hate you," loud enough for him to hear.

Once they hit the highway, Byron felt some tension drain from his body. The last stretch of road was long, tedious, and never-ending. As the day began to fade, the city finally came into view. A tinge of pink mixed with the last blue of day and the early black of night. Towering buildings created a kaleidoscope of lights. It was probably the only thing he liked about the place: The scenery. And the beaches: The sultry breeze of the Atlantic and lasting fragrance of baked sand.

He welcomed the momentary lapse. His mind had been in overdrive for the past few days, ready to explode at any moment. Lately, all of his thoughts were occupied with bombs. *Explode: Burst or shatter violently and noisily as a result of rapid combustion; excessive internal pressure, or other process.* Claire never elaborated on her dream, but if she could be believed, he would explode into lifelessness.

The vision she had of Ellie on the swing was perilously close to how that scene played out in real life. Until now, he had tried to write it off as mind manipulation. He had seen the *America's Got Talent* clip in which all four judges did or thought of the exact thing the mentalist had expected of them. If Claire was a mentalist, she had boggled his brain. She was brilliant.

Byron found himself at a constant tipping point. One moment he would lean towards the she-can-see-the-future side and the next, he would try to find some logic to prove the contrary. His overactive imagination made him drive right past the entrance to his apartment building.

He turned into the mall's parking lot across the road, Claire's car would have to stay there until he could find another space. He had considered arranging for another parking but had decided it was too traceable. Life was one hell of a mess. He slammed his head against the steering wheel, causing a loud hoot to erupt. *Erupt: To burst out suddenly and explode. Get your mind off your impending death, idiot! You will surely go insane.*

Like a Mexican wave, people pivoted to follow the sound. All he could do was wave an apology in return. He wheeled into the first empty spot and pulled out his phone to check the time. The passenger door opened and before he could respond, Claire was out of the car. His eyes searched the perimeter, but he couldn't spot her. Certain she had taken her window to escape, he scrolled to Trevor's number when an abrupt knock on the window made him jump.

The face he wasn't sure he wanted to see stared back at him.

He opened.

"You know," Claire started, "I really don't have to be here. I came here to help you." Her voice was overflowing with exasperation. "Who were you calling? Trevor?"

"You know Trevor?" He raced through his memories, trying to recall whether he had let the name slip. Nothing came to mind.

"Yes, I've heard the name." *In the future, she must have meant.* Her hands formed tight fists on her hips. "I had to stretch my legs, then bent down to tie my shoelace, but you're so desperate for me to be gone, you decided I ran."

Damn, this girl. No one, except Erica, had ever spoken to him that way.

"Sorry, you're right. Assumptions are the root of all evil."

"Why won't you believe me? Why are you like this?" She relaxed slightly, but her frustration hovered.

"It's just the way I am, okay. I can't help it." He closed his eyes, exhaled, and opened the door. "Let's go."

"Where to?" She stared at the mall as if it were a mountain she would have to climb.

"To my building. You must leave your car here for now."

Claire blinked as if to say: "Excuse me?"

"I don't have another spot. Don't worry, it's safe. I'll make a plan tomorrow."

Her tense shoulders sagged slightly. "Where's your building?"

He pointed across the road. "Do you know what my apartment looks like?" Byron asked out of curiosity.

"Studio. Cold. Italian cabinetry, dark furniture. It screams wealthy bachelor."

Well, she'd hit the nail on the head. "You can sleep in my

room. I'll take the couch."

"Uh-huh."

This time she didn't argue and didn't comment. He couldn't help but feel a tad disappointed. He had become used to her witty comebacks. She didn't like the way he treated her and wouldn't have any of it. *An accomplice. A colleague. Nothing more, nothing less.* Even if she wanted to leave, she wouldn't. Claire was good-hearted and well raised. If she felt he wasn't worth saving, there were other people to think about. But she could somehow see him, the real man behind the seven layers of concrete walls, and it terrified him. The constant stress and apprehension sickened him.

They made the quick walk across the road and used the hidden side entrance. He ushered her into his bedroom, cleared some space in the closet, and fled not just from his new invader, but from everything. His shambles of a life sent him sprinting down the road and on to the beach. The crashing sound of the waves was meditative, and the briny air, familiar. Soothing.

Upon return, he found a bright, smiling Penn in the hall, about to knock on his door. "What are you doing here?"

"Sorry, I've been tracking you. Thought I'd surprise you. I brought Chinese and wine. We can work on the case."

The case. Yeah right. He didn't feel comfortable being tracked without good reason.

"You should be more careful."

Penn cocked an eyebrow in challenge. "Are you doubting my abilities?"

Not really. Penn aced phantomism. She was well-trained and lethal. "No, it's just... No." He didn't like surprises and Claire was inside.

"This isn't a good time?" she asked, her smile faltering. Her usually confident tone dithered.

"Look, Taylor, I appreciate all of this, but it's been a long weekend. I actually just wanted to shower and watch a movie or something." Only the shower part was true. "Tomorrow I'll be operating at full steam again."

"Wow, you are human," she quipped. "Hoff's freaking out."

"I know, he called. Twice. Listen, I don't think we should discuss this out here." *Women.* He clenched his jaw. Even if she was a cold-hearted spy, he had now hurt the remnants of her feelings.

"Can I watch the movie with you?"

There wasn't a way of weaseling himself out of the request. They were partners, friends in her mind. Friends occasionally watched movies together. The question wasn't inordinate, merely invasive, since he wasn't really planning to watch anything.

"Sure," he agreed, hoping Claire had overheard their conversation and made herself scarce.

Please, Claire, he willed her to hear the words, like she possessed telepathy as well. *Please stay in my room.*

Squeezing his eyes shut, he slowly opened the door. No trace of another person. Maybe Claire had been a dream.

"I'm just gonna take a quick shower. Make yourself at home," he said on his way to the bedroom. Penn had been there many times before and she knew how to help herself. When he opened the closet door, he found Claire hiding inside.

"Did you hear us? She won't come in here. You can come out."

"No," Claire shook her head. "She knocked on the door and that led me here."

Byron assumed by "here" she meant the closet. "Good thinking. Sorry about this. I know it's not ideal." Another crack in his concrete.

"It's okay. I knew what I was getting myself into."

There's no way she could know what she's getting herself into. Without a response, he reached for a pair of blue jeans and a navy Polo shirt.

After his shower, he found Penn on the couch, remote in hand. Two glasses of pinot noir brimmed on coasters atop the sleek glass coffee table. The containers were all open beside two plates and chopsticks. He didn't understand what the woman was trying to pull, but the scene reminded him of every one of those soppy romances that Erica had forced him to watch when they were younger.

"What are you in the mood for?" Penn asked.

"Maybe it's better if we just work on the case. I'm behind."

She gave him an 'Oh-really?' look. "You work every chance you get and sleep three, maximum four hours a night."

Of course, she was right, although he worked on matters unrelated to the case, too. "Yeah, but I'm agitated. I think we've been overlooking the boutique hotels."

"What makes you say that?"

Claire had revealed that little fact, but he didn't have all the data he needed to get into the detail.

"Just a gut feeling. You said yourself that he's hiding it well. It might be worth a try."

"I see. How's the occupation rate coming along?"

It was nowhere near what Hoff required it to be. "Getting there."

At least he had wormed his way out of the treacly date-like affair. They worked through one of the boutique hotel's ledgers for the last year. Nothing out of the ordinary, except rather large loans from the bigger hotels, which they were struggling to pay back. If he was the actual operations manager, he would have gone all Gordon Ramsay on them. No matter the size of the business, proper management is essential.

10

Claire

Tuesday, 8 June 2020, 6 am

Byron poked around the salad on his plate. Claire observed him from the other side of the dining table, wondering if there was a problem. "Is it the food?"

"No." He looked up. "It's work. I had to cheat to get all the hotels to 100% occupancy. There was no other way. I feel really bad about it, but I suppose a lot of companies do it."

"Sure." Claire brought her fork to her mouth and chewed. "Any advertising is cheating. They tell you you'll lose 10 pounds in two weeks, and does that ever happen?"

"Guess you're right. I've just always sworn to be the exact opposite of my father. He lies and cheats for a living." He took a large gulp of the whiskey he had poured himself.

"All lawyers do."

"No, my dad's much more complicated than that."

She turned cold inside, as if she could feel his emo-tions, then changed the subject. "Tell me about it. The cheating, I mean."

"I opened a competition for an all-expenses-paid wedding worth $50,000. To enter, couples had to book one of our venues with accommodation for their guests. Only, there won't be a winner."

When Claire opened her eyes, a cup of coffee stood next to the bed. She took a sip. Exactly the way she liked it, only cold. Byron's constant mood swings gave her whiplash. One moment he was alienating and rude, and the next, he brought her coffee in bed. Not exactly the man from her dreams.

Then again, the dream from a few nights ago didn't pan out as it was supposed to at all. She had dreamt of Penn and Byron looking into the smaller hotels, as they had the night before. Except everything was different: The scene, the details, and the discussion. Perhaps the minor details she had revealed to him had altered its course. Claire sat up and spotted a note on the nightstand that she hadn't noticed before.

Claire,

Going to gym, we have to work out the details of the letter when I get back. I wanted to discuss it last night, but you were already asleep.

B

She scrunched it into a ball and threw it against the wall. "Ugh!" Leanne and Brent had been right, her head was filled with fantasies. The reality of the situation was nowhere near pleasant. *You're saving a lot of lives here*, she reminded herself.

Claire had also dreamt about the bomb blast again. For the second time, she witnessed him dying and her heart broke. It shattered, just like Byron's would in the blast.

"Claire." Byron knocked. "Can I come in?"

Usually, she would feel self-conscious, but Byron had already seen her in all stages of waking, in sleepwear, with bedhead and swollen eyes. "Yes," she called back.

"Good, you're awake." The edges of his mouth curled up, probably pleased he didn't have to wake her.

"I read your note. Thanks for the coffee." She wasn't really thankful, though. She needed to get him on her side before she could feel any form of gratitude.

"You're welcome. I've been thinking this thing over for the last... basically since you told me, and I can't wrap my mind around it."

Claire's dexterity was letting her down. How did she get him to believe her? She didn't have any more material to build on. "I lied," she blurted.

"What?" He let out a sigh and touched his heart with relief. "Why would you do something like that? What are you after?"

"No, not about the dreams or the explosion. When you asked me before if I knew how to boost a hotel's occupation rate, I lied."

He stared at her blankly, anticipating further elaboration.

The vision wasn't that difficult to explain, and yet she couldn't find words that wouldn't leave him suspicious. "I dreamt of it last night. You cheat."

"What do you mean: 'I cheat?'"

"You told me that out of desperation, you hosted a fake

competition with no real winner."

Byron looked away, almost as if embarrassed, then squeezed some water out of the bottle onto his tongue. Lightly, he chuckled. "You really can see the future, huh?"

"That's what I've been telling you."

"That thought popped into my head this morning. Would you allow me to pull your medical records?"

Claire bit her lip, narrowed her eyes. She didn't like people poking into her business. "Only if you swear you won't tell a soul."

"I swear," he said, giving her the scout's honor sign. "Okay, so here's the plan: I think it would be best to drop the letter at reception. You must go to the mall and buy a wig and a dress. Buy it from any department store that you can find across the country. Keep your head down at all times. At all times," he reiterated. "Do you have a scarf and sunglasses?"

Claire frowned. For an investigator, his observation skills seemed oddly lacking.

"Does it look like I own a scarf?"

"Hoodie?"

"Yup."

"Good, hide your face, and look down."

She counted on her fingers. "Hide my face. Drop the letter at reception. Got it."

"I wish I could help you... "

"I'll be fine." She wasn't some helpless little girl. Even if she had never camouflaged herself, she could pull it off. The mall was the most terrifying part of all.

Byron turned to face the closet. "Oh, and one more thing: Change your usual posture."

"Okay."

"I'm gonna get ready, then I'll be out of your hair."

I'll be out of your hair. She didn't want him gone not like she needed him but being alone in his apartment was somewhat terrifying. Something she would have to get used to rapidly. "Can I get a job?" she uttered, biting into her thumbnail.

"I thought you didn't like strangers?"

"I was a barista before. I got used to my coworkers, or they got used to me. And I always wore gloves. Serving people from behind a counter was fine. I paid special attention to no-touching."

"Claire." His face appeared pained. "It's not a good idea. I'll buy you some books, or anything you can busy yourself with, but try to focus on solving the mystery."

"Sure. It was a silly idea. Can I make breakfast?"

"Yes, there's cereal. Help yourself."

Although she knew there wouldn't be any decent food, since he couldn't cook, she'd been looking forward to bacon and eggs. "Thanks," she said, heading for the kitchen.

Once Byron left, she readied herself for Operation Letter Delivery. Just as he had explained, she pulled on a pair of black skinny jeans, a T-shirt, and the only hoodie she had brought with her: A plain olive-green one. She tightened the straps around her face, secured her sunglasses, then hid the cash and letter under her clothes. As an extra, she drew a beauty mark on her right cheek, above her lip.

Her hands started trembling; a pit of doom formed in her stomach. *You've got this.* Did she, though? She activated the alarm before heading out. Focusing on her posture, Claire slumped more than usual, keeping her face down. Halfway down the stairs, she found a good rhythm. To avoid reception, she left through the hidden side door they had used the previous day.

Her legs and feet opened up into a power walk, desperate to get it over. Her heartbeat skyrocketed and beads of sweat covered her skin not only because of her nerves but the humidity, too. In her warm clothes, she stuck out like a prom queen among goths.

Even though it was a weekday, the mall was buzzing, mostly with surgically-modified housewives, kids, and tourists. She had three things to focus on: No touching, head down, and slouching posture.

Gazing around Macy's, Claire found a knee-length maternity sundress that looked exactly like something Leanne would choose: White, with big, pink floral patterns. Instead of a wig, she decided on an ostentatious sun hat. To complete the look, she bought sandals, sunglasses, a scarf, and jewelry, all from different stores. Paying was difficult. She tried her best to avoid eye contact while not seeming like a lion that had escaped from the zoo. It felt oddly satisfying to spend Byron's money after the way he had treated her.

Once the whole outfit was attained, she followed the signs to the nearest bathroom and changed. Sunny Sandra stared back at her in the mirror. Claire had used her own clothes to create a pregnant belly. It had been difficult to perfect and uncomfortable, but it was worth it. A final check revealed no more beauty spot and no hair sticking out from under the hat.

Sunny Sandra's posture would be different. She would be crying about something. Bright pink lip-gloss, rosy cheeks, and artificial bronzer enhanced her persona. Unrecognizable. *You are brilliant,* she thought with a devilish grin.

Waddling through the parking lot, Claire (or rather, Sandra) approached a group of teenagers. "Hey girls," she sniffed into a Kleenex. "You wanna make a quick hundred bucks each?" The spot seemed out of any camera's line of vision.

The girls' faces mirrored that of her own when confronted by strangers: *Our parents warned us not to talk to you.*

"You see," Claire let out a crocodile tear under her oversized Ralph Lauren sunglasses. "I think my boyfriend is cheating on me and I'm trying to trap him. I just need someone to write in the card and deliver this gift to the front desk of our apartment building. It's just across the road. But no worries, I'll find another way." She turned on her heel, pretending to leave.

"Wait!" One of them stopped her.

Through the dark lenses, she noticed their expressions change from animosity to empathy in seconds. Preppy teenage girls enjoyed nothing more than drama.

"So, we just have to hand it in at reception?" the black girl with wild hair asked.

"Yes, just tell the clerk it's for Mr. Bob Schroeder, apartment A6."

"And you say it's just across the road?" the leggy brunette confirmed.

"Yes, right there." Claire pointed to the building. "Le Luxe. You can just say that someone paid you to deliver the package."

The African American girl seemed absorbed in Claire's story. "So, what's your plan?"

"Well, if he tells me about it, he'll assume it's from me, and then he probably has nothing to hide. If he doesn't, I'll know I have something to worry about." It wasn't a foolproof plan, but a plan nonetheless.

"Why do you think he's cheating on you?"

"If you don't mind, it's rather personal." The fake tears

surfaced again.

"Is it his?" The shorter brunette gestured to her belly, braving the question she knew was on all of their lips.

"Of course." Claire rubbed a hand over her minor bump and backed away slightly to avoid any touch. "So, you'll do it?"

"Hell, yeah!" The black girl whipped her neck from left to right with attitude.

"Thanks, guys." Claire removed the still-wrapped card from the bag. "Do you have a pen?"

All three of them simultaneously opened their bags, rummaging through cosmetics and make-up.

"Got it!" The shorter one produced a fluffy, pink object that looked more like a Barbie than a pen.

Claire opened the heart-covered card with great care, focusing on not touching the contents. Everything she was about to hand over had either been touched with a Kleenex or the sleeve of her hoodie.

The girl holding the pen took it from her and placed it in on the hood of her car. "What should I write?"

"Anything. Pretend it's a boy you like."

The brunette's smile spread from ear to ear as she bounded the card with words of love and probably lust, too, given the mischievous streak in teenagers nowadays. Her friends giggled while their eyes followed the lines. Claire couldn't care less about the seductive nonsense written inside, as long as his name was on the front of that envelope in handwriting other than her own.

"Do you want to read?" She held it out to Claire.

Claire waved her hand dismissively. The girl gave her a 'too bad' shrug and brought the envelope to her tongue.

"No, don't do that!" Claire protested.

At that, their smiles gave way to frowns.

"He's got a cop friend. Just now he sends it for analysis." The girls' fingerprints were already all over the card, but Byron might be able to take care of that, saliva was a completely different story.

"Oh," they said in unison, their heads bobbing like puppets on a string.

"What's his name again?" The writer-girl asked, setting it back down.

"Bob Schroeder." The name didn't fit him. It even felt like a lie rolling off her tongue. Claire handed the gift bag to the black girl whom, she sensed, was eager to snoop. All she would find inside was aftershave, a bottle of wine, and chocolate body paint. The actual letter was tucked away at the bottom, under layers of tissue paper a precaution against prying eyes. From the front of her dress, she produced three hundred-dollar bills and paid her debt to each of them.

All three showed their disapproval at carrying money in a bra with raised eyebrows, but accepted the generous payment with: "Aaah it's not necessary," and "We just want to help you."

"A deal's a deal." Claire scooted them off. She stood at the edge of the parking lot, following their movements like a predator gauging its prey. They became pixels once they reached the doors, and she took that as her cue to disappear. After changing back into her own attire, she did some grocery shopping and hurried back to Byron's apartment.

With nothing else to do, she started writing down as many of the dreams as she could remember, trying to build them together, like a puzzle. Even the one that had since changed. Claire had no way to contact Byron to ask for permission, so she started cooking when the hunger became unbearable.

He arrived just after 7 pm.

"Claire."

"I'm right here." She looked up from the couch to see him striding inside, his laptop bag slung over one shoulder, the gift bag in the other hand.

"I cooked. Yours is in the oven."

"That feels weirdly domestic, but thanks. You don't have to cook for me. Penn and I live on take-out. She'll get suspicious if we stop our ritual." His free hand rubbed at the back of his neck. "Make whatever you like, just hide all the evidence."

Claire bit down the urge to lecture him on fast foods. "I can't imagine living like that."

"Did you do this?" He held up the gift bag.

The pride in his voice automatically switched on her smile. "Yes, I paid some teenage girls to deliver it. You might want to get rid of their fingerprints."

"You spoke to people?" Byron's neck muscles visibly tensed.

"Relax, they won't recognize me. I wore a big hat that concealed my hair, huge dark glasses, and I kept a hand in front of my face. I was pretending to cry."

"You sure?"

"Yes, oh and the best part is, I was pregnant. I didn't write the card, either."

"You watch a lot of *CSI*?"

"No, I read a lot of horrors and thrillers."

He came to sit next to her on the couch. "I took care of the footage in the building. I have access to the security cameras. No one will see you leave or come back."

"Good. So, I've been trying to make sense of my dreams." She gestured with her head to the table.

Byron ran over her notes. "Anything new?"

"Not really."

With a quick nod, he said, "I won't be home tonight. Penn and I are going on a stake-out. But keep going, this looks good." Claire couldn't hide the knock of disappointment, which must have spread to her face.

"I'm sorry, I know you must feel like a prisoner here."

"Sometimes you treat me like one."

"You were at first, but now I just have to continue living my life like nothing has changed."

It was either manipulation, or he had finally started to trust her. "What made you change your mind about me?"

"Sometimes I'm still wary, but it's you. I did a complete background check, and everything you say is true. Especially your medical records. Your parents thought you had epilepsy, right?"

"Uh-huh. It just sucks being stuck here. I wish I was with my friends on their trip to Bend."

"Your friends are going to Bend?" He appeared blown away by that information.

"Yes, why is that so weird?"

"That's where Hoff and I are going. He's branching out, diversifying. He's looking to buy a ski lodge."

Claire wrinkled her nose. "I've never had any dreams of you in Bend."

Byron let out a chuckle. "That's good news. Maybe I'm not dying after all."

"Maybe." Both of them knew that wasn't true.

That was the end of their five-minute conversation.

"I have to go. Guess I'll see you later."

Five minutes of human interaction a day would be her life

for the foreseeable future, possibly the rest of her life.

11

Byron

On his way out, Byron glanced at Claire over his shoulder. She was still in the same spot with her fingertips on her temples. He had no idea why, but the thought of leaving her to fend for herself made him uneasy. He had already learnt that she did not appreciate being idle. The smell of disinfectant was distinct as he entered the door, a clear sign she had been cleaning. Her words and reactions gave him the notion that she felt isolated and trapped. She would probably never admit it, but Claire wore her emotions on her sleeve. Or perhaps he was just highly skilled at interpreting body language.

He had decided to trust her, but not completely. The easy comfort she felt around him as opposed to other people was fascinating. At each stop they had made on the road, he had sensed her anxiety until she was in his presence. Even his hostility didn't faze her. Layer by layer, she had destroyed his barriers.

"Bye, Claire." He paused, his hand on the door handle.

"Bye, Byron. Good luck."

"Got any help for me?"

"Nope, sorry."

* * *

"Love the wig," Byron mocked Penn as she jumped into the back of the spy van parked down the road from the restaurant they were surveilling.

"Shut up," she panted, handing him a set of earphones. "You have any more news?"

"No, I guess my feeling about the boutique hotels was wrong." Claire had never claimed that there was any evidence. According to her vision, he had simply expressed the idea to his partner.

"I've got worse news, though." He handed her the gift bag.

Penn's expression morphed into one of confusion. "What's this?"

"Marlon at reception gave it to me when I got home. He said some teenage girls dropped it off. Someone apparently paid them to deliver it. At first I thought it was from you."

She peeked inside. "Black, why would you assume this is from me?"

"Really, Taylor?" He had grown tired of her little flirtations. It was time to put a stop to it. "The 'date' last night?" He air-quoted with his fingers. "The indirect hints you sometimes drop?"

She grew still and her face went blank. It was too dark to see, but there was almost certainly a deep red-rose blush to her cheeks.

"It's okay," he went on. "I get it. We spend a lot of time together. You may have mistaken some... " Unable to say the word "feelings", he instead went with, "stuff". "We can move on like nothing has happened. That's not the point anyway. Look deeper."

Her grimace grew more intense with each item she removed, until her eyes finally landed on the piece of paper in question. If she was shocked before, it was nothing compared to the fear her eyes revealed as they moved over the words. He had known Taylor Penn for quite some time and had never seen anything scare her. Until now.

"Is this legit?" she asked.

"I don't know, but someone went through a hell of a lot of trouble to get it to me."

She read it again. He had the words memorized.

```
I heard conversations between my employer and an
accomplice. Plans to attack US cities with nuclear
power. Not a hoax. Thousands of lives at stake. Be
in touch with more info soon.
```

"Why you?"

"No idea."

"Ah Denton, please sit." Hoff's voice boomed through the earphones.

"Jon, good to see you, it's been a while." Denton Bays, his trusted attorney said.

"We'll get into it later," Byron told Penn before closing his eyes to focus on the dialogue in his ear.

"Well, I guess you didn't ask me here to find out if my putting has improved." Denton joked.

Hoff snickered. "Has it?"

"Working on it."

"Good, we'll have to take on a few holes soon."

"Sure. So, why has the great Jon Hoff summoned me?"

"Attorney-client privilege, right?"

The attorney cleared his throat. "Right."

"How do I get out of giving my wife 50% of my estate if I file for divorce?"

Now it was Denton's turn to laugh. "Why did you marry her without a prenup?"

"I didn't have anything at the time and I loved her."

"Ah, there's that one word we all fear love. Look, my friend, if you can catch her cheating, the court might swing your way, but you'll have to cut your losses on this one. Florida State doesn't really care what happened during the marriage."

The conversation caused Byron to frown. He would never have used "Hoff" and "love" in the same sentence. He couldn't even imagine himself writing those two words next to each other in the report.

Denton gulped. "Why?"

"Why do all men want to divorce their wives? They become prunes who sleep with the entire city except you."

The way Hoff described his wife didn't exude the hatred Byron had been expecting. He still loved her, but she didn't reciprocate his feelings. "It's his wife," Byron declared, removing his earphones.

"What now?" Penn shot him a look.

"I know Hoff is a major jackass, but I think it's her. She made him this way."

Penn's frown deepened. "That's a little farfetched."

"Perhaps, but it's worth a look. I'll try to get him drunk this weekend and fish for information."

"Wait, you're saying it's not Hoff that's embezzling? It's her?"

"Exactly."

The crease between her brows remained as she mulled over the information. "How would she even do that?"

"You women are creative creatures." The thought of Claire with a pregnant belly came to mind.

They tended to the rest of Hoff's conversation, but as Byron had expected, it steered more towards politics and business, since they were in public. Nothing more significant. He felt a searing urgency to get home to Claire and ask her input on his theory, but he had a hanging conversation with Penn that required his attention first.

When the men left, he turned towards her. "So, the letter?"

"Yes, there's one thing telling me it's real."

"Yeah, what's that?"

"It's unspecified."

"You mean why would someone write a letter telling us nothing?" If it had convinced her in seconds, they were on the right path.

"The person that sent it knows nothing, that's why he didn't elaborate. It's a whistleblower. He hid his identity out of fear. I don't know why it was sent to you, though. Who else knows that you're an agent?"

That was the one confusing part. "Just Erica. Not even her husband."

"What about your dad?"

"Haven't spoken to him since I paid him back the last cent of my college fund."

Penn tilted her head to the side, bit her bottom lip. "He has money and resources. He could be involved. Maybe he's trying to get your attention, or…" Her right index digit pointed to the roof as if she was asking for permission to speak in class. "If you're right about Tanya Hoff, she's trying to throw us off course. She knows."

"I'm not ignoring it. I'm showing it to Trevor," he said through gritted teeth. "If this is real, it's life-or-death serious,"

"Jeez, keep your pants on, Black. Of course, you should."

Keep your cool. The situation was too close to home to botch. He had to remain impartial, yet immersed enough to assist and throw them off Claire's track. Since he wasn't working for the terrorism departments or the CIA, he would have to ask for special permission to assist with the case. "Maybe it was sent to me because the person knows of infiltrators in the Bureau?"

Penn nodded. "It's possible."

Byron took his phone out of his suit pocket and dialed their supervising agent's number. Trevor answered immediately. "Black, you got something?"

"A theory, I'll file the report just now and investigate. That's not why I'm calling."

"You guys better get a move on with this case. So, why are you calling?"

Byron took a deep breath, willing all of his muscles into relaxation. "I received a suspicious gift when I came home tonight. It was full of romantic shit, but hidden at the bottom was a letter written in cut-outs stating someone is threatening with nukes."

"You're shitting me. Bring it in. Right now."

"Yes, Sir." He hung up.

He did as instructed and told the driver of the surveillance van to transport them back to the office. His head started swimming and his palms turned sweaty. The truth and gravity of that letter was his responsibility to convey. Claire was counting on it, innocent citizens were counting it, he was counting on it. They had to buy it. If he had the skills and equipment, he would investigate the threat himself, but there was no way he would be able to pull it off.

They walked through the sliding doors of the elegant building. On the outside Byron appeared detached, a man reporting information to his boss. Inwardly, he was certain his blood pressure had reached an all-time high and he felt a migraine starting at the back of his neck.

"Let's see it." Special Agent Trevor waved them in, unhooking his reading glasses.

Byron placed the package on the desk. His superior slipped on a set of rubber gloves before grabbing the card at the top. "You read this, Black?"

"Yes, Sir."

"Wish someone would send me a card like this." The fully grey 50-something old smirked and tossed it to the side, producing some quiet laughter in the room. One by one he removed and scrutinized each item.

"This says nothing," he concluded after reading the note four or five times.

Byron bit his lip. He wanted to scream the importance of it and force them to take action. Instead, he remained silent and waited for Agent Trevor to speak again.

"Penn, you get this analyzed." He pushed all the contents towards her. "Black, tell me everything."

"Yes, Sir," Penn said, collecting the evidence with gloved

hands.

"I went home to get a few things for the stake-out," Byron started. "I got off the elevator and greeted Marlon, like any other day, then he called me back and said that some teenage girls had been asked to deliver this gift for me. Apparently it's from a secret admirer."

"Uh-huh, you have secret admirers?"

Byron huffed. "Not that I know of. I hardly ever go out or talk to any girls."

Trevor's nod was unconvinced. "You talk to boys perhaps? Anyone in your building or at the office maybe?"

"I pay no attention to flirting, Sir. I don't have the time or place for that in my life." He swallowed hard since his next words were a betrayal of his partner. "Penn, she has been sending me some signals. When I first opened it, I thought it was from her."

His superior pursed his lips, with a popping sound, he said, "It happens often in our line of work, when people spend a lot of time in each other's presence. I doubt it's her."

"So do I. I really think this is legit. Penn and I both considered a whistleblower."

Byron studied Trevor's face, but it revealed nothing. He seemed utterly unfazed by it.

"File a report," Trevor continued. "Include everyone you can think of who might want to get your attention. I think your cover might be compromised and they're trying to throw you off." He removed his glasses and chewed on one end, deep in thought. "For now, you'll remain on the case. If we find any evidence to prove my suspicion, you'll be taken off immediately. Be more careful, watch your back every step of the way. I know you already work around the clock, but now you'll have to work smarter. Due to this glitch, you have only one week to solve this case."

"Yes, Sir," he nodded. "Are you going to investigate the threat? I would like to assist where I can."

"Terrorism units constantly monitor all other countries with nuclear power. We have people on the inside. I'll put out word of the letter, but we look out for these things all the time. When the people with power can't contain themselves on social media, then we get involved."

The answer did not instill any peace of mind. In fact, it left Byron feeling cold and empty. *I'm dead.* The realization pounced like a silent attacker at night. It had been on his mind since the words left Claire's mouth, but for the first time, it felt true. *I'm dead.* It was a moment of clarity and he felt the desire to pray, even though he had never been religious.

Trevor didn't wait for a response. "We will investigate the source, though." It sounded like a threat and Byron sensed he may have been an open book. "You'll have to help with that."

"Of course, Sir."

"One week, Agent Black."

"One week, Sir." He left the office and found Penn waiting for him outside.

"And?" She fell into step beside him.

His headache evolved at a rapid pace. "They'll investigate the source. He thinks I'm being stalked."

"So, he doesn't deem it to be real?" Penn stated the obvious.

"Not from what I can gather. He said we have one week to finalize the case."

"Shit." Worry crossed her face for a moment before she composed herself. "We can pull it off."

"Uh-huh," he agreed, knowing the case was the least of

his worries. Byron closed his eyes, sighed, and bumped into someone. When he looked up, he didn't recognize the object of his clumsiness. "Sorry, didn't see you there."

"Agent Black, right?" said the Asian man, Indian perhaps, as he held out a hand. "I'm Nakul Kaur, or just Kaur if you prefer."

Byron shook the man's hand with as much enthusiasm as the situation allowed. He could be a rookie agent or from another department. "Nice to meet you."

Penn paid Kaur no attention. "We'll start tonight. Meet you at your place?"

"Sure." Any other answer would have been frowned upon, and he wished for a way to contact Claire to give her a heads-up.

12

Claire

Tuesday, 14 June 2022, 11 pm

Claire had nodded off while watching an architecture show on Netflix. A quarrel at the front door woke her. A female voice spiked a rush of adrenaline, prompting her to shut off the TV and crawl to the sliding door in seconds. Byron stalled, gave her time to slip out on to the balcony. Once outside and in the clear, her latest dream returned.

> *"Dad," Byron answered the phone. "I thought I made it clear we have nothing more to say to each other."*
>
> *She could only hear Byron's side of the discussion.*
>
> *"How do you know?"*
>
> *"What?"*
>
> *"I don't care."*
>
> *"She's nothing to me."*
>
> *"I said I don't care. Bye." He ended the call.*
>
> *"What was that all about?" Claire asked.*
>
> *"It was my dad. My mom, she came back because she's dying," he said as if updating Claire on the current*

basketball score.

"Oh. I'm so sorry."

"I don't have a mother," he hissed.

"Byron," Claire looked down, not sure whether she was crossing some boundary. "Maybe this is your chance at closure. You should go see her before it's too late. Confront her."

"She'll just give me some sugarcoated version of the truth."

"If you don't, you'll regret it." She hugged him. "I'm really sorry."

"You're right. Will you come with me?"

"Where else would I go?"

Penn's booming voice brought Claire back from her reverie. "This place reeks of disinfectant."

"The cleaning service was here today."

"Well, they did a damn good job."

Claire couldn't help the feeling of pride. She deserved the credit for that statement. With not much else to do, she swept and scrubbed until it shone. Through the tiny opening in the curtain, she noticed Byron pinching the bridge of his nose. "Taylor," she heard him say, but the rest was inaudible.

Penn's head snapped in his direction. "You okay?"

His lips moved, yet she couldn't make out the words. Penn wheeled him toward the couch to sit down. A fusion of jealousy and concern overcame Claire as she watched the woman scurry towards the kitchen in search of medicine, she supposed. He didn't look good. He was as pale as winter in Oregon and sweat glistened on his forehead. Penn handed him tablets and some water before checking his temperature.

"No fever," she said. The whole sentence was blurry, except for the word "ER."

"No!" Byron objected.

The effort of drowning out the cicadas and other city buzzes was futile when they spoke in low tones. Penn sat down next to him. They were having a serious conversation of which she only caught a word or two. As Claire watched, she was losing an internal battle between running inside to take care of him and staying put.

The next moment Penn picked a strand of blonde hair from the couch cushion. "Uh, Byron... Girl over?"

Shit. Claire felt the life drain from her. Her knees numbed, causing her feet to shuffle.

"You hear that?" Penn's head twisted in her direction.

"No," Byron replied. "Probably a cat. They're here all the time."

Unfortunately, Penn wasn't that easily dissuaded. "I'll just have a look. You know, stalker and all."

Claire's heart hammered. She stepped away from the window and stood with her back against the wall. It wasn't a good cover in the slightest, but she didn't have any other option. Jumping down would cause even more mayhem. The woman came closer, her hand on the lever.

"Taylor," Byron's voice came through the glass. "I think I'm gonna be sick."

Thank you, Byron. Claire finally managed to breathe when the footsteps turned around. Her ears were attuned to the movements inside. As soon as they were both in the guest bathroom, she squeezed through a narrow opening in the door and skulked to the bedroom. Fear of being caught prompted her to hide in the shower. Even her best attempts at being strong couldn't fend off the tears that threatened her eyes.

After a few minutes of peace, she heard the bedroom door open, then the closet doors squeaked.

"Byron," Penn said sympathetically.

"Do you mind? I'm getting dressed." The closet doors slammed shut.

"Sorry, I just... I was worried."

"It's okay, thanks for helping. I'm just gonna call it a night."

"Yeah, sure. You want me to stay?" The hope emanating from Penn's voice made Claire uncomfortable.

"Taylor, we've talked about this." There was a resounding silence for a few moments before Byron spoke again. "After this case, I think we should switch partners."

"I didn't mean it like that."

"Yes, you did. Look, I understand, you and I, we make a good team. You're a brilliant cop, smart, attentive, and strong..."

Penn didn't allow him to finish. "But there's someone else."

Claire's neck went stiff and she could imagine the expression on Byron's face when he said, "Excuse me?"

"I'm a smart, attentive cop, right? That blonde hair, that's not the cleaner's. This room smells like a woman, I caught a glimpse of the clothes before you shut the closet door and there was actual food in your fridge. So, where is she?"

Claire Baxter, you idiot! She fought an impulse to bang her head against the shower wall.

"I would like to keep my private life private," Byron insisted.

"Fine." The bedroom door creaked. "I'll see you tomorrow. I know my way out."

Claire gave Penn a moment to leave before she braved the bedroom. Byron groaned when she entered, his head cradled in his hands.

"I'm so sorry," she whispered.

"It's not your fault," he said in an aloof 'it-is-your-fault' kind of way. "She stuck her nose in where it doesn't belong."

"Are you feeling better?"

"No, I'm going to sleep." He yanked a shirt over his head and escaped.

Claire decided to let him be. The news about his mother's impending death would have to wait. She crawled under the sheets and picked up her phone, anxious to speak to a familiar voice.

The phone barely rang. "Finally, how are you? We've been worried sick!" Leanne's eagerness was welcoming.

The tears Claire had been trying to contain found their way to the surface.

"Oh, honey, what's wrong?" Leanne asked.

"Everything's a mess," she lamented.

"Claire, calm down, tell me everything."

"I can't."

"Breath, hun. In and out, in and out."

Claire followed her friend's prompts until she was able to form a sentence.

"How are you guys?"

"We're good, all packed and ready to go. It won't be the same without you, though. You okay?"

"I'm with Byron. He's taking care of me. I'm fine, mostly."

"Is he like your dreams?"

"A little more serious. He can be quite an asshole, actually. We're working together on a plan." She purposely omitted the adversities she was facing, but her sobs had already given those away. "He's going to Bend this weekend, too.

"Are you coming with him? Maybe we could meet up?"

The idea had never crossed her mind. "I'll ask him. That would be great."

"Oh, does he cut your meat now, too?"

"No, L, but I can't do whatever I want. We have to st..." A clamorous sound of breaking glass interrupted her. "Sorry, have to go. Love you, bye."

Claire peeped out the door, still nervous about Penn's presence. When she noticed an empty hallway, she crept to the sitting room. "Byron," she murmured. No response. "Byron." His motionless body on the kitchen floor came into view. "Byron!"

She rushed forward and knelt beside him. He was surrounded by shattered glass and liquid that smelt potently of alcohol.

"Byron, wake up!" She slapped his cheeks. If it wasn't for the short rise and falls of his chest, Claire would have assumed him dead.

From the nearest counter, she grabbed a cloth and dampened it.

"Please, please, please, wake up!" With vehemence, she pushed the wet rag against his soaked skin. When that didn't work, she pulled a glass from the cupboard, filled it with water, and splashed it onto his face.

His eyes slowly flickered to life, prompting a relieved laugh from her lungs. "What happened?"

"Huh?"

"I think you fainted."

"I'm fine." He struggled to sit up.

"Here, let me help you to the couch." With his support, she was able to move him. He was too heavy for her scrawny arms alone.

"Would you mind getting me something dry to wear?"

Claire returned with some sleep shorts and a T-shirt. "Thanks." He took the clothes from her. "Go to bed, I'm okay now."

Claire's exasperation, which had been bubbling under the surface, eventually burst into flames. "No! You can't go on like this. You eat unhealthy food, you barely sleep, you work day and night, you were just about to mix alcohol with medicine, and you keep pushing me away."

"We have neighbors, you know." His face was stern and his nostrils flared. "And I heard you. I'm an asshole, right? Why do you care? Turns out I won't be able to save those people after all. Trevor didn't take the letter seriously."

At that, everything clicked into place. "If we have to save them ourselves, then so be it."

"We can't."

"We have my dreams, which is a helluva lot more than they do. Look at me." She turned his face towards hers. "I. Won't. Let. You. Die. Even if you are an asshole."

A faltering smile traced his lips. "I'm sorry, you don't deserve that."

"Damn right I don't. I gave up everything to be here, to save you and everyone else, and I won't allow that to be in vain."

He turned to look away. "How do you do that?"

"What?"

"Get me to believe you so easily?"

The answer was simple. "I feel like I know you from my dreams."

"You can't come to Bend with me." He had definitely been eavesdropping on her conversation. "We're flying in Hoff's private jet."

"You're flying again?"

The smile that had now reached his eyes made him seem vulnerable and human. "Sometimes, when you speak, it's like you're my narrator. I don't like flying, no, but I have to."

"I'll miss you." The words just slipped out.

"Go to bed, Claire," Byron ordered. "I'll clean up in the morning."

13

Byron

Saturday, 18 June 2022, 12 pm

Despite Claire's evil eye, Byron had been working on the case non-stop. Trevor had only given him one more week and failure didn't exist in his universe. His prick of a father had made sure of that. He was certain of one thing: Tanya Hoff was a greedy fraud who lived in the limelight of her husband's success. She had it all: Timeless beauty, three decent kids, mansions, cars, elite friends, and countless charities. Why anyone would want more than that was puzzling. She was a heartless black widow with no shard of care for the victims she claimed. Especially not her husband.

Penn's clever spying tactics had revealed the truth of Tanya's infidelities. The only thing still a mystery was the embezzlement. Byron knew it to be true, but he hadn't stumbled upon the proof, and he only had three more days until the case would be shut down.

At least one of his to-do list entries had been ticked off. Claire had helped him set up the competition. No pride came from the deceitful way in which they achieved 100%

occupancy, but he was desperate to gain Hoff's trust to help solve the case.

To win the prize, participants had to share the hotel group's social media pages, then book one of their venues and accommodation. Regrettably, the winner would be a fake profile that Claire had created herself. If Hoff was willing to grant an actual reward, it could have been a great concept.

Other areas of his life were still grim: No news on the nuclear front from either Trevor or Claire. The Bureau was frantically searching for the source of the package. As far as his knowledge stretched, they hadn't made a move to inform intelligence agencies or to tighten the missile defense system. Typical. Search for the 'who' and not the 'what', when more often the 'what' would lead to the 'who'. They had questioned Marlon and analyzed the contents, but so far nothing had turned up. Even if they were to find the delivery girls, Claire assured him they wouldn't be able to trace it back to her.

At least Penn was still Penn less the subtle affections. He had been expecting a Harley Quinn situation, since hell hath no fury like a woman scorned, but she was a professional, unaffected by her personal life.

The car swerved on to a gravel road that led to the lodge, surrounded by crystal-clear blue lakes, vast, white mountain ranges, and furry greens. Weather services had predicted an overcast day, but the sky was a soft blue, patched with clouds. It was cold, though, even for summer, not at all the heat to which he had grown accustomed over the past couple of weeks.

"You're awfully quiet," Hoff remarked.

"Just tired, I guess."

"Your hard work paid off. That sneaky tactic of yours exceeded even my expectations."

"Thank you, Sir."

"Please, call me Jon."

Byron nodded and smiled. It was exactly the type of relationship he required.

At the lodge, the current owners greeted them warmly. Byron peered around the lobby: The furniture, floors, trusses, and panes were all wooden, studiously crafted, with large windows, fiery maroon walls, and a hefty stone fireplace in the middle of the room. He couldn't ignore the at-home feeling.

Once they settled into their respective rooms, he opened the blinds and was met by tall pine trees and a fresh, earthy breeze. Byron grinned. He wouldn't mind spending his last days right there. With alternative company, of course. He'd want to be surrounded by his sister's incessant chatter, his nieces' giggles, and Claire's strength.

He had finally arrived at a place where he outright trusted Claire. She was eager and willing to help with everything. *She's hiding something, though.* He wiped a hand over his face. *But she has to tell me.*

He needed to check in with her. To dodge another mishap, he had bought them each a burner phone, which was meant only for communication with the other.

Byron: Hey, we've arrived. How are you? Any news? You should see this place. It's extraordinary.

Claire: I know. I'm from there, remember? Glad you're safe. Nothing new.

Byron: No, you stayed in Portland and Eugene, not Bend. There's a difference. Keep me posted.

Claire: (Eye-roll emoji). Will do. Have fun.

There was a knock at the door. He hid the phone before crossing the room to answer.

"Hope I'm not interrupting," Hoff said as Byron opened. "Russel has invited us to a local restaurant tonight. He wants to show us all the gems this place has to offer."

Byron chuckled. "Of course, he does, but if you're not buying it, I might."

Hoff nodded with a lopsided grin. "Let's first find out if the investment is as awesome as the beauty."

He already knew it was. Before the trip, Byron had done a detailed analysis of the turnover, profit margins, and growth of the lodge. The death of the main shareholder was the only reason they wanted to sell. His son, Russel, and the late shareholder's wife had no interest in continuing the business. The only thing left to do was convince them to lower their price. But unless Claire figured out the origins of those bombs, Byron's in-depth investigation would be in vain.

"Should I meet you in the lobby?" Byron asked. "What time?"

"At 6 pm. Wear something casual. Apparently, there's a local band playing."

Perfect, Byron thought. That would give him the opportunity to loosen Hoff's lips about Tanya. "See you then." He closed the door. It was time to get ready.

* * *

The restaurant's interior was very much the same as that of the lodge: Cozy with dimmed lighting, yet lively with excitement for the band. His stomach announced its hunger when he picked up the inviting smell of fresh-baked pizza.

Russel and Heather, his mother, were already seated at a reserved table as they approached. Both stood to greet them. Something about Russel made Byron wary. He was dressed down, no longer wearing the same Armani suit as earlier. His bald head gleamed and his dark eyes radiated malice. Since Claire came into his life, he had re-evaluated his mistrusting nature, but this guy raised his arm hair.

Heather seemed amiable. Her reason for selling was clear: She wanted to travel, and the place reminded her too much of her late husband. She brushed a lock of silver hair from her face a face that didn't belong to her age.

Byron slid a blue folder across the table. "I did a valuation of my own, based on the financial information you sent. We believe the price you're asking is way too high." Wasting time with small talk wasn't in his nature. He pushed straight to business.

Russel opened it and surveyed the pages. "I understand, but this is based on historical information. Our current data shows a steep incline in bookings."

"Sure, I get that," Hoff interrupted in his usual, careful business demeanor. "But unfortunately, we cannot place value on uncorroborated figures."

"You're welcome to take a look at the current books," Russell countered with a sly smile.

"It's unaudited," Byron reminded him.

Heather leaned forward. "Mr. Schroeder, I can see you are someone who does your homework. You seem like a good and honest person. I can assure you our current staff is of the same caliber. We handpick them from the most elite the workforce has to offer after extensive background checks."

It's not your workers I'm worried about, it's your son. "With all due respect, Ma'am, we cannot take your word for it. We require some sort of verification. The growth you've shown for the current year is considerably higher than previous years and, although not impossible, it's unlikely."

Byron wasn't sure whether he imagined a flicker of acknowledgment in her eyes. Perhaps she wasn't as oblivious to Russel's shenanigans as he had imagined. The conversation continued like a tennis match, both parties reluctant to back down. Eventually, Russel suggested they take the next few days meaning the length of the itinerary to decide. He did not hesitate to add that they needed an answer soon because he had other interested buyers.

Heather excused herself, saying her ears were too old for the loud music that was about to commence. Russel stayed for a while, until some supermodel-type blondes lured him away. Once he and Hoff were alone, he took his gap. "Another round?"

"Sure," Hoff agreed. "It's not every day we get to mix business with pleasure."

"How about a shot to celebrate?"

"Well, you sure deserve one. Your determination with the meeting, and everything else..." He threw his arms in the air. "Ah, what the hell, let's do it!"

Byron smiled. The waiter returned with their drinks. "Here's to you and a long career at the Losier Hotel Group." Hoff toasted.

"Sir."

"A-ah." Hoff rejected the use of the word 'Sir'. He motioned for Byron to raise his glass.

"Sorry, Jon. I can't take all the credit." Some of it had to go to Penn and Claire, but 'the boss' couldn't know that.

"Modesty is never the best policy. Now drink."

"I only did my job, but thank you." Byron drank the tequila, then spat the alcohol back into his almost empty craft beer bottle. He had to be on high alert for this conversation. Pretending to read a message, he opened the voice recorder on his phone.

"Holy cow!" A girl to his left yelled. "Byron?"

He instantly recognized her as Leanne. Claire had shown him pictures of her friends. Byron gave her a stern look, trying to convey a message. Undeterred, she came closer.

"Sorry," he said. "You must have the wrong person. I'm Bob Schroeder." He held out his hand in greeting.

The girl gave him a once-over and a knowing look crossed her face. She shook his hand. "My mistake. Leanne Sanchez."

"No problem." He smiled and whispered, "Come find me later."

Hoff must have interpreted the interaction as flirting. When Byron turned back, his head bobbed with pride. "She's pretty."

"I guess," he shrugged.

"You can be a little more enthusiastic. Unless you're not into girls."

It was the second time someone had questioned whether he was gay. "I'm into girls."

Before he could elaborate, Hoff held up his hands in apology. "Nowadays, you never know. Usually, I would commend your dedication to your work, but sometimes we have to let go. And that girl is someone with whom you can let go!"

"Well, I learn from the best. You seem to be married to your work, too. Does that not bother your wife?" His boss turned his head away. "Sorry, I didn't mean to pry. It's none of my business."

"No, that's okay. My wife has her own life. I think she prefers it that way."

The conversation was headed exactly where Byron had hoped. "Really? Actually, there's a girl at home. I've been neglecting her too. I'm starting to think you can only have a career or a love life, not both."

A flash of sympathy crossed the older man's face. "You may be right. Like the old saying goes: Money can't buy happiness. Now, we make the money and they get happiness and it's usually with someone else. Do you love her?"

"Very much. I just can't seem to keep both balls in the air." The way Byron delivered the line made him consider the notion that he could have had a successful acting career. He had never experienced romantic love, but still a believable amount of emotion and regret filled his voice.

"Make a choice, my friend. Our lives revolve around our work. So, either love her or love your work and take girls like that Latina home once in a while. Otherwise, you'll find yourself in my situation soon." Hoff's egotism surfaced. Even though Byron had deduced he may not be responsible for the embezzlement, he was still awful.

Byron furrowed his brow, playing along. "What situation?"

"We'll need another shot for this conversation." Hoff waved the waiter over to their table. He ordered two more tequilas and another round of drinks. "Money changes people. It changed my wife. Now I can't get rid of her without giving her half of what I own."

"You don't love her anymore?" Byron watched as the gold

liquid slid from the shot glass down his boss's throat.

"I still love the person she used to be. Rarely, she appears, but I'm just a bank and an image to her. The group funds all of her charities. She feigns a happy family for publicity and lives a life of single leisure behind closed doors."

The revelations grew in direct proportion to the amount of alcohol consumed. Byron learned that Tanya was blackmailing him with undisclosed information. Before Hoff called it a night, Byron had a lot more details than before. He sent the recording to Penn, asking her to investigate. Not for lack of trying, he couldn't avoid all the liquor which the older man had loaded their table with.

He found himself in a slightly drunken haze as he caught Leanne's eye on the restaurant's impromptu dance floor. She waited for his nod before making her way towards him with her two friends in tow. Taking a seat next to him, she asked, "How is she?"

"She's good. Been a major help."

The brunette had a murderous glint in her eye as she spat, "What? Now you're using her for information."

Even if he wanted to deny it, there was a certain truth to her accusation. "Not exactly. We're partners."

Before she could continue, the Asian boy, Brent, held his hand up to stop her and cut in. "Calm down, Leanne. He by no means kidnapped her, this was Claire's choice." He turned to face Byron. "Any advancement on the bombs?"

"Unfortunately, not. As soon as we solve this case, we can focus more on that. She is really well. A little lonely and homesick perhaps." Whether she was happy, he couldn't be sure, but he refused to let her go not only because of her special abilities but also the hope and the strength she offered him when he called 'game over'.

"The Bureau thinks it's a hoax. They won't give the warning the time of day. So, I need her."

Claire's three friends stared at him and he wasn't sure why. Leanne stood to leave. "Take care of her." Her words were suddenly tender.

"I will, I promise. By the way, how'd you recognize me?"

The tall, blonde guy, Ted, smirked. "Clairy does not only draw bridges and buildings." He winked.

It took a moment for the realization to settle in. "You recognized me from a drawing?"

"Several actually," Brent concurred. "Claire, she's, umm, a little obsessed with you." This resulted in a hard slap on the shoulder from Leanne. "Sorry, but it's true."

"That's okay, she told me everything herself. Except about the pictures." Byron slapped his hands on his thighs. "Well, I better call a cab."

They said goodbye and returned to their fun while he made his way back to the lodge. In the back of the cab, a terrifying idea bombarded his mind. As soon as he reached the room, he called Claire the time difference be damned.

"Hello," her voice came over the speaker in a throaty croak.

"Hey, it's me. Sorry for waking you, but I needed to tell you that I met your friends."

"At four in the morning?" A bite in her voice, but not entirely unfriendly.

He laughed. "Actually, I didn't expect you to wake up. Not even a bomb can wake you."

"Funny," she mocked. "How are they?"

"I think they miss you." The next words at the back of his throat struggled to make it to his lips. "I, uh... Do you... Do you wanna come home? We can still talk on the phone, it will be harder but, you know, we're all good now. We have an agreement and can sort the bombs out remotely."

"You want me to go? If you want your bed back, I can sleep on the couch."

The disappointment in her voice spurred a relieved exhalation from his lungs. She didn't want to leave. "No, no, not at all. I just thought maybe you'd want to leave. And you can keep the bed. I'm good on the couch."

"Okay." Her relief was audible. "Going back to sleep now. Bye, Byron."

"Bye, Claire." He ended the call and crawled into bed, unwilling to admit that he dreaded the day when they would part ways, even if by death. It was inevitable.

14

Penn

Sunday, 19 June 2022, 4 am

Taylor Penn looked at the message from her partner. It was the drunken conversation he had planned for Hoff. Something had been off about him since the visit to his sister's home. After spending most of their time together for months, she had learned to read him; she had studied him intently. Her first concern was that he had driven back home and slept over at a hotel. At the time, she'd thought nothing of it. He wasn't up to flying again, had grown tired on the road, and needed sleep. Now, a lot of things didn't stack up.

When she had contacted the hotel, claiming to be his PA, Penn had learned that the booking was for a double room. Surely, if he had brought the girlfriend back with him, they would have shared a bed. But there was undoubtedly someone either living with him or spending time with him. He also worked a lot more on his own at home. His sister's presence in Williamsville disproved the notion that she was his tenant. Byron Black had no other familial relationships, as far as she knew. Then there was the letter and his response to it.

DNA tests on the parcel had come up blank, but Penn had video footage of the girls in the foyer. They were mere pawns in the game, but still worth questioning.

"Sir," Penn peeked into Agent Trevor's office upon finding the light still on. It wasn't odd for any agent to work this late or early on occasion. "Do you have a minute?"

He looked up, pleased to see her. "Sure, what's this about?"

"It's about Agent Black. I think he's hiding something." She stepped inside. Deceiving Byron was as odd as snow in July.

"Uh-huh. And you want permission to investigate him? Only, you already have." Her superior was always one step ahead. "May I ask why, Penn?"

"Certain things about him don't add up. I could be wrong, but I rarely am."

He leaned forward with an intimidating stare. Actually, all of his stares were intimidating, as if he could read your mind. "Did you send the package?"

Penn scoffed in disbelief. "Excuse me?"

"It has come to my attention that there might be more than a professional relationship between you two."

Without wavering, she looked him straight in the eye. If honesty was what he needed in order to grant her the permission she sought, she would gladly comply. "My feelings may have overstepped their bounds, but I never acted on them. Our relationship remains professional. I did not send the letter, nor is it a reason for my request."

Agent Trevor nodded, seemingly pleased with her response. "Good. Send me a report with the proof you have gained to date. If I deem it reasonable, you may proceed."

"Thank you, Sir. On the other case, we're making good

headway. Black just sent me a recording of his conversation with Hoff."

"Good. You have two more days. Now go home and get some rest." He cocked his head in the direction of the door with a hint of a smile.

Gnawed by guilt, she drove home. As she passed Byron's apartment, a shallow glow, like a bedside lamp, came from the bedroom. *Who's living with him?* Even his mood had changed inexplicably. One day he appeared more upbeat, and the next, he seemed strained. He was no longer the permanently miserable, brooding workhorse she knew.

Back at home, Penn slipped under the sheets. She didn't know why Trevor had questioned their relationship, but the most likely answer was that Byron had informed him. He was wrong, though. He mistook her attempts at friendship for something more. Perhaps it was more. Byron seemed as screwed up as she was, perhaps her mind had ventured into emotional territory. It was a disaster. She had needed a friend, or just a person in general, and he was good to her. If she was completely honest with herself, perhaps an intimate courthouse wedding and a life surrounded by take-out containers and thrilling case details was the logical next step.

Relationships, in general, were not her forte. All of her life, she had meant nothing to her parents but an aid to their next fix. The foster homes were no different, and the only way she had survived after she'd run away was to use what her parents had taught her. Even Detective Tanner, who had helped her out of trouble, died shortly after rescuing Penn from the streets. No one had ever cared about her in the way Byron seemed to care, but apparently she had misconstrued that, too.

The trip down memory lane made her skin itch. Sentiments and emotions were for fools. Humans disappointed it was the only thing at which they excelled. She pressed play on the recording to distract her mind from the wrong turn it had taken.

Byron played his part well, yet there was a solemnity to his acting that she couldn't deny. Alcohol had loosened the tight bolts on a lot of secrets, yet there was nothing incriminating. One thing stood out: A girl called Leanne Sanchez recognized him as Byron. It could be an old college friend or someone insignificant. Still worth a snoop.

* * *

Monday, 20 June 2022, 7 am

When she got into the office, Penn focused on the more time-sensitive case, although her fingers burnt with the desire to continue her search for the Latin-American woman from the recording. She assessed every charity that the Losier Hotel Group funded, looking for any inconsistencies.

The letter "B" flitted across the screen when Byron called. To avoid anyone overhearing, she hid in Hoff's empty office. "Hey," she answered. "How's your holiday?"

"Well, this place is great. Wish I was on holiday. Listen, you found anything yet?"

"No," she sighed. "I mean apart from the fact that we donate a lot, nothing seems out of the ordinary."

Her partner barely gave her time to finish before he responded with a whisper, "I need you to check out an NPO in Africa called the Thuto Foundation."

Penn frowned. She didn't recognize the name. "Why? I don't think it's one of the charities on the list. What gave you that idea?"

"It doesn't matter. Just do it, please."

Another glitch in his behavior: Pretending to be busy while hiding significant information. "Okay," she agreed politely, to avoid putting him on the alert.

"Thanks. Let me know what you find."

"Will do. Bye."

Penn returned to her desk and started a search for the foundation he mentioned. She found an amateur website which explained that their main function was education support activities (in collaboration with iDream) to underprivileged kids. It listed two main donors, an email address as a contact, and nothing else. When that led to a wall, Penn searched for the non-profit company's details on the Bureau's company database, which verified that it was registered in South Africa, with three directors. One of the names, Benjamin Duminy, switched on a pale light in her mind.

She sat back in her chair, a pen between her teeth. *Where have I heard that name before?* The FBI had no file on him, so she turned to social media. Four LinkedIn profiles popped up, three with photos she didn't recognize. Seemingly, it wasn't a popular name because there was only one Facebook profile that matched one of the three she had found on LinkedIn.

When the online search proved a fruitless effort, Penn scanned all of her reports on the case. "Bingo," she whispered, spotting the name. He was one of Tanya Hoff's friends. They had met the previous day while she was undercover at a charity event. The information established a connection, but there was no proof of fraud. Yet.

Before typing an email to her team, she searched for iDream. She discovered that it was an American corporation that provided psychometric testing to large companies and university and school students. It supposedly tested personality; modalities; aptitudes; interests; and environmental needs to develop learning modules, study techniques, and ADD/ADHD assistance, among others.

To: agentbblack@fbi.gov.us; agentbtrevor@fbi.gov.us

Subject: Case update

Good day,

I have established a link between Tanya Hoff and one of the African recipients of her donations. Benjamin Duminy, who was more than cozy with her at the Trinity fundraiser. He is one of the three directors of the Thuto Foundation. This organization provides education support to underprivileged children, in collaboration with iDream.

Right now, it's not much, but I would need company records and documentation for further investigation. Would it be possible to obtain a search warrant or subpoena to secure such data as soon as possible?

Regards,

Penn

While waiting for feedback, Penn sated her earlier curiosity by searching for Leanne Sanchez. Unfortunately, there were a lot of people with that name in the world. She carefully surveyed every Facebook profile, narrowing down her search one by one. Some profiles weren't public, but the education or employment information and a few photographs were visible. The girl on the recording had an American accent, which ruled out any foreigners, and she whittled the list down to three.

Feeling smug, Penn tapped the pen on her desk. *What're you up to, Black?* Then her pseudo-boss called, bursting her haughty bubble with banal duties. At his request, she drew the financial reports and sent them to him, shifted two meetings, and responded to unimportant emails. *Only a few more days,* she told herself. They couldn't pass soon enough.

15

Claire

Monday, 20 June 2022, 11 am

All around the world, people were starving without shelter or education, which is why Claire scolded herself for her own self-pity about her isolation and boredom. It was the midwife to all evil, her mother always said. In the pit of her stomach, a weed of uncertainty sprouted bigger and stronger each day. She often found herself feeling like a bundle of nerves and starved for human contact. Not physical, obviously. Even when Byron was in Miami, he was always working. He had told her to limit her phone calls, just in case. This was pushing her rapidly toward hermit status.

With Byron nearby, her dreams of the case had been increasing, but they contained nothing more on the bombs. Prayers and yoga were the only answer to all her current qualms. They had become her companion, her relaxant, and inspiration. Every time Claire felt the enamel around her teeth grinding away, she turned to the downward dog on YouTube. Never had she given the meditative exercise much thought, but desperate times called for desperate measures and she now enjoyed the serenity of it.

The standard ringtone on her burner phone announced Byron's call. Without a second thought, she disrupted her plank stance and almost tumbled to the ground, trying to pause the video.

"Hi," she answered, out of breath.

"Hey, how are you?" he asked in his usual pared tone.

"Well, you know. Alone. Bored."

"Claire," he sighed.

"Yeah, I know." It wasn't all his fault. He had given her the opportunity to return home, but she knew that then they wouldn't get much done and it might hinder the current flood of dreams. "So, why are you calling?"

"Just checking up."

"No, you're not." Byron never called to make small talk. "You wanna know more about the dream. What did you find out?"

"I just received an email from Penn. The foundation you dreamt of is spot on. One of the directors is also Tanya's lover. So, there's a connection."

Claire didn't allow him to finish the sentence. "But you still don't know how they're embezzling. Am I getting paid for all the work I do?"

"I pay you. You get a place to stay and everything you need. Come on, Claire, this is serious and you're acting like a spoilt little brat."

She bowed her head in shame. "Yeah, I know. I'm just feeling sorry for myself. What do you need?"

"The Thuto Foundation collaborates with iDream. Does that ring any bells?"

Claire scratched her head, unsure if she could be of any

help. "No, but like I told you, I only caught a word or two of your conversation with Penn in my dream, since I was eavesdropping."

"I know, but it was worth a shot. We're waiting for a subpoena to get both companies' records. They are tending to it urgently. Even so, it might take a while."

"I'll see what I can do."

"Thank you." His voice turned sympathetic.

"Don't thank me yet."

"Just in general. For all of your help."

"You're welcome."

Since the call had interrupted her routine, she decided it wasn't worth trying to find her inner peace again. Instead, she lay down on the couch and tried to conjure up the previous night's dream. It wasn't as easy as she thought. She squeezed her eyes shut and focused on tapping into the memory.

> *Shouts came from the living room. Claire had never heard the partners fighting that intensely before, but the stakes had been raised. She placed an ear against the door. Byron would not appreciate her prying, but curiosity had no regard for common courtesy.*

Straining her mind, she struggled to recall the details.

> *"It's the Thuto Foundation," Byron shouted.*
>
> *"Thuto Foundation... educational development... less privileged kids." Claire only caught a few words of Penn's retort.*
>
> *"Taylor, listen to me. Tanya is smart... other grants much bigger... they're American... well structured. Ob-*

*viously it's a ruse... common audit practice to target
more significant amounts."*

"Black, time is running out... On your hunch."

If Claire understood correctly, Byron wanted to investigate
one of the smaller donation recipients, but Penn considered it
a waste of time.

The dream had no links to the current situation, although
with her slight push, they had gained a lot more information
than they would have otherwise had. None the wiser, she
searched through Tanya Hoff's many social pages. Her
tweets were typical of a philanthropist socialite: Gender
disparity; socio-economic concerns; videos of the changes
her foundations had made in the lives of others. On paper,
she appeared to be a modern-day Mother Teresa, but in the
dark corners of reality, the woman was a sociopath. Claire
recoiled with the horrifying realization. She touched a photo
of Tanya's face on the screen...

*"So, how did she do it exactly?" Claire asked, staring at
the television screen. Tanya followed her attorney with
her head down, while thousands of reporters awaited
her outside the court's doors.*

*"You know, this info is supposed to be confidential,"
Byron argued between bites of cereal from his spot at
the kitchen bar.*

*Claire laughed. "Right. You still don't trust me,
huh?"*

*He smiled; an unusual emotion that made him seem
so much younger. "A lady in iDream's accounts department created fake invoices for the Thuto Foundation.*

They paid her a lot of money to do it. As a single mom with a sick child, the temptation was too much to resist."

Claire kept staring, like a little girl engrossed in a fairytale of a princess defeating a dragon.

"Anyway, she would Photoshop the original invoice she created with a different service department and PayPal account, so when the actual invoice was paid by the Thuto Foundation, the money was paid into iDream's account, but when the fake invoice was paid, Tanya and Ben's fake PayPal account increased with stolen loot."

"How did no one pick up on it, though?"

"Well, nothing showed on iDream's side and Benjamin controlled the whole foundation's system: Projects, bank accounts, payments, everything. And he obviously pulled the wool over everyone's eyes with the good work he does."

"It's clever." Claire shrugged. "I mean awful, but smart... using an African foundation as a vessel. I'm proud of you for solving this."

Claire was shaking as she came back to reality. There it was, the final answer, the solution to the equation. The only difficulty no points were awarded in Math if the correct steps weren't provided. How would they explain this one? Claire grabbed her burner phone from the coffee table and texted Byron.

Claire: Call me as soon as you can, it's urgent!

She waited around for hours, nibbling her fingernails in

anticipation of Byron's response. Nothing. She made chicken à la king, slamming the knife into the chicken breasts and peppers as if they were responsible for her recent state. Excitement weaved together with dread and fear, but mostly impatience. Her head spun with the number of theories she had cooked up as fake reasons for why they would know such crucial information. None of them held any weight.

16

Byron

Monday, 20 June 2022, 6 pm

Byron grinned his way through all of the activities: From mountain biking up the gnarly green hills, to canoeing down the lazy river, to the current chatter around the bonfire. On any other day, it would have been a phenomenal experience but today his mind was fixated on more serious issues. Beer in hand, he laughed at the jokes Hoff and Russel made, although he only caught the punchlines as he planned his escape.

They were on the brink of a breakthrough and his bones rattled to respond to Claire's urgent text messages. Something was horribly wrong, or she had discovered vital answers. Either way, he wanted to get to her. His mind proffered several excuses, but none of them seemed viable until the girlfriend-lie he had told the previous night blessed his thoughts.

"Would you excuse me for a while?" he asked his companions. "My girlfriend is on my case. She says it's urgent." He waved his phone in the air.

Both men laughed.

"Ah, the old ball and chain." Russel mocked.

Ignoring the tired, old comment, he hurried up the stone path, along beautifully kept gardens to the lodge's entrance. As soon he found the privacy of his room, he called her.

"Finally!" she shouted, so loudly that he had to pull the phone away from his ear.

"Sorry, I couldn't get away. What's going on?"

"I had another vision."

Silence.

"Yeah, and?" Byron prompted with wild hand gestures, as if she could see him through the phone.

"I know what they're doing. In my dream you told me the whole story."

"What?" he swallowed, almost not believing her. "How?"

"A lady in iDream's Accounts Department is creating fake invoices for the African foundation. She copies the real ones and changes a few details on them."

"Wait, wait, slow down. So, the foundation pays these fake invoices as well as the real ones?"

"Yup, she puts a different PayPal account on them, as if they're a different department or something."

Byron laced a hand through his sticky hair and felt 10 pounds lighter. "That's great, you're great. Brilliant."

"Byron," she said, her voice suddenly somber. "How are we going to explain this to Penn and Trevor?"

"I don't know." He sobered up from the momentous elation. "I'll think of something... tell them it's a hunch. Penn already knows they collaborate with iDream."

"Maybe you should wait until they subpoena the documents?"

"Yeah, probably, but the foundation's handover will take longer, as it's not US-based. And they'll try to fight it. Claire,

133

thank you. Now we can direct all our energy on your dream." Nothing's more important than saving who-knows-how-many lives. With no help from the Bureau, it would be an Everest to climb.

He ended the call and retrieved his contacts, only to find it was the wrong phone. He shook his head at his brief lapse of judgment, hid the burner phone, and dialed Penn.

"Where have you been? iDream's been more than forthcoming. They received the subpoena with poise and said that all of their documentation is in order."

"Sorry," his hands balled into fists and his feet prickled to get back on the case. "I was occupied, so what have you found?"

"Nothing yet. We've just received the data. You can work through the soft copies. I'll compile a team this side."

He barely heard a word while planning an approach in his head. "Listen, Penn, iDream wouldn't have been so helpful if they had something to hide. And they're conveniently located in Miami. Tanya may have some of the employees in her pocket."

"Maybe they're trying so hard to hide the fact that they do have something to hide. Don't worry, Trevor has granted an extension because of our progress."

Determined to lead her down the right path, he said, "It's worth a try, don't you think? Just asking the employees a few questions?"

"Sure, if we find nothing out of the ordinary in the data they've provided."

Why does she always have to follow her own damn mind? "Why wait? I'll be on the first plane back and we can question them in the morning. I'll go through the files on the way."

There was silence for a few seconds before she responded, "Okay, see you soon then."

Byron ended the call, ran down the stairs, and back out to where the party was in full swing. Orange and red sparked from the center of the laughing guests. Panting, Byron reached Hoff, who was in conversation with an unfamiliar guy. "Jon, it's an emergency. I have to get back home."

"What's wrong?"

"My girlfriend's been admitted to hospital."

"But what about the investment? Doesn't she have someone else to take care of her?" Typical. His entire universe orbited around his empire.

Byron shook his head. "Her parents don't stay in Miami. She has no one else."

"Bob," Hoff pulled him closer and whispered, "I really need you on this. Russel's intimidated by you, even if he doesn't show it. You're smarter than him, and he knows it."

Byron turned and started for the lodge, no longer caring about Jonathon Hoff's opinion. "I'm sorry. Guess I choose love!" he called over his shoulder.

He packed his sparse luggage and booked an Uber to Redmond Airport. On the way, he texted Claire to let her know he was coming home. He had promised Penn to work through the documents, so he did. Perhaps he would find something to prove his 'theory'.

The half-hour trip took forever and a week. The vehicle had barely parked before he'd paid and bolted to the nearest counter. His haste was likely ridiculous, considering the limited number of flights out. He really needed to be on the next one. "I need the earliest flight to Miami, please."

"Sure, let me check." The attendant smiled a full, white

smile, and he noticed her eyeing him from head to toe. Knowing it would get the job done, he leaned in and returned her flirty grin.

She typed something into the computer and turned the screen towards him. "The next flight leaves at 10.55 pm, with a two-and-a-half-hour layover in Chicago. Arrival time in Miami, 11:31 am. That's all I've got," she pouted.

"Fuck!" He slammed his fist on the table, realized his mistake, and waved an apologetic hand. "Sorry, not your fault." He pulled out his wallet and handed her a credit card.

Byron paid, bought a Coke from the vending machine, and continued his search through the files. If there was something to find, the auditors would have somehow picked up on it. Not that it was a given. External auditors had a limited scope, which was why they provided limited assurance, and corruption within accounting firms couldn't be ignored.

He checked his watch frequently, and every announcement at the small, almost deserted municipal airport had him on high alert. His acrophobia kicked in every time he neared a plane, although the urge to get back to the case trumped his phobia six-love. Over time, he had learnt to control it, but he would never overcome it.

His forehead gave way to sweat when the boarding call came. Dread devoured his virility as he approached the gate. Every muscle in his body spasmed, as if clinging to a limp branch in the face of rugged tusks. *This is ridiculous, you've done this more than once.* He swallowed the fear down with an over-the-counter sedative Claire had given him before the flight to Bend. It was time to go home, slam a solved stamp on the case file, and get to the bottom of the damn bombs. With the constant chaos in his life, he sometimes forgot he was going to die. It was a much-needed distraction from the true terror that dominated his existence, but it was still a reality. Only, he couldn't frequent that train of thought or the hyperventilation would kill him before the investigation had even started.

* * *

Tuesday, 21 June 2022, 12 pm

"Ladies and gentlemen, please take your seats and fasten your seatbelts for the final descent," the captain called as they neared Miami International Airport. Once his safety belt was secured, Byron rubbed his hands together. Thousands of figurative ants had him bouncing on his toes in anticipation.

He was the first passenger to approach the nearest exit. Small suitcase in hand, he called Penn to let her know he was on his way home.

"Honey, I'm home," he joked as he entered the apartment door. Before he could register anything, Claire charged towards him and threw herself into his arms. He had no choice but to catch her.

The embrace lasted a few moments too long before she pulled away. "Oh, uh, sorry, I've been lonely. It's good to see you."

Her dreams, support, presence, or something else, had somehow shapeshifted their status. "It's fine, Claire. I missed you too."

She looked up, her brows furrowed. "You did?"

"I mean, I've gotten used to having you around."

"You must be an imposter." She playfully pulled at his hair, checking for a wig.

"Ha-ha. Hilarious, but I'm on my way again."

"Oh, not an imposter."

Byron showered and changed as swiftly as he imagined the Flash would, then drove to the field office. He found Penn in one of the boardrooms with a group of other people, their heads deep in boxes and files.

"Hi," he greeted them.

"Hey," Penn looked up. "You made it."

"Yup, I'm still alive." *For now,* came the silent sneer. "Are you ready?"

"Yeah, sure. Let me just grab my bag and equipment."

"Okay, meet you outside."

Byron returned to his car and Penn followed a few minutes later. On the way, he relayed all of the special activities and Bend's magnificence, in an attempt to close the uncomfortable rift between them.

"So," he asked, "did you miss me?"

"Not at all," she joked, and he was glad to have his old no-crush partner back.

"Listen, I made a rash decision before. Like we've established, we make a great team, and I think we should remain partners, if Trevor agrees."

"Sure." Penn smiled, though it seemed forced.

"What's with the one-word answers?"

"Ah, I'm stressed about this case. We've found nothing so far. You seem all chipper. Perhaps a holiday was all you needed."

"Yeah, maybe. But the end is in sight and I can just feel a win coming on. For now."

"For now?" Penn shot him a deep, concerned glance.

"I'm still worried about that letter."

"Why, Black?" She lifted a shoulder in confusion. "Nothing

may come of it, and the Bureau's dealing with it."

"Really?" he huffed, clenching the steering wheel. "They're making it out to be a hoax when it could mean the end of thousands of people."

"You have arrived at your destination," the GPS interrupted before the fear took over and made a spectacle of him.

Byron turned into iDream's parking lot and pulled a ticket from the machine at the boom. "You've arranged with them, right?"

"Yes, and they've assured me that they are more than willing to help. I get the idea their Accounting manager despises frauds."

17

Penn

Tuesday, 21 June 2022, 2 pm

Penn swallowed the urge to question Byron about his sudden change in mood with tight-lipped smiles and nods. His insistence on interrogating the employees set off booming alarms in her mind. Not that it was an unorthodox method, but he had insisted before they gained any input from the documents. At least a team of analysts were scanning through them while they embarked on a possible fool's errand.

The reception area did not differ from any other corporate building. It even had that particular commercial smell. The logo was engraved on the wall behind a large, wooden reception desk, manned by a stylish brunette male with earphones attached to his head. A warm smile graced his lips as they approached, and he held up a finger to signal that he was on a call. Telephones rang at unbidden speeds. It was a shrill sound that Penn was sure sent the poor man home with a headache each night.

Smile still in place, he removed the earphones. "Welcome to iDream, how can I assist you?"

"We have an appointment with Mrs. Bell from the Finance department," Penn explained, while Byron fidgeted with his fingers and phone beside her.

"Please, have a seat." He motioned to the blue velvet couches to his left. "I'll call and let her know you're here."

"Thank you," Penn said, following his instructions. She sat down, but Byron remained standing, his back to her, staring at the receptionist, as if his glaring would speed up the process. "Did you down a six-pack of energy drinks?"

He turned around. "No, but I'm about done with this case. You should've seen Hoff's face when I ran out on him."

Curiosity sparked. "Yeah?"

"Flabbergasted, like he couldn't tell left from right. Man, I should've snapped a shot."

"No, you should've spilled your drink on him," she snorted.

"Well, you never know. We might need him again. We've discerned that he's a douche, but I think there's more to him than meets the eye."

Penn blinked, almost choking on her own saliva. "What?"

Byron held up his hands in faux defeat. "Just an observation. Don't attack me."

His behavior grew more mysterious by the day. Everything about the man she had come to know was diverging. It was something on which she could write a book. Two, maybe. Penn bit her tongue, trying not to expose any of her suspicions. Luckily, Mrs. Bell saved her.

"Good afternoon, I'm Desha Bell." The well-dressed African American woman, perhaps in her early 40s, extended a hand. Her hair was cropped short and a pair of black-rimmed glasses perched on her nose.

"I'm Special Agent Penn, and this is my partner, Special

Agent Black. Pleased to meet you."

Byron stepped forward, eagerly greeting the woman. "Thank you so much for your willing assistance on this case."

"Anything we can do to help," she said with a stoic expression. "I've arranged for you to use one of our consultation rooms. There are only three employees that work directly with the Thuto Foundation, and me, who oversees the process. I assume that makes me a suspect, too."

"No, no," Penn appeased her. "No one is a suspect. We just want to find out if anyone has ever noticed anything odd."

"Yes," Byron agreed. "This is solely to peruse information that we may not find in the documents."

"I see." Mrs. Bell delivered a short nod as they followed her to the room: Small, with plain white walls and furniture. It contained only a table with six chairs tucked under it and a whiteboard. Bright noon sunlight streamed in from the two, large windows. "You can set up while I call the first employee."

Penn pulled out a small digital camera and positioned it on the table between her and Byron. The first employee entered, a bald black man sporting a lavish grey suit.

"This is Lionel Baird," Mrs. Bell said as the man stepped forward to shake their hands. "He is the sales executive working on the account."

The broad-shouldered man sat down across from them. As soon as Mrs. Bell left the room, they asked standard questions, all of which he seemed to answer truthfully and transparently. The beads of sweat on his forehead exposed his nerves through his arrogant exterior, but no more than any other person being questioned by federal agents.

"Woof, that was intense," Lionel said, getting to his feet. "I hope you got everything you needed."

"Thank you," Byron responded, not giving anything away in his expression. "Would you please ask Mrs. Bell to send in the next employee?"

"Sure," he smiled, heading for the door.

Mrs. Bell ushered in the next person, whom she introduced as Tina May. Uncomfortable, the needle-thin, platinum blonde hovered in the room as soon as her superior left.

"Please, have a seat." Penn gestured to the seat across from her.

Dark rings encircled the young woman's eyes, poorly covered by a dash of foundation. The tiles shrieked in complaint as she pulled out the chair to sit down.

"Relax," Penn said, trying to calm her visible nerves. "This is purely for information."

"What's your name?" Byron started with easy questions.

"Tina May."

"What is your position at the company?"

"I'm a debtor's clerk."

"What does the position entail?" Penn asked.

"Customer order processing; invoicing; the allocation of payments; statements and the reconciliation of debtor accounts," she counted the functions on her fingers, as if it were a rehearsed speech.

Penn noticed she was in the ideal position to adjust customer accounts. "How long have you worked for the company?"

"Going on seven years."

"How long have you worked with the Thuto Foundation's account?" Byron asked.

"More or less five years."

"Is there anything odd about the account?"

Tina lifted her shoulders and took a deep breath. "No, they

pay their account on time every month."

Byron leaned forward, slightly intimidating. "For what type of work do you invoice them?"

A pause.

"They order tests from us and we sometimes do consultations and training for them."

"How often is 'sometimes'?" Byron pressed.

Another pause, but the woman didn't answer the question and her face paled to snow. Suddenly, she shot to her feet and bolted out of the door. Penn was right behind her. Checking the hall, she saw Tina on the right, rounding a corner.

Penn raced in pursuit, but as she turned, the woman was nowhere in sight. Tina had been a part of the company for seven years, so she probably knew the layout by heart. She closed her eyes and tried to zoom in on footfalls, but the office buzz was too loud. Searching every closed door would take too long. Tina would most likely head for an exit and Byron should have alerted security by now.

Penn started for the underground parking lot, where a security guard stopped her. She showed her badge. Not without reluctance, he allowed her to pass. Close to the wall, she circled the inside building, mimicking a camouflaged gecko ambushing a cricket. Hyper aware of her surroundings, she reached for her gun and scoured the rows of cars in the dim light. When she heard a small noise somewhere behind her, she carried forward.

Penn rounded the corner, her ears adjusted to the source of the noise. Short breaths were barely audible. "Miss May, I know you're in here."

No sound.

"There's no use hiding. Security will be surrounding this

place soon." Penn shifted in the direction of the earlier sound.

Still nothing.

"Perhaps we can help each other," she tried again when the door that led to the building clicked. Penn held her focus. A few rows down there was movement, quickly followed by heavy steps. Penn chased after her. There was no way out for the escapee. The footfalls grew louder and more desperate. It took Penn only a few seconds to reach her. She aimed her gun at the woman's back. "Freeze, hands in the air."

A loud sniffle escaped from Tina's lungs as her knees dropped to the ground. She raised her hands. "If I help you, will you help me? Please, I need to take care of my son."

Penn's own eyes widened at the sudden admission. "I'm sure that can be arranged."

"I want proof of the agreement first," Tina demanded with a quivering lip.

"That's not up to us," Byron explained when he reached the scene. "The DA will probably offer you a plea bargain."

"Then I'm not saying anything else without an attorney present."

Byron nodded in Penn's direction. She moved forward and cuffed Tina's hands behind her back. "You have the right to remain silent." She trailed off, listing the woman's rights.

Byron escorted Tina to the car while Penn thanked Mrs. Bell for her help. She breathed deeply as Byron turned on to the road. They finally had a crucial part of the puzzle, but even that victory opened up a myriad of questions.

They brought the suspect into an interrogation room and awaited a prosecutor. Penn and Byron stood behind the glass window, peering at the woman who steadied her head on her folded hands on the table.

"How'd you know?" Penn studied Byron's face.

"How'd I know what?" A deep crease formed between his brows.

"Where to look? What questions to ask? You went off script and that's when she cracked."

"I told you before, iDream was too forthcoming to have anything to hide. My next logical conclusion was that it could be an employee working for Tanya Hoff. And with her," he pointed to the witness, "I read the body language."

"I see." Never a good idea to try to cheat a cheat. "Good spy skills, partner."

"Thank you." He ducked his head with a bashful half-smile.

* * *

Tuesday, 21 June 2022, 7 pm

Despite the win, Agent Trevor still wore his signature surly expression when Penn and Byron sat down at his desk. She had no idea why they had been called in, but she secretly hoped they weren't being asked to further investigate Tanya Hoff's affairs.

"Well done, both of you," he said. "With Tanya Hoff and her African friend behind bars, the DA will take over from here. But I'm sure that one charity is merely a drop in the bucket. Take the rest of the day off. I need both of you rested for your next assignment."

Penn's insides buzzed with the prospect of a fresh mission. No more corporate dresses or answering telephones, unless it was a similar undercover job, but that was unlikely.

"Sir," Byron spoke up. "Do you have any info on the nuclear threat?"

146

"That's no concern of yours. I'll ask for help if I need any, and I'm sure I don't have to remind you that you work in the white-collar unit."

"Sorry, Sir. It just haunts me."

Penn kept her calm intact, although Byron's obsession with the nuclear threat irked her. *Is he on drugs?*

Trevor ignored Byron's statement. "I'll see you tomorrow at 8 am sharp. Get some rest. Agent Penn, I'd like to talk to you for a second."

With a sharp nod, Byron left. Trevor gave him a moment to leave before he spoke.

"I read your report and you have a point. Agent Black's behavior is anomalous. You are free to investigate, as long as it doesn't disrupt the next case."

"Of course, Sir."

"Keep me updated. I cannot have a rogue agent in my sphere."

Penn nodded and left the room with an undeniable eagerness to excavate the case. Still, she couldn't help but worry about Byron. Despite her misgivings about her partner, she cared for his wellbeing.

* * *

The kettle howled. Penn turned off the gas and added water to the cup. Stretching her neck, she walked to the small corner of the dining room she had converted into an office and took a seat at the desk. With Byron's 'inside info', she had grown even more distrustful. Having gained permission to work on the case, she was able to obtain footage from the mall across from Byron's apartment building. The security had sent her all the video files they had from the day the letter was delivered. If three teenage girls were involved, they were likely recruited at a mall.

Penn pressed play, sat back, and sipped on her tea, knowing it would be a long night. She paused and zoomed in on anything that seemed even a tad conspicuous. Once her eyes could no longer focus on the distorted film, she reverted to her investigation of Leanne Sanchez.

She searched for the three narrowed-down possibilities on Twitter the social media platform with the least red tape and all three had matching accounts: One of them, a lawyer; one a singer, and the other, a student at the University of Oregon. Penn scanned her tweets. The girl was highly opinionated on a range of topics, including fashion, television, and feminism.

One particular tweet caught her eye: A photo of herself and two guys standing against the backdrop of a high zip line.

It was captioned: "We conquered it."

Penn clicked on the comments and read one from @teddy-bear23: "Too bad @clairebaxter decided to ditch us."

She clicked on the handle. Claire Baxter's profile resembled a deserted island: An occasional retweet of an article on buildings or books, but she was obviously not a social media enthusiast. Even her profile picture was a Metallica logo. There was no phot of Claire, herself. Ted Barnes, the commenter, had retweeted Leanne's picture with the words: "Bend is a blast." That proved Penn had found the right person. She was several years younger than Byron and lived in Oregon. *What's the connection?*

She found the allegedly missing Claire Baxter on Instagram, and at last discovered a photo of the tall, scrawny blonde. Penn sighed and rolled her tense neck. She was running on a treadmill with no destination in sight. Her eyes drooped. With no more evidence to be found at that moment, she decided that it was time for bed.

18

Claire

Claire used two dish towels to pull the lasagna from the oven since Byron didn't have any oven mittens. In fact, it was a blessing he had any cookware at all. She imagined someone had set up the apartment for him a decorator of some sort. He had no home. For him, it was a place to sleep and shower in between the busyness of his life.

Setting the dish down to cool, she cleared the sleek glass dining room table, which had never been used for such a purpose. Careful not to jumble up any of his work, she placed the documents neatly in their original piles on the couch.

She wiped the table clean and set two places with plates, wine glasses, and cutlery. With her bottom lip clenched between her teeth, she studied her handiwork. *No, he'll get the wrong idea.* Then she thought it more pragmatic to leave everything in the kitchen where they could dish up and eat on the couch, as they had done before his trip to Bend. He had promised they would celebrate, and a sit-down dinner resonated celebration. Still, Byron had to be handled like silk.

If anything seemed remotely date-like, he would clamp up again and send her back home.

As she carried the glasses back to the kitchen, the door unlocked. *Oops.* She looked between the table and the kitchen, unsure of her next move. It was too late. Claire squeezed her eyes shut and her heart pounded in her chest. If Byron walked through that door and noticed the set table, he wouldn't be impressed.

"I brought champagne," he said on his way inside and paused when his eyes landed on the table. "What's this?"

Claire tensed up. "Wait, before you freak out, it's not what it looks like. You said we'd celebrate, and I thought it would be nice to have an actual dinner at the table, but we don't have to. It was a silly idea... "

Byron chuckled. "You are so cute."

Claire swallowed hard. She stared at him, in a quandary about how to respond. "I'm cute?"

"I'll pour the champagne, you get the food and we'll have dinner."

She did. Still, her heart would not calm down as she scurried through the kitchen. She carried the lasagna and salad to the table, causing more noise than necessary with her trembling hands.

"Sit, Claire, calm down."

"You're not mad?"

"No," he shook his head. "I am an idiot, though."

"Can't argue with that," she joked, raising her champagne glass. "I don't want you to get the wrong idea. We have work to do, and if I go back home, then it probably won't get done."

Byron scooped a healthy portion of food onto his plate and pushed the lasagna towards her. "I'm not gonna send you away unless you want to go."

"But you told Penn you didn't want to be her partner anymore when she did the same thing," Claire argued, helping herself to a much smaller portion.

"Okay. One, Penn's not you, and two, I need you a lot more than I need her." He wiped a hand over his face. "No, that came out wrong. I mean, I need Penn.. "

"I know what you mean."

A silence followed, broken only by the clinking of cutlery.

"She used to be a con woman," Byron spoke up. "That's how she came to work for the FBI. She's proven herself, but I've never truly learnt to trust her. I don't mean to speak badly of her, it's just that she wears a mask, never lets you in."

"Maybe you've never given her the opportunity?" Claire raised an eyebrow in challenge.

"Fair point, but a true person lets you see them without you having to ask for permission. Like you."

Claire gulped and wiped her mouth with a napkin. "Me?"

"Yes, you say that you hide and that you fear people, yet you're not scared to show your emotions."

She wasn't sure what he meant by that, nor what to shoot back. As a result, she ogled her plate, pretending to be absorbed in her food while trying to decipher his sentiment.

"When you're angry, you show it," he continued. "You sulk and you pout and you scold. And when you're happy, you run into my arms like a silly teenager."

Claire felt her insides constrict with shame. Her face heated to boiling point. "Sorry, I didn't realize I was such a mess."

"You're not, you're a person. A real one." Byron sipped on his champagne. "You know how ignoring someone infuriates them more than backlash?"

What a weird question. "Sure, why?"

"You wouldn't accept the way I acted, and you reacted strongly in ways that caught my attention."

Claire studied him. He looked tired; his eyes were so puffy that they'd sunken deep into his face. His hair curled in all directions at the end, pleading for a haircut. Regardless of the big chunk of burden that had been removed from his plate, lines of worry charted his face, along with two-day-old stubble.

"Byron," she whispered. "Maybe you should get some rest before we discuss my dreams."

"See, Claire. You worry about me," he teased, grinning. "But no, tomorrow we start another case and I'll be lost in it before we've made any progress."

"Ugh." She stuck her tongue out and rolled her eyes back. "Here we go again."

"See, you express your emotions."

"Okay, I get it. I'm an open book and I care about you."

He laughed, a sound she hadn't yet heard. In real life, at least. They finished their meal and moved to the living room while Claire grabbed the flashcards from the bedroom. It had been more difficult than building a 1 000-piece puzzle, since her last few dreams had completely changed after revealing a few snippets.

"Okay," she placed them on the table. "It's weird, some dreams I've had multiple times, others only once. And they differ remarkably. Some are significant moments in your life. Others, only of your face." As she spoke, a recollection appeared in her mind's eye. "Lately they've become more lifelike, like I'm living them with you."

"Start with the first one." He motioned to the cards.

"That would be where you almost drowned. I've had that dream so many times." She positioned it in first place. "Then your graduation, and your sister's wedding and a holiday you took with the Klein's." Claire arranged them all in order.

"Something's bothering me here." Byron gestured towards the dreams of current events. "Trevor gave us a week to complete the case, yet these dreams run past that timeline. I mean, he granted an extension in the end, but that was because of the sudden progress."

"I know," Claire nodded. "I thought about that, too, but he cut the time because of the bomb threat, right? So, maybe he wouldn't have done that if we hadn't intervened."

"Hell, if I know how your gift works." He fiddled with his fingers, lost in thought. "Okay, that means we still have a bit of time, because that would've happened at least a few days into the future. I was only set to return from Bend tomorrow morning."

"Yes, now I've had the... "

"What's this?" Byron cut her off, reaching for the vision she hadn't told him about. "Is this what you've been hiding?" He looked at her, his eyes pleading to be wrong.

Claire bit her lip, already feeling him pull away. "I wanted to tell you, but you were so busy and stressed."

"My mom's dying?" He stared blankly at the card in front of him. "She's still out there somewhere?"

"I'm so sorry, Byron." Claire reached for his shoulder. He swatted her hand away. "In my dream you didn't push me away when I tried to comfort you."

"Sorry, it's not your fault." He blinked, shaking his head. "I can't dwell on this now."

"Okay." She left it for the moment, knowing that he would

have to face it sometime soon. She took the card from him and placed it in sequence. "So, if my calculations are correct, we have about a month left."

"Can you give me any details on the location of the bomb?"

Claire closed her eyes. By then she had the dream of the bomb memorized, as if she would have to write a qualifying exam on the subject. The second dream of the explosion added more detail, but not nearly enough yet. "We're together, in a stairwell or something. I'm standing at a big window and I see this huge puff of smoke in the distance. I'm calling for you. Everything is shaking and then the building collapses."

"And that's it? What else do you see outside the window?"

"Buildings, but I don't recognize them."

"Could it be this apartment building?"

She shook her head. None of Claire's surroundings in the vision appeared the least bit familiar.

II

Dilemmas

19

Byron

Wednesday, 22 June 2022, 6 pm

Byron had hoped the new case would send him back to New York, but apparently, he was to remain stationed in Miami for the time being. At least he wouldn't be working undercover. Those cases only happened on rare occasions.

Since he was now on an assignment instigated by a company itself, they already had all the information they needed. The case only required a deeper investigation.

It was a slower day now that he was no longer an operations manager, too. He considered the term 'slow' loosely. He simply didn't have to do two jobs any longer. Still, he had a monster of a riddle to solve. On his way home, the phone rang from an unknown number. He pressed the button to answer, "Hello."

"I should have known," the familiar voice said.

Byron's mouth curled upwards involuntarily. "Jon. Good to hear from you."

"You know, fighting crime is very noble, but my hotels need you more. I'm calling to say thank you. You are my hero. No other way to put it."

It was odd how often Jonathan Hoff thanked him nowadays. "How so?"

"Well, you imprisoned my wife and convinced Heather to accept my offer on the lodge."

The acknowledgment gave him some confidence to utter the question that had been at the back of his mind for the past few days. "Glad I could help, but I have to ask: Did you tip off the FBI initially?"

"A successful man never reveals his secrets. Your desk is waiting for you whenever you're ready to return."

Pride tugged at his heart, but he wasn't built for a desk job. "Thanks, but I'm more suited to danger than improving service."

Hoff chuckled. "Well, if you ever change your mind or need a golfing partner... "

"You'll be the first person I call."

His smile still intact, he ended the call. If he didn't know he was dying, he would have thought his life was falling into place. But after Claire's declaration that he only had one month left, he had no time to waste not to find a solution, nor to live. He came to a stop in front of the flower shop and hurried inside.

Byron didn't have a romantic bone in his body. Flowers, chocolates, and dates were all foreign concepts. With very little sand left in the hourglass, he attempted to act on the unbidden feelings that Claire stirred within him. Granted, it could be owing to her gift, but she understood him on levels no one else ever had. He looked around, trying to find the right flowers. The shop was full of roses that wouldn't make the grade. Roses, one flower he knew, thanks to the hype of Valentine's Day.

"Can I help you?" an older lady asked.

"Yes, what type of flowers say, 'Sorry for being a jackass and I might like you'?"

Despite the woman's composure, she burst out laughing. "Said every man ever. What is she like?"

Byron shrugged. "Beautiful. Smart. Strong. She puts me in my place when I need it."

"I think you need gladiolus." She gestured towards a bunch of pink, bear-claw-like flowers behind him. It was a petite bundle. Perfect.

"Thank you." He paid and returned to the car. Byron was gently placing the flowers on the passenger seat when the object caught his eye. It blended into the black interior, like a snake in a tree. If he wasn't an FBI agent, he'd never have noticed it. It was perfectly positioned behind the steering wheel, out of the usual line of sight. The only thing he could think of in that moment was Claire.

Byron jerked the car into gear and sped off. As fast as suburban roads allowed, he raced home. His hands shivered as the panic clawed its way from the pit of his stomach to the rest of his body. Every stop sign and traffic light was yet another thorn stinging his sides. He had to get to her.

When he finally made it home, he jumped from the car and sprinted up the stairs. In one swift motion, he unlocked the door and threw it open. There she was, standing behind the kitchen counter with a deep frown between her brows. "What's going on?"

Byron closed the door and pressed a finger to his lips. She nodded in slow motion and followed him to the bedroom. Hidden cameras and bugs could be anywhere, but at least he had some counter-spy gear. He retrieved a small device from his drawer and swiped across the apartment. Nothing. *So, just the car then.*

Just in case, he checked again. When the second sweep came up clear, he pulled Claire towards the couch. "We have one of two choices now: You either tell the FBI or another authority about what you know, or we have to get the hell out of here."

Distressed, Claire looked down at her hands. Her mouth opened and closed several times as she struggled with what must be one of the hardest decisions of her life.

"Either way, I'll take care of you," Byron assured her, gently squeezing her shoulder. It was Claire's gift and her future. He didn't trust anyone either, so he empathized with her uncertainty.

"Ever since I was a little girl, my parents have warned me not to tell anyone. They said that people could either exploit it or try to kill me."

"I know, but Claire you have to decide soon. I don't know who knows what, but if you decide not to trust the authorities, we have to leave before they find out we know they're looking into us."

Claire nodded. "I'm sorry for involving you in this."

"What?" It was the most ridiculous thing he'd ever heard. "You had to involve me. What if we hide until we know more? I'm hoping your dreams will increase, as they did with the case. Once we have an answer, we can force Trevor to listen."

"And what if that's the wrong decision? What if I'm meant to collaborate with them?"

He took her hands in his. "You promised me once that you won't let me die. I believed you then and I believe you now."

A smile threatened her lips, despite the inner turbulence he knew she felt. "Okay. Where will we go?"

"You're not gonna like it." Her determined glare prodded the answer from him. "We'll have to ask Hoff for help. He has resources cars and houses we can use."

"Jonathon Hoff?" Claire's eyes bulged. "You wanna ask someone you hate for help?"

"Look, he's a lot of things, but he owes me, and I think he'll help us."

"Is there no one else?"

Byron looked at the roof, as if it would provide him with the answers he sought. The only other person he could think of was his father, and Jonathon Hoff seemed to be the lesser of the two evils. "I don't have a lot of friends and I'm not involving Erica in this. I don't like it either, but life doesn't always fall at our feet. He's our only option right now."

With a less-than-pleased sigh, Claire agreed. Byron took out his burner phone and made the dreaded call, but there was no answer. "Okay, let's pack what we need. We'll take your car for now. At the first truck stop, we'll steal a car."

She rolled her eyes and then jumped up. "Okay, let's go."

Byron already had a survival pack containing clothes, cash, and camping equipment at the bottom of his closet. He watched as Claire struggled to pack her supplies. Everything kept dropping from her trembling hands and sweaty palms, and she failed to secure the zipper on her backpack. He had mad respect for her thrown into a situation that required a bravery most people wouldn't possess, and she trudged the path with a valiant dignity.

Once dark, they slipped through the sliding doors on to the balcony. When he was certain the coast was clear, Byron shimmied down the pillar and signaled for Claire to jump into his arms. It wasn't that high, but a loud clunk on the ground would stir unwanted attention. They snuck through the garden and out of the gates toward the parking space he had rented for her car.

20

Penn

Wednesday, 22 June 2022, 9 pm

Penn's eyes burnt from the strain of focus. In what seemed to be another futile attempt, she had explored the video footage for the past hour. In fact, she was starting to think she had imagined everything wrong with her partner. Perhaps he had simply been stressed about their previous case and the realization of her feelings for him. It had never been her intention to make them known, but the sharp spy within him had sensed it.

When they started their new case, there was a normalcy to their partnership that Penn had to admit she had missed. It was possible that her suspicions were an aftermath of jealousy, an emotion over which she had no grasp. Byron was the only living person who cared and made her feel safe. And, after all, she was human.

His earlier conversation with Hoff in the car had proved to be nothing more than a friendly chat between two men who had become better acquainted during a weekend away. Bugs weren't protocol, but Trevor had insisted. About to write the video footage off as an abominable-snowman chase, her eye caught something on the screen: A woman with oversized sunglasses coming out of the ladies' toilets. She had been watching the recording non-stop and had never spotted the person entering the restroom.

Penn zoomed in. The woman's face was hidden by a Kleenex and dark lenses, but the shape of her mouth nagged at Penn. She had seen the person before. She scrutinized the visible parts of her face, squeezing her eyes shut, in search of the owner.

She scanned through her reports on Tanya Hoff's case, but couldn't find anything related to the woman in the video. With no particular expectation, she turned to her social media search from the previous night and there it was. The woman in that video was Claire Baxter Leanne Sanchez's friend, who had been absent from their Bend trip, according to a comment on her Twitter photo. Somewhere, dots were connecting, bringing a sardonic smile to her lips. She followed the woman through the footage as she went outside, then returned to the restroom a while later and never re-emerged.

* * *

Thursday, 23 June 2022, 9 am

Agent Penn had used facial recognition software to find the teenage delivery girls. She texted Byron to let him know she would be late as she had to run a personal errand. It would buy her time to question each of the girls individually. All three were from the same wealthy, suburban neighborhood. The first lived in a rather small two-story home with alternating white and stone walls. Penn made her way up the paved driveway towards the soft-blue door that stood out against the earthy colors of the exterior.

A short, white woman answered. Her dark hair was neatly tied into a ponytail. A typical tracksuit mom, no doubt. "Morning. Can I help you?"

Penn nodded politely and showed the woman her badge. "Morning, I'm Special Agent Penn of the FBI. Relax, you have nothing to worry about, but I believe your daughter may have been conned into assisting a rebel. I just need some info from her."

The woman's eyes widened with each word she spoke. The word "relax" was no consolation to the woman, and equivocation had never been Penn's strong suit.

"Is she in trouble?"

"Not that we know of, but I do need to ask her a few questions."

"She's still asleep. I'll go wake her." Fear remained stamped in the woman's face as she turned towards the stairs.

Penn waited in the doorway for a full 15 minutes before the girl and her mother returned. They looked very much alike, except the girl's hair was shaved on the one side and longer on the other.

"Caroline," the mother pushed her forward, "this is the FBI agent... "

"Special Agent Penn." She stepped forward and stuck out her hand. "And you are Caroline Reed, I assume."

The girl breathed heavily and shook Penn's hand. Her eyes betrayed her apprehension. "Carrie, if you don't mind."

Penn assumed the girl had done something she shouldn't have done and that she expected trouble. To set her at ease, Penn removed the photo of a disguised Claire Baxter from the file and held it out to her. "Do you recognize this woman?"

"Yes," she nodded.

"Please," Mrs. Reed pointed through an archway to the living room, "let's sit down. Can I get you something to drink?"

"I'm fine, thank you. I don't wish to take up any more of your time than necessary." She followed behind them and sat down across from Carrie. "Can you tell me where you know her from?"

"I was at The Village Walk Mall with my friends when she approached us."

Suddenly Penn's heart felt heavy. It confirmed her suspicions. Byron might be involved in some conspiracy. Involving what, she wasn't sure. "Why did she approach you?"

"She told us she suspected her boyfriend of cheating and wanted us to deliver a gift to their front desk to catch him." She shook her head. "Did we do something wrong?"

"No, not at all. This woman is a con artist. She used you to deliver a gift that held other hidden contents. I'm trying to find her, but I cannot do that without your help."

Carrie's hand went straight to her mouth, she gasped. "What contents?"

"Agent Penn," Mrs. Reed interrupted. "Is Caroline in any danger?"

Penn didn't even know the nature of the situation she was dealing with herself, but if these conspirators knew that Penn was using the girls as witnesses, they could be in jeopardy.

"Possibly."

Caroline looked to her mother in shock. "I didn't know, I swear. She looked so innocent, she was crying, and she was pregnant."

"I know, sweetheart." Her mother hugged her against her chest. "It'll be all right. We'll take care of you."

Penn nodded at the woman. "Do you have family that you can visit until we catch these people, or should we arrange for witness protection?"

"No, we'll take her somewhere safe."

Penn asked the girl a few more questions about the incident and learnt that Claire Baxter was familiar with Byron's alias. The other two girls' testimonies validated her story. While she had no idea if or how Byron was involved, Claire Baxter was either a spy, a whistleblower, or a pawn of some sort. The only way to know was to find her.

It troubled her that on paper, Claire seemed to be an innocent college student. She could have been recruited by a rebel corporation straight from college, though, or perhaps she was being used to pay off a drug debt. Anything was possible and until Penn could talk to her directly, it would remain a mystery.

On her way back to the office, Agent Trevor called.

"Sir," she answered via Bluetooth.

"Penn, any idea of Agent Black's whereabouts?"

"Is he not at the office?" With her busy morning, she hadn't checked in with him, apart from the text.

"No, his phone's off, and I cannot pick up a signal. His car's still at the apartment."

"Shit." She clenched her jaw. "I found the person who sent the letter, I think he might be in trouble. Can you send some back-up? I'll head to the apartment straight away."

"Fine."

She turned the car around and raced to his building. At first, she knocked, but there was no answer, so she was forced to arrange with Marlon to gain entry. That same acute disinfectant smell hung in the air as they entered, but the place was deserted. They found an untouched chicken pie in the oven and cooked vegetables on the stove. The apartment had been vacated in a haste.

Everything was neat and orderly. The bed still made, no clothes lying around, and all of the couch cushions were perfectly arranged. Besides the suspicious food and cleanliness, nothing appeared to be out of order. They swept the place for hair and fingerprints. Deep inside, Penn hoped they had abducted Byron, although she knew all of the evidence pointed to him harboring the girl who had sent that letter. DNA evidence was a mere formality. As she stared at the familiar apartment, she knew. Only, she didn't know why.

21

Claire

Thursday, 23 June 2022, 8 pm

They had been on the road for 24 hours and Byron still hadn't been able to get hold of Jonathon Hoff. He had written it off to the man being busy, but Claire was losing hope. Without his help, they had no land of milk and honey. For now, they lived in her car, taking turns at the wheel while the other slept. Pretty soon they would have to get rid of the car, though.

Claire stared ahead. There was still a drop of orange on the horizon, but night had taken hold. Encased in darkness, they drifted somewhere outside of Georgia, no town in sight, barely even a car. Nothing but the open road in front of her. Even the moon was resting behind a drape of clouds. Her heart raced with the idea that 'they' would find them, or worse, her family. A tear slipped from her eye. Everyone close to her was now a target.

Her intentions were to save people, not to hurt them, but her selfish fears had created one mother of a mess. Every time she entertained the possibility of explaining the situation to the FBI, her parents' words resonated in her mind: "They might not believe you and they'll lock you away for treason," her mother had said.

"Or they will believe you and they'll study your brain to figure out why you possess this gift," her father had warned.

Their words remained engrained deep in her consciousness. Her parents had raised her with qualms that shattered any chance of building a bridge of trust between herself and the authorities. No, she could never share her secret with anyone. The possible negative outcome was too great to contemplate.

Byron's light snoring interrupted her fretting. She sneaked a glance at him. He barely knew her and had risked everything to hide her. Claire reached out her right hand to touch his arm. With the illicit emotions she felt in his presence, she yearned to touch him. He was beautiful, in a masculine kind of way, especially while he slept. A coppery bulk of muscle. He stirred and she yanked her arm back.

"Hey," he said in a sleep-heavy voice. "Is it my turn?"

Guiltily, she looked straight ahead. "No, you can take over from the next stop."

He sat up. "Claire, it'll be all right."

"I know. It always is."

He didn't push, which she appreciated, although now she knew he could read her better than she sometimes understood herself. Apart from her dreams, she didn't possess the ability to unscramble his code. He had turned marshmallowy since his return from Bend, and there was no logic to it. Byron was an enigma only the Einsteins of the world could fathom.

"Hey," he said, staring ahead. "I'll get a hold of Hoff. Don't worry."

She only nodded. The road sign indicated that the next travel stop was 15 miles ahead. Claire had postponed the car-stealing for way too long since it flustered her. But if 'they' knew about her, 'they' would be searching for her car.

"We're not literally gonna steal a car, Claire." Byron must have picked up her unease.

"I don't follow."

"Stealing wouldn't be very smart. They'll report it and bring the police to us. We find a garage, break your car and take it in for repairs. Then we'll tell the owner that we desperately need to borrow one."

Claire raised her eyebrow, as if to say: "Are you kidding me?".

"And they'll just lend us a car?"

"We'll have to sound really desperate."

She frowned, given her lack of criminal knowledge. "Do you really think people are that gullible? I have 24-hour roadside assist."

"Everyone's gullible when money talks. It won't be a fancy car, but any car will do."

She swallowed hard. It wasn't that she cared about her car, but the underhandedness of it all felt like bathing in mud. "How much money do you have?"

"A lot. I've always feared a situation like this and made sure to keep a big enough stash to survive. Why?"

She shook her head. "Just wondering why you would have enough cash to buy a car."

"Let's just get some food and fuel for now. We'll find a garage tomorrow."

Wordlessly, Claire followed the road to the entrance and parked in a spot far enough away from sight. An extreme heat plunged into her skin as the car door opened and the humidity engulfed her. As she looked up to the heavy sky, a drop of rain fell on her nose. Having been stuck in Byron's airconditioned apartment all day, she hadn't acclimatized to the warmth. Even in summer, Oregon was never blazing hot. The air wrapped around her, like a wild force strong enough to strangle her.

"There's only a McDonald's." Byron pointed to the familiar "M" sign. "Unless you want to get something from the shop?"

"No, McDonald's is fine," she sighed. At this point, what food she ate was the least of her worries. Faces hidden, they hurried inside, steering clear of anything that resembled a camera. Twenty minutes later, they were back on the road, fueled up and chomping on burgers. With a full belly and the light pitter-patter on the windows, Claire reclined her seat and drifted off easily.

"So glad you made it." A man who looked to be an older, grayer version of Byron opened the door.

"Dad," Byron nodded, then pointed to her. "This is my girlfriend, Claire. And my dad, Douglas Black."

Claire had to be polite, but she wanted to strangle the man in front of her. Byron had told her stories about how he used to turn whiskey-ward and beat him.

"Well, you are ravishing, my dear." Doug pulled her in for a hug. The action repulsed Claire, nevertheless, she leaned in non-committally.

From the corner of her eye, she noticed Byron grimace.

"Your mother's resting," his father continued. "She's getting weaker by the day."

Instead of responding to Doug, he gestured with his head to Claire to follow him inside. The living room was pale and unworn, with no sign of life. Only minimalistic traces of expensive art and furniture. The halls were a different story altogether. Claire felt like she had stepped into a graphic family novel. The photos started from the twins' birth and followed every important occasion in their lives, Erica's on the left and Byron's on the right.

She studied each photo she passed: Birthdays, awards, high school, and college graduations. Erica had one, Byron had several: College, grad school, Quantico. She wondered where Doug had found the later photos of Byron. Probably Erica, if any line of contact still existed between the pair.

They ambled down hardwood halls until Byron paused. He gripped the knob and squeezed, white-knuckled. He pushed the door open. It screeched, as if waking up from years in a coma. Claire entered first and was fascinated by the glimpse of teenaged Byron through his old bedroom.

A look around revealed that his father hadn't changed the room. A few photos and basketball shirts were displayed on the dark-grey walls. Behind a large desk hung a calendar and a map of the world. Next to it stood a large bookshelf, proffering mostly biographies, textbooks, and trophies.

"What were you like?" Claire asked, placing her bag down on the bed.

"Pretty much the same douche I am now, just less educated. And maybe hotter," he smiled.

Claire looked around at the certificates and photos.

"Nah, you weren't that hot."

Friday, 24 June 2022, 2 am

Her eyes fluttered open and she took a moment to ingest her surroundings. Each dream was becoming more cinematic. It had to be her growing connection to Byron that added color to the backdrop.

"New York," she groaned. "We're going to New York."

"What?" Byron gave her a quick glance before averting his eyes to the road.

"I had a dream. We went to your father's place."

"Really?" He pinched the bridge of his nose with his free hand. "I'd rather die than face my old man again."

"Byron, don't make jokes like that."

"Sorry." He wiped at his eyes. "Listen, you'll have to take over. I can't keep my eyes open any longer."

"Sure, what time is it? And where are we?"

"It's just past 2 am, in Mississippi. I just drove, aimlessly. Still haven't heard anything from Hoff."

"Damn it." Claire clicked her tongue. "I think that dream meant we must ask your dad for help."

"Yup, guess you're right. New York it is, then."

Claire drove through the night with the rock station on a whisper. She hummed along to the songs she knew while analyzing all of her dreams. In the far-off distance, she noticed the sun dusting clouds with pink, and the clock read 5.49 am. For another hour she steered east until they neared a gas station and decided it was time for breakfast and to swap out the car.

"Byron," she gently shook his shoulder. "Wake up." He blinked and stretched, then sat up straight. *Ugh, morning people.* She was envious. "It's time."

He nodded and gestured for her to pull over to the side of the road. Despite the early hour, it was boiling hot outside. She watched as Byron opened the hood and fiddled around. She hoped he knew what he was doing. Still, his acumen was often intimidating. Claire had always considered herself smart. She had done well in school and college, but compared to him, she sometimes felt notably uninformed.

"That should do it," he said, slamming the cover with one hand. "We'll have to walk from here and make up a story."

"What if we can't pull this off?"

"Then we hike," he said, as if deciding what to cook for dinner. Even if she wanted to, Claire couldn't shut down the idea. It was her own doing that had brought them to their current perplexity. She had no option but to mask her terror with a fearless face.

"Come here." Byron pulled her by the arm. "I know all of this is terrifying, but we can pull it off."

One side of her mouth pulled into a half-smile as he hugged her against his side. "Okay." He smelled like sweat and his T-shirt was dark with damp patches. It didn't take much for him to ooze his intense body heat. "You need a shower," she said, playfully scrunching up her nose.

He huffed out a laugh. "And you smell like vanilla."

"I'm surprised you know what vanilla smells like."

They removed everything they needed from the car and walked the few miles to a lonely, red sign against the road. The fresh air would have been welcoming if she hadn't felt like she was trapped in a sauna. Just like their relationship cover for Dan and Erica, they agreed on a few plot points for the lie and would elaborate from there.

Inside a ghostly little shop, the remaining food choices were frustrating. Each one was less appetizing than the last:

Crumpled-up, stale sandwiches, canned food, and sweets. Barf. She had to eat, though, and picked a bag of chips and protein bars. The tire center across the road had a roadside assistance service for broken-down trucks. Byron arranged for the car to be towed to the nearest garage. For a fee, of course.

"You use money to fix everything," she scowled as they hustled toward the pick-up that would deliver them to her car.

"Would you rather hike your way to New York?"

"No, but... "

"No 'buts', Claire. Right now, we need money to wiggle ourselves out of this situation. So, I'd say it's a good thing I saved a lot."

"You know, you are so sad. You work yourself to a pulp and you don't even spend the money you make from it."

"I'm spending it now. Besides, the reward of a thing well done is having done it."

Claire chuckled. "You read that in one of your many fortune cookies?"

"I'm helping you. What the hell is wrong with you?"

She had no answer to that. Byron was spending his hard-earned, honest money to help her and she was questioning his methods.

"Sorry, I'm an idiot sometimes. Why do you put up with me?"

"Same reason you put up with me." She didn't know exactly what that statement meant, only that they were on the same page willing to sacrifice everything for the cause.

That was the easy part. The truck driver drove them back to her car and towed it toward the nearest garage. They approached a big, open grass lot filled with cars in all states of disrepair. Claire thought it the perfect place to 'steal' a car.

A sturdy, tan woman approached as the tow truck released the vehicle on to an open space on the lawn. Her dark hair was cropped short around a face that carried the trouble lines of her early 30s. "Can I help ya?" she said in a deep Southern accent.

"Yes," Byron stepped out. "Our car broke down a few miles from here and we're on our way to my mother's funeral."

They had agreed to stick to as much of the truth as possible, and since his mother was already dying, her burial seemed appropriate. Still, it pushed on Claire's heart as he said the words. It couldn't have been easy for him.

"Uh-huh, so it's urgent, then?"

"Very urgent," Claire pressed. "Can you help us?"

The woman eyed her up and down. Claire pushed her hands down into her jean pockets, the way she usually did in the presence of strangers. Byron noticed it too and raised his eyebrows in her direction. Smirking, the woman asked Claire to open the hood and scratched around inside for a few minutes. "Start the car for me, will ya, luv?" she shouted.

Claire turned the key in the ignition. No sound.

"I'll, uh, have to take a deeper look."

That was the cue for their performance. With Byron's undercover experience, he had agreed to take the lead. "Ma'am, we have to get to North Carolina by tonight."

"Well, then y'all will have to arrange for someone to take you," she said with her head still deep into the engine.

"What about another car? Do you have one available that we can borrow? We can pay you for it?"

That caught her attention. She stood and turned towards

him. "Sure we do, but it'll cost ya."

"How much?"

The woman looked to Claire who was still in the driver's side of the car. "I wouldn't mind a kiss from your pretty little lady here, but let's settle on $2,000."

"A day?" Byron's eyes began to water and his Adam's apple bobbed with a loud gulp.

"No, mister, I'm not in the car rental business, but I have a few you can buy."

Claire looked at him. Buying wasn't the plan and $2,000 was a lot of money. Even though it looked like the transaction was going smoothly, her stomach swooshed with nerves. Her temperature rose higher than the heat, yet she had to keep her cool or risk botching their plan. Relieved puppet was her role to portray.

"I got two cars that're just taking up space." The woman gestured to them to follow and led them to the back of the garage where two men worked on other vehicles. "I've got this Ford Taurus," she tapped on a worn, faded blue car's door, "and the Honda Accord over there." Her finger pointed to the white model, which looked to be in a better condition, though still a few years old.

"Which do you suggest?" Byron asked. "I'm clueless about cars."

"This one." She tapped on the car again. "Don't let her age fool you, she won't give you any problems. Sturdy horse, I tell you."

"Thank you, then we'll take that one."

She led them to a small office and opened a receipt book lying on the desk. "Can I see a driver's license, please?"

Claire's pulse sped to a sprint. They were on the edge of

being caught, she could already feel the shackles around her arms. Byron noticed, squeezed her hand, and handed the woman a card. She placed it on the table and read the details.

Byron said, "The address is old. We've recently moved and I haven't replaced it yet."

Paying him no attention, she continued filling in the details on a standard bill of sale. Claire looked down at the table, noticing the name on the card. Samuel Lautner. She wondered whether it was an old alias. If so, it meant the FBI would know.

"We only accept cash." She stood, searched through a filing cabinet, and retrieved a document from it. "This is the title. You have seven days to register the vehicle."

"Thank you." Byron removed his wallet, counting as he dropped the hundred-dollar bills on the table. She nodded, pleased, and both of them signed the document she had prepared.

In return, the woman gave him the top part of the receipt, the bill, and the title, then reached for a key from the large, steel holder against the wall. "I'll pull her out for you and y'all can meet me out front."

Before long, they were back on the road in a much less conspicuous vehicle. Well, without plates. Claire let out a breath. "The driver's license, was it an old alias?"

"Yes," he said, eyes steadfast on the road.

"But... they'll..."

"Yes, but they already know I'm gone. If they find your car, they'll find the place. At least this gives us a head start."

22

Penn

Friday, 24 June 2022, 11 am

Penn threw the reports down on her desk. "Ugh," she groaned, staring out the office window, as if the sky would somehow change the proof on those papers. But DNA evidence didn't lie. It placed Claire Baxter all over Byron's apartment. She still didn't know how or why they were linked. Her mind concocted many reasons why Claire would have sent that letter, then run away. Every notion led to a brick wall. Her main theory was that the girl was in some sort of trouble and had asked Byron for help.

Penn considered contacting her friends and family until she found out Claire's father had filed a missing person's report. They didn't know where she was, either. The only lead she had was the details of her car. Penn had informed the Portland PD that they were investigating the girl and asked them to keep the investigation discreet for the time being. Readying herself, she bundled all the documents for the meeting into a file and breathed deeply. Laptop under arm and file in hand, she aimed for the door. Her rubber soles squeaked down the polished linoleum on her way to the boardroom.

Owing to the severity of the threat, Trevor had brought in the CIA to assist with their spy tactics and equipment. Most of the team were already seated when she entered. A few last members came in and the room quieted down in her presence. It was her first time as a team leader. All of her other cases had been with a single partner and no one had ever before reported to her.

"Morning," she addressed the room. "Some of you might know the details of the case, but not everyone, so I will... "

The door clicked open and in walked Agent Trevor. A control freak, he didn't even trust her enough to conduct one meeting by herself. All eyes followed him from the door to the first available seat.

"As I said," she continued. "I'll relay the specifics of the case for those of you that aren't up to speed with it yet." Penn plugged her laptop into the projector and turned off the light. She opened the file on her computer which contained all the case documents, then clicked on the letter Byron had received about the bombs. She looked to the wall and saw the words that now held a little more meaning than before.

```
I heard conversations between my employer and an
accomplice. Plans to attack US cities with nuclear
power. Not a hoax. Millions of lives at stake. Be
in touch with more info soon.
```

"A few weeks ago, Agent Byron Black received an anonymous gift. At the bottom, the sender buried this letter. Given that only countries constantly monitored by the authorities hold nuclear weapons, we didn't give it much thought." Penn started pacing the front of the room, only for something to do while she spoke. "However, Agent Black couldn't put the subject to rest. This suggests that he knows something that we don't."

Penn pulled up the photo of Claire. "Because of his odd behavior, I did some digging into Agent Black and the person responsible for the letter and found that this woman, Claire Baxter, sent the letter via three teenaged girls. The girls have confirmed it." She handed out copies of the forensic reports to every member.

"I noticed that someone had been staying with him for a while, and the tests have confirmed it to be the same Claire Baxter. Agent Black never showed up for work yesterday, his apartment was abandoned and his phone is untraceable, although his car is still parked in the lot."

A rookie CIA agent raised his hand, Penn pinpointed the Asian man as Nakul Kaur, his black curls elegantly styled around trendy, squared glasses that rimmed his eyes. "Yes, Agent Kaur?"

"Have you established the relationship between Agent Black and Claire Baxter?"

"No, not yet, but they knew each other. One of Claire's friends recognized him while he was in Bend on business." She moved on to the photograph of the car. "We believe they drove away in a silver Ford Fiesta, 2015 model, Oregon license plate 843 JDH."

"Do we know how and when Miss Baxter arrived in Miami?" Agent Trevor asked.

"Yes, she came back with him from his sister's house the

weekend before we received the letter. I haven't contacted Erica Klein yet, but I'm certain that is the last place they'll go."

Agent Trevor removed his glasses. "And what makes you so certain?"

"I know Agent Black, Sir. He would never risk his sister's safety."

"Maybe that's exactly why he would go there. He knows it's the last place you'll look."

She fought down a bark of ridicule. "With all due respect, Sir, Erica has two little girls. He would keep any trouble as far away from them as possible."

With the tip of his glasses in his mouth, Agent Trevor nodded. "I understand, but when you run out of options, I think it's worth pursuing."

Penn issued a faint nod and continued her speech. "Agent Black is smart, his intelligence is astounding. He thinks like a criminal and a cop. He would avoid any cameras on the road and at travel stops. But they will need fuel and food. Assuming they'll get rid of the car, our priority should be finding them." She clasped her hands together. "Your job is to search every nook and cranny of this country. You are Big Brother. Check social media, cameras, taxi drivers, and anything else that could be helpful. I'll divide you into teams of two for each region. Failure is not an option."

"Do you have any clues as to where they could be headed?" a blonde woman she recognized as Agent Bisset spoke up.

"Byron," she clicked her tongue. "I mean Agent Black has always been a lone wolf. I wasn't aware that he had any other relationships, apart from his sister. I'm sure he has friends, even if he doesn't talk to them very often. We need to find college roommates, basketball teammates, girlfriends, and anyone with whom he's ever had a connection. Any questions?"

"What about his father?" Trevor asked.

"He hasn't spoken to his father in years, but I guess it's worth looking into. I'll put someone on his trail. Anyone else?" She looked around the room to find only heads shaking from left to right. "Very well then, I'll send out an email with the teams." At that, Penn packed up her laptop and returned to her office.

Byron's desk stood empty across from her own. She rummaged through the drawers and files, trying to locate anything that could be useful, but found no personal items or anything related to Claire. Memories flooded her as she stared at the vacant chair. Despite the current circumstances, she missed the jerk. At that moment, Penn realized she had never truly missed anyone in her life before.

With no time to open a box of nostalgia, she sat down at her own desk and searched for Byron's father. Luckily, the internet was flooded with information on renowned defense attorney Douglas Black. She made a few calls and arranged for a spy to bug his phones and car and to keep an eye on him. Pursing her lips, she glanced at the unoccupied desk again. "What have you gotten yourself into, Black?"

23

Byron

Friday, 24 June 2022, 2 pm

Luscious pine trees, farms, and trucks became overwhelming, and since the 'stolen' car's airconditioning didn't work, Byron was on the verge of exploding. Several times he had considered taking off his shirt, which clung to him like cheap spandex. Moisture poured from every inch of his skin. *Why did I even suggest this?* If he opened the window, the clutter of cars combating the wind was too loud. Then again, the hot air that flowed in didn't bring much solace either. At least they were in a region that had no signal to Claire's noisy radio station.

The thought prompted him to peek at her. With her head leaning against the window, she stared at the same scenery they had seen for the past two days. He wondered whether she thought of the bombs as much as he did. His fear grew each day, each hour, and each minute. People weren't supposed to know how they were going to die. Every time she closed her eyes, he hoped she would open them with news on the bombs, much as she had with Tanya Hoff's case. So far, there was nothing. And with their current lack of technology, they couldn't dig. If they made it to his father's place, he would research every news article, every suggestive tweet... anything that could provide a clue to the source of the threat.

Byron leaned back into the seat, trying to fan himself with his hands the when familiar guitar chords of *Take Me Home, Country Roads* started on the radio. He turned it up and started singing.

Claire flipped her head back to look at him. "What? You sing? Country of all things!"

"Join me. You know you want to..."

It didn't take much convincing. "West Virginia..." she sang from deep within her chest. "It's so weird, completely fitting, aren't those the Blueridge Mountains?" she pointed to the emerald hills in the distance.

"Indeed. They're beautiful. Pity we can't explore them."

"Yeah, someday we will."

He turned the music down. "Glad you've found that glimmer of hope again. I'm scared too, you know," he admitted.

"Of what exactly?"

Fearing that she would see the magnitude of terror in his eyes, he focused on the road. "Of everything; of getting caught before we find anything, but mostly of dying." She touched his shoulder and increased her grip. "What are you doing?"

"I got the vision of Tanya's arrest from touching the screen with her photo. I'm trying to do the same now, so let me focus."

Claire closed her eyes, and he left her to work her magic, even though he was uncomfortable with her touching his sweat-soaked shirt. He tried to keep his attention on the road ahead, but curiosity caused him to squint every few seconds.

"Stop staring," she scowled. "I'm trying to concentrate."

Byron opened his mouth to apologize when he saw the object flying through the sky towards them. He swerved left to avoid it, but it was too late. Glass splintered as the wooden plank smashed against Claire's side of the windshield. She jumped back into the seat, her eyes wide with shock.

"Woah!"

He evened his own breathing before slowly veering back into lane. "It fell off the back of a truck that passed us. Are you okay?"

"I'm fine. That woman didn't lie. The windshield's still intact. Sturdy horse, indeed," she mocked in a shaky Southern accent.

Byron wiped a hand across his face. "If the cops see this, they'll pull us over."

The realization settled in Claire's eyes. She turned quiet, banging her head back against the headrest.

"We'll camp out for the night," he said. "Let's get some food and a shower, then we'll head to a campground."

"Won't they ask for ID?"

"Not the free campgrounds."

A map at the gas station told him a main freeway lay between them and the closest national park. A little too exposed. Dangerous. The broken screen was more visible and risky, though. It would have to be the former. Another hour on the road brought them to a rest stop. Claire hopped out to stretch her legs once they had parked. Byron tried calling Hoff again. Turning on the burner phone was a perilous gamble since the signals could be traced. Too bad. It would take 'them' a while to discern that he was the owner of the phone anyway. His hope for support from Hoff, instead of his father, hadn't waned, so he risked it. Just as before, it rang and rang without answer.

With their caps secured and their heads down, they ambled inside and paid for a shower. He needed one desperately. Since all the bathrooms were occupied, the lady at the counter handed them a queue number. While waiting, they joined the IHop line for some food. His stomach growled as the smell of sizzling pancake batter hit him. They hadn't eaten anything since that morning. Buying food while avoiding cameras was more daunting than basketing three consecutive free throws. He had to scope and circumvent them with his head in a menu or his nose on the phone. He spoke downwards, too, pretending to be an intense introvert.

Claire stuck to his side, as if a controlled minion or submissive. She carefully eluded people, fearing that she would touch someone by accident. As he had noticed before, she stood with her hands in her pockets, shifting uncomfortably from one foot to the other. She really did not like strangers. It was a solemn situation, though he couldn't help but find it comical. They each ordered a turkey and avocado wrap for take-out, then returned to the shop to wait their turn.

Byron unlocked the door to a clean and neat beige-tiled bathroom. Wasting no time, he yanked off his sweat-ridden clothes and stepped into the cold water. Even if they had to hurry, he took a moment to savor the chill a drink of water in the desert which was over all too quickly before he washed and dressed. Outside, he found Claire's door still locked and knocked to hurry her along.

The lady at the counter gave them a map and directions to the free campground nearby. She probably assumed they were RV campers. If only she had known the truth. With her concise guidelines, he effortlessly found the sign that read "Corojo

Campground".

Surrounded by an overhang of trees, they followed the dirt road to the camping spots. The crowded site surprised Byron: Cars, tents, RVs, and picnic tables littered nature's purest charms. Despite the throng of campers, it was silent, save for quiet laughter, the final note of bird songs, and the rippling of a nearby stream.

"Let's try to find a secluded spot," he told Claire.

She turned to look on the right side of the road while he searched the left.

"Here," she said, pointing to a small clearing with two tall pine trees in the center. The space was too small to accommodate an RV, but their two-man tent would fit like Cinderella's slipper.

24

Claire

Friday, 24 June 2022, 6 pm

While Byron built a small rock structure for a fire between the two trees, Claire rustled through the bushes in search of dead branches. It wasn't a difficult task as they lay scattered across the dirt. She stopped at the stream and closed her eyes. For a moment she pretended she wasn't being hunted by the authorities or anyone else and absorbed her tranquil surroundings: Fresh air, babbling water, and the smell of pine and smoke...

Cackling laughs and whistling interrupted her serenity. She looked around but couldn't find the source of the noise. She bent down, placed her pile of branches on the ground, and watched as the translucent water flowed along its muddy, rock path. Claire cupped a handful of water to her mouth and sipped before splashing the coolness onto her face.

"Claire!" She heard Byron's voice behind her.

With a shy smile, she turned to face him. "Sorry, I got a little carried away."

As he moved closer, she noticed his stoic expression. "It's

not safe out here alone."

She followed him back to camp. He remained rigid on the walk, which made her wish for the gift of telepathy, too. In the past, she would have preferred that gift 'instead', but she now knew that what she had previously considered a curse had been given to her to stop a catastrophic occurrence. Why her? She would never know. Plain, average Claire Baxter. Nothing justified God's decision.

She looked up at the man in front of her as she coaxed her thoughts back to the trail. His mood swings were unpredictable, with no pattern or algorithm. Earlier he had sung in the car, which had helped her to relax somewhat. Now, he was once more grave.

When they reached the clearing, Claire placed the firewood within the circle of stones. Byron lit it with a match. They sat down on opposite sides. A party with guitars and loud chatter could be heard somewhere in the distance. They both stared deep into the crackling flames, as if they were complete strangers forced together by circumstance. Granted, that wasn't far from reality, but they had grown closer over time. Now, he made it impossible to reach him.

"Must be locals," Byron finally said. "It only started just now. I got worried. That's why I came to look for you."

"Uh-huh." She kept her eyes trained on the merging of orange and gold flames.

"Claire, come on. Not this again."

"What do you want from me? You're the one closing up again."

He gave her a stern look, as if she were a student who hadn't been paying attention in class. "You cannot act like a child while we're in this situation. We have to stick together if we're

193

gonna succeed."

"Then you have to talk to me, like you did earlier," she spat, keeping her voice low, although she was sure no one could hear anything above the raucousness of the party. "You can read my body language, but I'm not a spy. I don't know what you're thinking or feeling."

"Sorry, I'm not good with this, okay. I'm useless with people." And then Byron knocked her for a home run. He came to sit next to her and pulled her into his side. She stiffened into a statue. "Sorry, you don't like touching." He detached his arm and moved a few inches away.

"It's okay, you just caught me off guard, that's all. Your touch doesn't bother me."

Byron laughed. "So, I'm the only person in the universe who can touch you?"

Claire grimaced at the odd realization. "Guess so," she shrugged, tilting her head to the side. "Give me your hands."

He turned to face her and held out his arms, as instructed. She took his hands in hers and closed her eyes, focusing on the connection. For a few seconds she saw and felt nothing, but she used her desperation as persuasion.

> They ran down the stairs. The earth shook and trem-
> bled, as if a betrayed earthquake had returned for
> vengeance. Byron cleared five steps at a time. Claire
> followed in his footsteps, as far as she could reach.
> "What the hell is going on?"
>   "No time. We have to get to the basement."
>   "But what if the building collapses?"
>   "We have to get away from the nuclear fall-out,
> Claire. Just trust me."

The shaking blurred her vision, and everything started to move in slow motion. Bile shot up from her stomach into her throat, causing her to vomit on the spot. Byron grabbed her hand and pulled her down. She tripped and rolled down the steps onto the small landing. He stopped dead in his tracks and turned around. "Are you okay?"

"I'm fine," she nodded, getting to her feet. There was no time to consider scraped knees.

The basement door was right in front of them. Only a few more steps. Outside the window, a few buildings peeped through a cloud of vermilion smoke. From above them, two elderly people came struggling down the stairs. Byron rushed back up the stairs to help them when the tube light above his head crashed down. The building was crumbling to the ground. He turned around to run back, but it was too late. The stairwell above them shattered and a large piece of stone plunged him to the ground.

"Byron! No!" she cried. Blood was everywhere, turning the small space crimson. She started for him before a hand dragged her down.

"I see the bombs." She jumped up, startled by the vulgar image. She paced around the fire, dragging a hand through her messy curls. "All I see is the bombs," she shouted. Why was there nothing else? Why couldn't she see something useful, instead of horrifying?

"Quiet, Claire."

"Each time I see more details. This time it felt like I was the actor in a movie. You were trying to save an elderly couple when the stairwell above you collapsed. And someone saved me." She frowned, remembering the hand that dragged her down. "It can't happen, Byron. I refuse to watch you die."

His face was blank, although there was no way that what she had said had not affected him.

"Let's go to sleep. We'll get an early start tomorrow."

Claire crawled in first and lay on her back with a hand behind her head. Byron followed suit. His hand settled next to hers. She wanted to weave her fingers through his; a comfort for him or her she wasn't sure, but she didn't have the nerve. It was right there, burning in proximity.

"Hey, Claire," Byron spoke into the dark roof of the tent.

"Mm-hm."

"I, uh, I was actually, uh," he stuttered.

"What?"

"Never mind."

She turned on to her side, facing away from him, and closed her eyes, but sleep wouldn't come. Bugs buzzed, the music and chatter boomed, and the dream kept replaying in her mind. None of it provided any clues and only fueled her anxiety. If she wasn't determined before, that life-like glimpse kicked her into the high gear. She would save him.

25

Penn

Friday, 24 June 2022, 9 pm

Another day had passed. They were another 24 hours ahead without a trace. Penn had barely slept an hour or two on her desk, at most. There was no use trying, either. Every time she closed her eyes, an image of him out there besieged her mind. Finding them was the only thing that mattered, the only thing on which she would focus. How the hell did he get himself into such a mess?

The thought of him dying had crossed her mind a couple of times. Since she had no idea with whom he, or rather, Claire, associated, he could be lying somewhere in a ditch. Those thoughts stirred even deeper anger and despondency within her.

Penn had taken a deeper look into Douglas Black's affairs and learnt that he was something of a devil's advocate completely capable of getting Byron off on a technicality once they caught him.

She wiped at her burning eyes and scanned the missing person's report that Claire's parents had filed.

Claire Baxter, a 22-year-old female with chin-length blonde curls and blue eyes left on a trip in the middle of the night, informing none of her friends or family. She was in contact with her father daily until 15 June, at 8 pm. The daily texts confirming her safety stopped that day and her phone had been off ever since.

It confirmed everything that Penn already knew, except for an observation the detective made on the behavior of the parents. He described them as edgy, as if they were hiding something. He wrote that although he believed them to be highly concerned about their daughter's safety, he sensed that there was something they weren't disclosing. At once, Penn picked up the phone and dialed her team's extension.

"Agent Kaur," a rumbly voice answered.

"Kaur, can you get me all the communication between Claire Baxter and her parents from the day she left Eugene to the day she went missing?"

"That's not exactly legal."

"I know the law. Can you do it or not?"

"Sure, but I think you should come see this."

Penn dashed down the stairs to the team's open office. She refused to get her hopes up before anything proved to be a true lead. Agent Kaur waved her in when she got to the door, then turned the screen for her and his teammates to see.

"So, Claire's friends and family shared this missing person's post on all social media." The screen showed a flyer image on Instagram that had been liked and shared thousands of times. "But look at this comment." He clicked to open the comments and pointed to the one that read:

I'm pretty sure this girl stood in front of me at the Lexington truck

*stop's IHop earlier today. I remember thinking that her boyfriend
is hot but way too old for her. I can't be sure because she wore
glasses and a cap, but I think it was her.*

"Well done, Agent Kaur. Now, please get me those communi-
cations I asked for, and uh, get ready for a trip to Virginia."
The man was out for a promotion and right now, Penn was
exploiting his ambitions.

He nodded. "On it."

She hurried straight to Trevor's office and knocked.

"Come in!"

"Sir." She pushed the door open. "We've got something. I
need a helicopter to take us to Virginia straight away."

"Okay, I'll arrange it. Be ready in an hour."

* * *

Saturday, 25 June 2022, 12 am

A car waited outside the hospital where the helicopter had
dropped them. She flung the door open and jumped in, moving
up to allow Kaur to enter next to her. Time was of the essence.
They drove through the city toward the outskirts of town,
where the truck stop was located. Subconsciously, she leaned
forward, as if it would increase the car's speed.

They were barely parked when Penn shoved herself out the
door, heading straight to the front counter. "Good evening,
I'm Special Agent Penn of the FBI." She opened her badge.
"This is Agent Kaur. We have a warrant to look at your security
cameras."

The older woman frowned. "Um."

"Sorry, Ma'am, this is urgent. Please can you point me

toward your management office?"

She nodded, pointing toward a hallway next to the shelf holding car products. "What is this about? Perhaps I can help?"

Penn paused and turned back to face the woman. She pulled out her tablet and scrolled to a photo of Claire. "Have you seen this woman in here?"

Her eyes narrowed as she studied the photo, then shook her head.

"How 'bout this man?" Penn flicked to a photo of Byron.

The shop assistant blinked, the weathered wrinkles around her eyes increasing with concentration. "Yes, I think so." Her voice wavered.

"You think so?"

"I can't be sure it's him, but I think he asked me for a map earlier."

Penn looked down, thinking. "Is there a campground nearby?"

"Corojo. it's around the corner," she said with a circular gesture.

Penn looked at the rookie next to her. "Activate the drone. Let's go."

26

Byron

Saturday, 25 June 2022, 1.30 am

Byron opened his eyes, blinking at his surroundings. He was in the tent. Sleep wasn't the plan. He couldn't sleep while he knew they were being hunted, but he had nodded off for a moment, overwhelmed by exhaustion. When he'd checked, there was no weight next to him. Nervously, he zipped the tent open to look for Claire. A quick scan of the clearing revealed no sign of her. *Where is she?* He clenched his fists around the door flap. She infuriated, excited, and scared him more than any person ever had.

He grabbed his gun from behind him and crawled out of the cramped space. Weapon at the ready, he scouted the bushes. The earlier party had died down and calling Claire would wake their fellow-campers. Not an option. His head veered left and right into the trees, following his small flashlight. On high alert, he tracked the same path to the stream where he had found her earlier. *How could she be so careless?*

Apart from the flowing water, there was no sound around him. Looking about the ominous woods, his heart jumped into his throat. *What if someone took her?* The thought prompted a shiver down his spine. He cared about her, probably more than he should. A branch cracked behind him and he spun around in the direction of the noise. Carefully, he moved closer with a finger on the trigger. Step by step, he crept forward. He let out a quiet breath when the pale light exposed Penn's face.

"Drop it," she ordered.

"Where is she?" he demanded.

"I said drop the gun!"

He knew she wouldn't be alone. Soon he would be surrounded, but it was worth a chance. "Taylor, you don't understand. You need to let us go. Lives are in danger."

"You can explain when we get back."

Without thinking, he lunged forward and pushed her to the ground. He pulled her right arm into the air and wrenched the gun from her grip. With her left hand, she punched his cheek. The knuckle-on-bone thump rang through his ears as he bounced back. He reached for the gun that lay millimeters away. Penn was faster. She kicked him back down, but he caught her leg and twisted until she slammed face-first into the dirt. With a hair-width opportunity, he jumped up and grabbed the gun.

Still on her stomach, Penn kicked his legs out from under him, but he held tight and pinned all his focus on retaining his balance. As a result, he landed in a crouching tiger position. She turned around, stiffened. Aiming the gun straight at her head, he snarled, "Where is she?"

And then he felt the sting in his butt cheek. *Tranquilizer dart* was all he could think before the world spun and went blank. He was vaguely aware of being dragged, but his eyelids were too heavy to fight. They were caught. Game over.

* * *

Saturday, 25 June 2022, 5:30 am

Faint light streamed into the window. He felt sick, as if waking up after one hell of a college party. Byron hadn't woken up with a hangover in months. His eyes wouldn't open. *Too tired.* Something important gnawed at him, something for which he had to fight the sleep. He couldn't place a finger on it. His mouth felt bone-dry. *Water.* He needed water.

He didn't know where he was. He couldn't keep his eyes open long enough to look around. No link between his brain and body. He tried to remember something, anything, but his mind was a blank canvas. Then an elusive image of a tall, curly, blonde floated in. Big, mysterious, icy eyes. He knew her. Once again, he tried to open his lids. He blinked, pushing against the fatigue.

"Morning, sunshine," a voice sounded somewhere in the distance. "You awake?"

Trying to stay conscious was one thing, speaking was another matter altogether.

"Get some rest. We'll be there soon."

Eventually, he gave up the battle and succumbed to sleep.

* * *

Who knows how much time passed before his eyes fluttered open again. Coherence was still difficult, but at least he was awake. Byron looked around. He was in a car with tinted windows. All he could see was the back of the driver's head. Short, black hair no one he knew. Through the haze, he formed a plan, but something bothered him. What?

As noiselessly as possible, he tore off a piece of his shirt. It took a while, since he had to do it inch-by-inch as not to create any obvious noise. A gun clicked. His eyes widened and he shot upright.

"I wouldn't do that if I were you." The driver aimed the gun at the passenger seat.

He almost cried, crushed in the middle of fear and relief as the blonde curls came into view.

"Okay, easy." Byron raised his hands in surrender.

"Yeah, that's what I thought."

Claire giggled in her sleep.

"Is she okay?"

"Yes, and it'll stay that way as long as you behave."

He sat back in the seat. "Do you have some water?" The man fiddled with something in front, then tossed him a bottled water and a protein bar.

"Thank you." Manners should count for something.

"Before you think of another plan to kill me, I'm not who you think." He glanced at Byron in the rearview mirror. "My name's Jason Daniels."

"That supposed to mean something to me?"

"Yes."

Byron lifted an eyebrow, wondering whether he'd heard the name before. "Nope, sorry."

"I'll give you a hint. You're a hot topic around the coffee room at the office."

"Yeah, I bet." He ignored Jason and stared at Claire. The relief of her safety normalized his pulse to an acceptable level. He needed her. Only, now that they were caught, she'd be forced to share her secret, and who knows what they'd believe and do? Sighing, he slammed a fist into the seat behind him.

He'd screwed up by stopping for the night. They should have kept going. Then he realized what was bothering him: His free hands. No cuffs.

"Some girls were very sad to see you go," Jason interrupted his musings. "And apparently Hoff, too."

The bells went off in Byron's head. J. Daniels was the nametag at the Security desk he passed each morning en route to his office.

"Hoff sent you?"

Jason smiled, nodded. "He got your gift but couldn't answer it. The FBI's surveilling his every move. He told me to track the signal of the phone you were calling from, and here I am."

"Thank you." He didn't know what else to say. Finding them sure as hell couldn't have been easy. "Thank you," he said again, just as Claire stirred in her seat. He reached for her hand.

"Hey, we're safe."

Sleepily, she tried to smile, or scowl perhaps. "I know, he told me," she grumbled as those frosty blues opened.

"What happened to you?"

"I couldn't sleep and needed some fresh air. This guy grabbed me and threw me into the car when Penn showed up."

"So," Jason said. "You wanna tell me why the FBI's after you?"

Byron looked to Claire. He knew she trusted no one with her secret. "Not yet. Where are we headed, by the way?"

"Plymouth area. Hoff owns a little cottage on the lake."

Byron couldn't help the laugh that escaped him. "Never pegged him for a small-cottage-in-the-South kinda guy."

"Yeah, well, he's saving your ass, so you owe him big time."

At least they had a chance to save lives now. Albeit small, but a chance, nonetheless. And if they succeeded, he might have to quit the FBI and work for Hoff free of charge for the rest of his life. He squinted. The tranquilizer must have done considerable damage to the wires of his mind.

27

Claire

Saturday, 25 June 2022, 7 am

The cottage was a wooden marvel beside the cobalt water: Small and cozy, cradled between shortleaf pines. If Claire were ever on a reality dating show and they asked what her perfect holiday destination was, this cabin would be the answer. Not that she would even consider entering one of those ridiculous shows.

The small, refurbished wooden kitchen joined the parlor, which opened on to the back porch, overlooking the lake. There was even a boat on the dock, down the steps. It was like something out of a travel magazine. Inside, she buzzed with enough excitement to forget about the past 24 hours. *You're not here on holiday.*

Her shoulders slumped when the disappointing realization struck. *Damn, I could sure use a real holiday.* She turned around and traipsed back inside. They had tons of work to do.

"There are two bedrooms," said Jason, returning from the hallway. "You guys can take the double bed and I'll sleep on one of the singles."

"Does this place have a PC and wi-fi?" Byron asked, entering the front door. Claire was certain he hadn't heard their new cohort's suggestion.

"I brought along a laptop and there should be wi-fi, but I can't promise anything about the signal."

"Claire, can we talk for a sec?" Byron asked.

"Sure."

He steered her back outside and closed the sliding door. "We must tell him."

Her blood rose to boiling point in an instant. "Absolutely not, we know nothing about the guy."

Byron took a deep breath, staring up at the sky before releasing it into the ground. "I need a smoke." He pushed against the railing that surrounded the porch with enough force to rattle the frail steel.

"You want to break that?"

"No, I just... Claire, I took a leap of faith with you. We'll have to do the same with him."

Claire tilted her head and pursed her lips. The answer would always be no. "We tell him about the bombs, but not my dreams. Let's just say we have a trusted source."

Byron shook his head. "This guy found us in the middle of nowhere. He's smart. He won't accept 'a trusted source'."

"Yeah, well, we'll tell him he's in danger, too. It worked with you." There was no further discussion to be had. She didn't care how his fingers stiffened into claws. He wasn't the one who had to live with the consequences of having someone know about her superpower. "Deal with it."

"Fine," he kicked at the railing like a five-year-old who couldn't have candy before dinner. "I think you should get drunk."

"What?"

"Alcohol relieves us of our inhibitions. I think it might help prompt your dreams. Until then, let's search for anything that could lead to nuclear war."

Byron headed back inside without waiting for her. She didn't want to fight with him. He was her only certainty in their current predicament. Yet she couldn't ignore the small voice inside that told her not to trust anyone. Only if a vision revealed Jason's loyalty would she tell him the truth.

The men were outside when she returned, and Claire took the opportunity to explore the rest of the loft-style building with beige walls and gleaming wooden edges. It was cramped and smelled like dust, slightly cowed by the scent of fresh water. She peeked into the small bedrooms and found they weren't much different from those of motels: Sparsely furnished with plain white sheets. Still, she loved it.

"Claire," Byron called. When she turned, he was right behind her. "Hey, Jason's going into town to buy some food and supplies. You need anything? I mean we left all of our stuff at the campsite."

"The basics, I guess."

With half a nod, he darted back out. Byron seemed very trusting of someone he barely knew. She had thought the roles would be reversed, given his skeptical nature. Now she felt slightly off balance and outnumbered. Once she heard the car engine start outside, she rejoined Byron in the living room. He was setting up the laptop on the dining room table, which was squeezed into the far corner of the room. She read the screen over his shoulder: A Homeland Security article on terrorism and threats towards the US.

"So, you, uh, trust this guy?"

"No." He didn't look up. His eyes moved over the screen in speed-reading fashion.

"You seem to?"

"I don't, but I have no other choice," he barked. "Just like I had no other choice than to trust you. We'll have to work with him, and we can't do that without some form of mutual trust."

Without responding, she sat down next to him and read. The news feature held terms she didn't understand, but the gist of the article proved that the US's biggest threats were Iraq, Afghanistan, and violent, domestic extremists. Byron went on to search for articles that showed which countries had operational nuclear bombs. Russia posed the biggest threat, but the first article had explained the authorities' traditional espionage methods: Field officers and students acting as diplomats, or other crucial employees, in countries with the capacity to wage war.

Everything she read explained how well the US was protected. Just like the article she had read after her first nightmare of the bombs: Early detection systems; spy systems; anti- and counter-terrorism units and deployments units. These were considered to be an almost uncrackable shell. None of those measures would be able to protect against the hazard she had witnessed in ultra-high definition and surround sound.

Jason returned a few hours later with numerous bags in hand. He set them on the kitchen counter and unpacked. Food, clothing, and toiletries. *Who is this guy?*

"I didn't know your size." He handed her a pair of jeans. "But you're a toothpick, so I took the smallest they had."

"Yup, wish I could put on some weight."

"I thought you were anorexic or something."

"Definitely not. I'm a total foodie." Claire pulled the bags containing the food closer and perused the contents. Eggs, milk, and non-perishables. The mac-n-cheese packets caused her to cringe but she had eaten worse. "I'll whip something up."

"Did you buy alcohol?" Byron asked without looking at them. His face was glued to the screen. He was terrified. No other way to describe it. He would die and she wouldn't.

"Sure did." Jason held up a bottle of wine.

"Thanks," he called over his shoulder, fingers clicking away violently on the keyboard. "Claire, you should have some. Lots."

Jason raised an eyebrow paired with an amused smirk. "You trying to seduce her?"

"Actually, we're not together." Claire finally put the poor man out of his misery. A crinkle formed between his dark eyes while he rubbed at his ear. She estimated him to be around Byron's age early 30s. He was good looking with a wide, friendly face and full lips. She wasn't sure about his ethnicity owing to his darker skin.

"Oh, I assumed... "

"That's okay. Honest mistake."

Jason didn't seem convinced. She ignored his still-skeptical gaze and checked the cabinets for cookware. Whisking eggs and milk together in a bowl, she made omelets with cheese since that was the only filling she could find. Claire dished the first, perfect one on to a plate and took it to Byron.

"Thanks, just put it down there." He gestured with his eyes to a spot on the table.

"Just humor me. I'll drink the whole bottle of wine if you'll take a break and eat this."

Byron turned around in his seat. "You know for someone who lacks social interaction, you sure have people skills."

"Whatever, just eat the omelet."

Jason and Claire joined him at the table. As promised, she brought along a big glass of wine.

"You ever been drunk?" Byron asked, ravaging the food he initially didn't want.

"Yes, with my friends."

She noticed that he wanted to elaborate on the question, but closed his mouth when his eyes caught Jason's.

Byron then addressed him: "We've found out that someone will attack the US with nukes." For some reason, he'd chosen to casually sweep it into the conversation.

Jason's knife and fork dropped from his hands. All of the color drained from his face. "What? So why are the feds after you? Why aren't you working with them?"

"We tried to warn them, but they didn't buy it, and we can't reveal our source."

"Who will attack? What? Where?" He shook his head in utter disbelief. Or skepticism, Claire couldn't tell.

"Those are the missing parts of the equation," she said. "That's what we're trying to figure out. The source only knows that it will happen. Nothing more."

"And I suppose you can't reveal your source to me either?"

Byron glanced at Claire, giving her one last chance to speak up. She kept a straight face.

"No," Byron said. "This person will be in too much danger if it ever comes out."

Claire expected an objection, yet Jason said, "How the hell will the two of you figure this out on your own."

"We're still in contact with the source," Byron explained. "They'll provide us with more info when they have any. Once we have a strong case, we'll contact my supervising agent. But we can't sit around and wait, we have to look into matters ourselves."

Jason didn't protest. He offered to clean up and took the empty plates to the kitchen. Claire ignored him and sat down next to Byron again. He glared at her slow sips. In turn, she rolled her eyes and sped up the drinking process. Each mouthful tasted better. It was the dry, extravagant kind of wine that she wasn't used to. An acquired taste that poor students couldn't afford.

Byron created a fake social media account and searched the pages of political Twitter. The mouse and flimsy wooden table banged and clanged when the pages wouldn't load fast enough for his liking. Without engaging, he scanned every US civil debate. Comments were highly diverse. Some commended the president's efforts and others condemned him. Nothing new. Often Byron's jaw clenched and unclenched with fury.

Claire didn't pay enough attention to parliamentary shenanigans to give a damn. Even reading it now gave her a headache. Everyone needed someone to blame for the country's shortfalls. Racial issues, dollar price drops, and deficits were all pointed to some person or organization. She was in way over her head. Claire's strong suit was ensuring that a construction project had a resilient foundation, or adapting infrastructure for the growing population. Even making red wine reduction. Why on earth would God gift her, a nobody, with clairvoyance?

Day turned to night as the moon took its turn in the sky. Its pale light snuck into the curtain openings, as if curious about their investigation. A chill ran down her spine and Claire closed the windows.

They had learnt a lot about the US economy, national affairs, allies, and enemies. Nine countries had nuclear weapons in their arsenal. None of them currently seemed to have any negative relations with the US. Still, Byron had reminded her of the surprise attack at Pearl Harbor and 9/11. Anything could happen. Anything could change. They had been searching all day and were nowhere closer to an answer.

Byron finally stood to stretch his legs after hours cemented to the chair. "I think we must work with the authorities. They have the intelligence equipment. They can hack phone calls and emails. This won't work."

Fear shot up inside her. She imagined her face and neck turning crimson with the broiling anger. The alcohol wasn't helping either. She glared at him, grinding her teeth. Maybe she hadn't heard him correctly. After all, the liquor had taken away her ability to focus. "Can you repeat that?" she slurred.

"I said we'll have to go to the authorities."

With the liquid courage flowing through her veins, she slapped him across the face.

28

Penn

"Son of a gun!" Penn jumped from the chopper door onto the concrete platform. Byron had been in her grip. She had her hands around his throat until... *You idiot*, she scolded herself. She had to admit that the unusual girl's tranquilizer trick was brilliant. No question, Claire was far from a plain Jane. Throughout their rumble, Byron had cared only about her where she was. She had to be something remarkable (three nipples?) if he was willing to give up everything for her. But even in the dark, Penn had noticed a deep fear in his eyes when he'd told her lives were in danger. That girl had a shock collar around his neck.

Byron clearly still believed her story about the nuclear threat. Why? He was smarter than to trust some blonde bimbo who claimed to have proof. There had to be an underlying reason. Something else was going on. *If I could just catch them.* Her fists clenched in anger. The constant 'who', 'what' and 'whys' devoured her. The person she had fought in the bushes was a phony.

215

Once they reached the Bureau, Penn retreated to her own office for a moment alone. The call she had expected from Trevor hadn't arrived, and until she had another lead, she would avoid the lecture. She opened her laptop and retrieved the drone footage.

As back-up, she instructed the team to check all the license plates for stolen vehicles. She groaned, not looking forward to the tiresome exercise. Since the image was too dark to see clearly, she brightened it with video-enhancing software. Once ready, she watched as the camera swerved over the cars, RV's and trees.

Penn replayed the fight scene in slow motion and realized her mistake. She'd hesitated because Byron was her opponent. She could have shot him in the leg to cripple him, but she turned soft. He didn't care about her one bit. His only goal was to get her out of the way. *Time,* she reminded herself. No time to tarry over 'what ifs'.

Progressing to the shooter, Penn frowned. Originally, she had thought Claire had shot the darts, but the masked person did not fit her description. That person was too far away for her to see clearly, but the build didn't match. It was a man's build, tall and buff. Penn rewound to track his movements, but he avoided the drone like a trained art thief.

With a flicker of hope, she rejoined her team in the surveillance office. They tapped into all the cameras they had on the roads nearby, while others continued to search the drone's path for a car that could belong to the shooter. The vehicle Claire and Byron had stolen was still parked next to the camp when Penn and Kaur awoke, so they'd used a different getaway car.

Her phone rang. She didn't have to look at the screen to

216

know it was Agent Trevor.

"Sir."

"My office. Right now."

"Yes, Sir."

She wasn't some Sorry-Suzy. She squared her shoulders and approached the boss with her head held high.

"What happened?" he demanded the moment she entered.

"One of their allies shot us with tranquilizer darts. I had Byron; we were fighting for possession of the gun when I felt the sting."

Disinterested in the excuse, he glared at her. "So, now we know someone is helping them. My money is on Douglas Black or Jonathon Hoff."

"I have people surveilling both of them. Movements, calls, emails."

Trevor removed his glasses. "Agent Penn, Black knows everything you know. He won't be stupid enough to contact them directly, but he'll find a way. Check all their resources. Find their cars and properties and you'll find your fugitives."

He had a point, a good one. "Yes, Sir."

Penn did as asked and compiled a list of all their assets and those of close family. Both had a lot of investments, mostly stocks, and bonds. Two pieces of property attracted her attention, though. Doug had a beach house in the Hampton's and Hoff's mother owned a river house near Plymouth, North Carolina.

"Kaur," she called. Penn showed him the two properties in question. "We need to tap into our cameras in these areas and find out whether any of the cars present at the campsite were near these places."

She watched as he called up security footage of their surveillance cameras on roads and at shopping centers. Scanning through video was a prolonged, humdrum effort. At least it was easier to follow a specific vehicle via satellites than to backtrack and search for something unknown, as they had done until now.

Inwardly, she laughed, wondering how the cops had operated back in the day without social media and espionage technology. The CIA had some of the most innovative tools, although it was a mission to get approval for their use. If she sent a helicopter into the area, it would cause Byron to run, but she could deploy another drone. With that idea, Penn called Trevor to join them.

"Sir." She showed him her list of assets. "We've been trying to match any of the cars at the campground that night to the surveillance footage we have of these areas. No luck so far. Either we check it out ourselves or send in a drone."

"Send a drone. That's our best bet for now."

"Penn," Agent Kaur interrupted. "I managed to hack into Claire and her father's telephone calls. I think you better listen to this." He handed her a set of earphones and pressed play.

"Clairy," a deep male voice said. *"What are you doing?"*

"I saw people dying in a bomb explosion," the girl said. *"I have to warn... someone."*

"You know how many times your mother and I have begged you to keep your gift quiet. If the wrong people hear about this, you will be in trouble... "

She cut him off. The word "gift" lifted the hair at the back of Penn's neck.

"Daddy, I've heard the speech many times. I'm not going to the wrong person. I can trust this person, promise."

"Let me guess. A hunch?" The father grew angry. "Who is this person, Claire?"

"Daddy, you have to trust me. I'm doing the right thing." Claire's voice dripped with honey.

"Claire." Penn imagined his lip quivering. "I don't like this one bit. I want an update every day. If not, I'm calling the police. And honey, be careful. If you need anything, whatsoever, you call me... It's hard... Now that you're all grown up."

"'kay, Dad, I promise, I'll be fine."

Penn removed the earphones. With wide eyes and a hammering heart, she handed them to Trevor. "I think this girl may have been telling the truth."

Agent Trevor yanked them over his head while Kaur restarted the recording. His face yielded nothing. He brought a fist to his mouth a few times as if to shield a cough. His breathing remained calm. *Would he believe it or not?* Penn was more inclined toward not, given how he had immediately discarded the letter. But if Claire was telling the truth, it meant fatal repercussions for the country.

"Get someone to Oregon now. I wanna know everything about this girl's gift." Trevor's silent breaths erupted into heaves. Beads of sweat broke out over his pale face. "And Penn, you find her. All terrorism agencies have been looking into the matter and no country has indicated a threat. This operation suggests a high level of collusion."

"Sir, are you alright?"

Lips pursed tightly, he stared her down. "If that call wasn't staged, the US is in danger and she may be the only one that knows anything. I'll alert the director and the agencies. I don't care how many hares you have to pull out of how many hats, you find her. Is that clear?"

"Yes, Sir."

Penn made several calls to their offices near the highlighted areas. Since the case had received 'red-sticker status', she was free to use all available resources. It took a while to arrange for a drone search of the properties, but eventually she located agents with the proper tech and expertise.

The drone that flew over the beach house in the Hamptons detected some activity inside. A quick internet search showed that the house was available for rent on two holiday accommodation sites. She ran the license plates of the blue BMW parked outside. It belonged to Mr. Shaun Tanner, a teacher from Brooklyn. Negative.

The house in Plymouth, on the other hand, was a graveyard. The lights were out and the curtains drawn. No indications of life. The black of the night made it difficult to spot any movement through the windows. Her hopes were high, but apparently the collaborator had a better location to stow them. The camera circled the house, indicating no sign of occupants. Penn tapped her foot on the ground, her nose still deep in the screen. *Just a minor bump in the smooth road that leads to Claire and Byron ahead.*

"Hey," she spoke to the drone operator in her ear. "Can you turn on the thermal detection?"

29

Claire

Saturday, 19 June 2020, 9 pm

Even through Claire's heavy intoxication, she could see the hurt gleaming in Byron's eyes. Sure, they quarreled all the time, but they trusted and protected each other. Her hand burnt with guilt, although not as much as the betrayal in her heart. He had vowed to keep her safe, and turning her in was the epitome of forsaking that promise.

Ignoring him, she stumbled toward the hallway and into one of the twin beds. Feeling more wretched than ever, she curled up into a tiny ball and let the tears escape. The shower of tears she had suppressed over the past few weeks poured out of her. Claire cried, not caring how loud her sniffles were. When did her insignificant life become so utterly terrifying?

Moments later, she felt the hand on her back. His touch was careful, slow, and pacifying circles with no words. Byron lay down next to her and pulled her into his chest. He held her as she shook with terror. They didn't speak. The silent comfort was enough. Eventually, Claire drifted into an abyss of dreams.

"Morning, beautiful. Happy 4th of July," Byron breathed into her neck, pulling her closer. "Did you sleep well?"

"Mmm," she groaned, not ready to wake up. "Why are you so cheerful with everything going on?" She looked around at his old bedroom.

"You're here. I'm happy." He kissed her, moving down her ear and jaw. She knew it was a distraction, his perfect instrument of denial.

"Byron!" Claire nuzzled him away. "We're in your father's house."

"I don't care." He continued his ministrations. It was distracting, but Claire wasn't comfortable avoiding reality. She squirmed, trying to wriggle herself from his grip.

"Hey." Byron stopped and pressed a quick kiss to her lips. "My dad is probably downstairs in his study and my mom is sleeping."

Several objections formed in her throat and died on her lips until her eyes landed on the television screen in the corner. The sound was muted, although she read the description of the breaking news report: "Nuclear missile attack in San Diego and Washington". They showed the footage of the explosion, blood-red smoke erupting into a mushroom-shaped cloud. Her limbs numbed and her mouth dried up.

"Byron!" She rocked him, breathless. "Look at the screen."

Byron jerked backward at her sudden panic and turned to follow her pointing finger. He stared for all of one second. "Put on some clothes."

Claire jumped up and flung on the closest shirt and pair of skinnies she could find. Halfway dressed, Byron dragged her out the door, into the hallway, and down the stairs.

Sunday, 26 June 2022, 4 am

Screaming, Claire opened her eyes to a pitch-black room.

"Hey." Byron's hand snaked around her waist. He hadn't left her. "What's wrong?"

"The 4th of July," she huffed. "That's when they hit."

"They?" Byron frowned.

"San Diego first, then DC. Then, New York, I assume."

Before she could blink, he sat up. Worry lines mapped his face. "Tell me everything."

"We're at your father's house. It's early in the morning. You, uh... I saw the report on TV. Two bombs. Those were the bombs I saw in my first dream."

Byron stood, rubbing his temples. "The news report, did it say who was behind the attacks?"

"No, all I read was 'nuclear bomb attacks'. There was no sound."

A knock on the door startled her. "Is everything all right in there?"

"Fine," Byron yelled over his shoulder. "She just had a nightmare."

He knelt next to the bed. "Claire, I understand you're scared of working with the authorities, but I really think it's our best shot. Time is running out and your dreams haven't revealed all that much."

Not this again. "If you want to go back, I can't stop you, but I won't."

"This is bigger than both of us and you're being selfish."

Claire bit her tongue to stop the "Screw you" that had already formed in her head. "I don't care what you think, my answer won't change. I've had years to consider the consequences. All you think about is the 'right now'."

"You might be the only person who can stop this, but you need help. Of course, I think about right now." He threw his arms in the air, writhing with frustration. "We might be stopping World War III, and all you care about is yourself."

She sent him a deadly glare. "If I only cared about myself, I would have gone to Bend with my friends. I would have started my internship. Did I? No, I skipped town in the middle of the night to find you."

Byron relaxed and sat down next to her again. "Tell me, why are you so afraid?"

She wanted to help him. In fact, it was all she wanted to do, only the people he expected her to trust could be colluding with those responsible for the attacks. One wrong person was all it took for things to turn lethal.

"I've grown up considering every stranger a threat. Look at their reaction to the letter. They won't believe me. You didn't. And what happens after we stop the bombs, huh?"

"I didn't at first, but I do now, and they will, too."

Claire slowly shook her head. "You only fully trusted me after I shared with you dreams containing information that came true. And the point is that people will know. There will be a target on my back. I'll never be able to live a normal life again. I'll be their pit of information and looking over my shoulder all the time."

"They can't force you..."

"They can and they will."

Byron took her hand and held it in his. His touch prickled her skin. "Okay, I get it. Let's make a deal. We give it a few more days. If we're still non-the-wiser, we go to them."

"Okay."

"Yeah?"

She nodded, and he pulled her in for a hug when the first part of the dream returned with full force. Their intimacy strengthened her dreams. Claire could hear his fearful heart-beats, causing an incline in her own. In her vision, their relationship appeared to have moved on to the next level. She felt it happening in the present; the growing emotions and affections, and she ran.

Out into the living room. She was about to open the sliding door to the porch when the previous night's fear of an eye in the sky hit. She shook the frisson from her body and started a pot of coffee, but the fear loitered. It numbed her, choked her, and froze her. She couldn't breathe, couldn't speak, and couldn't think.

Reality pivoted with fantasy. Her surroundings turned to a slow-moving smog. The crickets and birds outside morphed into taunting skeletons. The aroma of brewing coffee gave way to a stench of tarmac and sludge. She was in the middle of a railway, with an oncoming train and no escape.

Claire gasped for a knife tip of air, yet her lungs seemed to have lost their power. When the corners of her eyes turned dark, she heard the distant sound of his voice as arms wrapped around her. "Breathe," he said.

She couldn't.

"Breathe, Claire. You're okay, just breathe."

Jason appeared in the kitchen, a thumb scratching against his forehead. "Panic attack? Let's take her back to bed."

"Claire," Byron turned toward her, "can you walk?"

She couldn't answer him. Jason rounded the kitchen counter and moved closer. Her chest tightened, causing a pain to erupt in her heart. Closer. His hand reached out to touch her.

"Don't," Byron shouted. "I've got her."

"I'm just tryin' to help, man."

"I said I'm fine."

Breathe, Claire, get your act together. A faint pulse started to beat in her brain. Byron pulled her arm over his shoulder, maneuvered her forward in the direction of the bedroom. Each step relaxed her, her pulse slowed and a sliver of air found an entry point to her lungs. She didn't remember much else before falling into a deep, dreamless sleep.

At some point, Jason woke her. "Hey, are you thirsty? I brought you some tea."

Daylight was trying to inch its way through the still-drawn curtains. She sat up and took the cup. "Thanks."

He hovered in the room. "How are you feeling?"

"I'm okay." She sipped on the tea. "Just tired. Where's Byron?"

"In front of the laptop, growing more frustrated by the hour." He sat down on the opposite bed. "I tried to help, to form some sort of plan, but he's not really interested in my opinion. So, uh, you really believe this, too?"

Instinctively, she moved closer to the wall next to her, clutching her cup. Invasive questions from strangers were not her forte. "It's gonna happen, whether you want to believe it or not." She suppressed a yawn and her eyelids drooped. In her frazzled state, fatigue was too strong to fight.

* * *

Monday, 27 June 2022, 4 am

Claire sat up, fully awake for once. She had slept most of the day away. *There had to be something in that tea.* She had been vaguely aware of Byron coming to check on her a couple of times. Once her eyes adjusted to the dark, she noticed his peaceful sleeping form on the other side of the room.

Her stomach hollered with hunger. She moved the blankets away and swung her feet to the ground when Jason burst into the room. Byron turned and wiped at his eyes.

"I have bad news. Just received a text from the burner phone you sent Hoff. They're looking into his assets. We gotta get outta here."

"Shit." Byron slumped his head down to his chest. "Why are you helping us?"

"I'm Hoff's eyes and ears, masquerading as a simple security guard. My mission is to protect and help you at all costs. I get paid to do it."

"Don't know how I'll ever repay him." Byron glanced at Claire. "If I get the chance to."

"When you get the chance to… " she reassured him. She wanted to drag the agony from within him and carry it herself. Regardless of his current qualms, she cared. She had always cared, no matter how hard she tried to deny it. Deep inside, she knew they could stop it, if he would just trust her. Soon the answers would appear to her. She could almost taste them on the tip of her tongue.

30

Byron

Monday, 27 June 2022, 4 am

The clock ticked. Byron rapidly stuffed clothes and supplies into his new backpack. He exhaled, zipping it closed. Hoff's unqualified help had brought a surge of both relief and despair. The man was way too atrocious to work with the FBI, or whatever agency was following them, but he couldn't help but wonder if there was more to Hoff's help.

Of course, Byron had helped him achieve the one goal he had written off as impossible, but was that enough to prompt Hoff to move mountains for him? He considered himself a good judge of character, and unless Jason was a master manipulator, the guy appeared to be in their corner. Albeit at Hoff's instruction. No bad vibes came from his direction. He was open and straight. No ear touching, eye movement, or elevated breathing when he spoke. He had been sent to protect them. Still, no one could ever be fully trusted.

Although asking questions wasted time, he needed an answer. So, he marched toward the kitchen where Jason was filling a bag with food. Byron caught a peek of the contents and noticed weapons and cash beneath the layer of sustenance. The guy had quite a collection of arms. "Why is he helping us?"

Jason's shoulders sagged with a sigh, as if tired of Byron's incessant distrust. "I don't like to admit it, but I've been trying to figure out how Tanya stole that money for years. You did it in a couple of weeks. Jonathon Hoff will swim the Atlantic for you." He continued stuffing protein bars into the bag. "Have to admit, I think you had inside info, and that girl, she's it. Is she part of some insidious mob, or a cult or something?"

Byron shook his head.

"You're gonna burn your fingers with her if you're not careful. She's dragging you down, and for what? I've seen girls way hotter than her perve over you. Have you met this source?"

"Yes," he nodded. "And I trust him. So far, all of his information's been legit."

"And you really think America's at risk of a nuke war? Have you seen our nuclear inventory?" Jason scoffed, his voice soaked with scorn. "I think she's the source. She helped you out with Tanya's case and now you believe her. And you're too blinded by love to see that she's using you."

Byron's hands balled into fists. *Keep cool. You can't give her secret away.* "You're wrong, but I appreciate the concern. And, uh, thanks for all your help."

Jason's suggestion lingered on his way back to the bedroom. His breath caught in his throat. The possibility existed that Claire had received the case info from someone and then fabricated a lie of the dream. *Could it all be a ploy? Could she be making up those dreams?* He had considered mentalism before. An unusual phenomenon, not impossible.

But Claire had had the perfect little American life before. There was no reason for her to get involved in illegalities. "Yeah, like that's any indication. Just look at your father and Tanya Hoff," he spoke into thin air.

"Who are you talking to?" Claire emerged from the bathroom behind him.

"Just myself." Suddenly, he was wary of her. The strong bond they had formed impaled by a few divisive words. Everything Jason had said was the truth, and he couldn't shake it. He was falling for her. Fast and hard. He believed everything she told him. Byron linked his hands above his head, stretching his elbows outward. Was he a fool for trusting her? Was she using him as a diversion to escape certain vices?

A gentle hand touched his shoulder. "We'll figure this out."

He had no words. Byron could no longer tell north from south. Nearby, a roaring engine switched off. He was still frozen, with no idea of his next move. Should he follow her into the 'lie' of the nukes, or should he hand her over to Penn?

"Byron, you're scaring me."

"I think they're already here," he managed. "We should slip out the back and take the boat." Claire looked paler than usual and she swallowed hard a lump, he imagined. "Go ahead, I'll be right there."

Eyes tapered with doubt, she headed for the door while Byron stayed behind. He looked from left to right. Penn or Claire? Then finally scribbled a quick note on a piece of paper and left it on the table.

He slung his backpack over his shoulder and vanished through the sliding door just as footsteps approached the front of the house. Pulse throbbing, he sprinted down the steps that led to the dock and leapt into the boat that Jason had already started. They veered toward the far side of the river. The buzzing engine was interrupted by ricocheting bullets. All three of them ducked, covering their heads with their hands. One bang after the other. Byron lost count of how many shots were fired. The small stretch of land seemed eons away. *Faster.*He rocked forward.

The verge grew larger as they propelled forward, yet the gunshots continued, piercing his eardrums. All of those shots meant it wasn't just the FBI chasing them. One by one, lights from the surrounding houses switched on and residents appeared in nightgowns. The boat rocked in the light wind and he felt Claire grab on to him for support. As the expanse of green approached, he murmured to her, "We can't dock, we'll have to jump and swim, okay?"

She nodded.

Counting, he held up one finger. He took a deep breath and snatched the bag that held the weapons. Two. They jumped. Water splashed in all directions with the numbing impact. A welcome chill. Perfecting a small dolphin dive, he swam toward the bushes. Feet still in the water, Byron stepped into the swamp. His nose burned with the amount of water it had taken in, initiating a snort. Claire puffed behind him. He turned around and pulled her toward him.

"Come on," he said, sloshing into the vast verdure. "They'll be here soon."

Where the water had dried up, tree roots erupted from the overgrown grass, like soldiers strategically positioned in an ancient warzone at night. Fleetingly, he helped himself to a lungful of the fresh, natured scent. Snakes lurked, he was certain of that. Up ahead, he heard the low buzzing noise. *Drone!* He looked at Claire and pointed toward the sky. She frowned in confusion. "Drone, they've got us surrounded."

Claire hugged herself as the water dripped from her soaking hair and clothes. "No, I won't give up," she snarled through chattering teeth.

31

Penn

Monday, 27 June 2022, 5 am

Like a herd of buffalo, they loped from the dock, back up to the cars. Penn hopped in and pushed her foot down on the gas. Siren blaring, she sped toward the other side of the river with the cavalry in tow. No margin for failure. They had to know what the girl had seen. At least there were no cars on the road in the early morning.

Speed was a necessity since the drone didn't have eyes everywhere. Penn didn't understand why Byron hadn't been able to tell her about Claire. Why hadn't they told the full truth in the first place? It hurt. She may have buried all of her emotions so deep in her chest that she struggled to find them, but she still had feelings. Her version of their partnership friendship was a lie. He hadn't trusted her enough to confide in her about something so crucial.

"I've spotted them," said the drone operator in her ear. "They're entering a small cabin."

"Thank you."

She brought the car to a stop in the road near the creek that encompassed the swamp. Careful not to make a sound, she opened the door. Agent Kaur trailed behind. All the hands on deck split into pairs, who would scour different parts of the bush. A small flashlight in one hand and her gun in the other, they scuttled through the trees. Since light would give them away, they kept their flashlights off and felt their path in the dark, bumping into underbrush and tripping over gnarly branches. Reptiles were her biggest concern.

As betrayal subsided, fury burnt in her chest. They were partners and should have had each other's backs at all times. She would find and ask him before that damn explosion, in case there was no 'after'. They still knew nothing about these visions to which the girl referred. Byron did not believe in superstitious mumbo-jumbo, which meant there had to be some truth to it.

If Penn didn't return with the pair of them in cuffs, she might as well turn in her badge. Trevor had practically had a panic attack after that phone conversation. It had hit a nerve for her, too. Another 9/11, she presumed. Thousands of people would die. In Claire's defense, she had tried to warn them, Trevor simply didn't deem such a threat to be serious. Penn didn't care much for her own life, only the citizens she had sworn to protect.

A small sound on her left derailed her thoughts. Both of them turned in its direction and slinked closer. "Hands in the air!" she yelled.

The man stepped out from behind the tree; arms above his head, as instructed. Penn nodded to Agent Kaur, instructing him to take care of the unknown man while she continued to search for Byron and Claire. Up ahead, she saw the cabin to which the operator had referred.

As prompt and cat-like as possible, she moved through the trees toward it. Wood cracked as she kicked at the door and lunged forward, aiming her weapon. "Byron, these woods are surrounded by UAVs and agents. You'll never make it out of here."

Her eyes scanned left and right. *This place is too small to hide*, she thought until she felt the blade against her throat, and the hand on her mouth. Byron's fingers tasted of metal residue. One inch of movement would cause the sharp edge of the knife to puncture her artery. Penn stood stock still and watched as Claire removed something from a bag and held it out. A grenade. A distraction. The girl in front of her looked determined and lethal as she took the gun from Penn's hands certainly not sweet and innocent.

She felt one of Byron's hands drop from her, ripping the car keys from her jacket pocket. He whispered, "I left you a note. Be in touch," and pushed her further into the cabin. She stumbled backward, landing against the wall with a thump. Still, she kept her balance and pressed herself toward the door.

Once outside, she saw Byron and Claire running to the street where the cars were parked. Penn had no choice but to follow. Everything fell into slow motion as she sprinted forth, racing to catch up. At least the flicker of morning light made sidestepping the undergrowth a tad easier. Both fugitives dodged the shots fired in their direction, but the mission was to keep Claire alive at all cost. Those shots were meant to scare, not kill. They needed her alive to find out what she had seen.

As they left the blanket of green, she heard the car alarm beep and they aimed straight for the car that lit up. In one swift movement, Byron detonated the grenade and threw it in the direction of the oncoming attack. Most agents scrambled for cover, including herself.

She dived to the ground, shielding her face and ears, and squeezed her eyes shut. The grenade erupted with violent force, sending a series of shock waves through her body. It didn't hit her. She shook her head while an ironic laugh broke out of her chest. The SOB had fooled her again.

Rolling her eyes, she pulled herself to her feet and searched for an available car. "Do you have a trail on them?" she asked the operator.

"Yes, ma'am, but they'll be out of range soon."

"Then tap into satellites. You cannot lose them."

32

Claire

Monday, 27 June 2022, 6 am

Claire whipped her head back. "They're right behind us."

"Thanks, Captain Obvious. Hell, Claire, I'm not Superman."

"Jeez, I'm just saying. But that was kind of a Superman move back there." She smiled despite their crisis.

He stayed quiet; she assumed trying to figure something out. This was a mess she had made. She was supposed to get them out of it. Byron veered left and right between the first morning traffic no indicator and no consideration for other drivers or the speed limit. It didn't matter how many cars they dodged; they couldn't shake the tail. Claire had seen this in movies many times, but being chased in real life was a whole other drug. She had grown so used to almost getting caught, it no longer affected her.

"Claire." He touched her leg. "I need you to do something for me."

"Okay."

"Get me a gun out of that bag and take the wheel."

She bit her lip. The feds had guns, too. If Byron opened

fire, surely they would retaliate. Their only advantage was the element of surprise. "What if they... "

"Just do it. I'm gonna shoot the tires. Take a sharp left up ahead to give me a better angle."

She gave a weak nod and pulled out what looked like a 9mm from the bag.

"I'll count to three, then you hop over to my side. One... two..."

Claire jumped to the driver's side when she heard the loud shattering of glass. She felt a warm liquid drop on to her leg and noticed the deep-red color. He was bleeding. She shook, not allowing herself to think about that. One after the other, the excruciating gunshots rang through her ears. Claire blocked it all out and floored the gas, swerving left, as he had asked. The car screeched around the corner, producing a potent, burning rubber smell.

She heard the strident sound of a crash and scraping metal, but could no longer see anything. *Dear God, please let them be okay.* Then, just as Byron pulled back, another vehicle with screeching sirens turned the corner. On instinct, Claire took the next left to get away. *We're so screwed.*

Byron half-pushed her back to the passenger side, reclaiming his position. Her whole body trembled, moving of its own accord. Sirens wailed, cars buzzed, and sweat pooled at the back of her neck as they tried to speed away from the car behind them. Each car dodge was more nail-biting than the next. They neared a red light where an array of fast-moving cars were crossing. A sudden idea formed in her mind based on a YouTube video Brent and Ted had once shown her.

"Wait for a small gap and go!"

Byron slowed down slightly. More gunshots rang out behind

her and she forgot how to breathe. He slipped through a glint of an opening between two cars, and they were free. For now.

Claire expected another chaser at any moment. An on-slaught of thunder roared in the distance. When she looked up, the sky had turned blustery and bleak, sending an unnerving shiver through her bones. They kept moving through the narrow town roads, trying to escape the labyrinth. Byron's sudden stop jerked her forward. She narrowed her eyes in his direction while he pulled into a parking space covered by a canopy of trees. He ignored her and grabbed the bag with the weapons. The blood around his hand had slightly dried and knotted, yet fresh blood still leaked from the wound. *It must hurt.*

She opened the door and followed him, presuming they would head to one of the nearby stores. Instead, he took out a knife and slashed it into the soft cover of the truck next to them, tearing a careful slit into the fabric. He gestured to her and she crawled through the narrow opening. The metal was cold against her skin as she lay down on her stomach. Byron struggled to fit, his muscular frame a touch too big for the small incision.

"Guess all that boxing has its cons, huh?"

"Yeah," he smiled, to her surprise, considering his solem-nity that morning. "Damn, I hope this works. I didn't see any drones, and I doubt they can see past all those trees. Move up." He pushed her against the other side of the truck. "We need to lie far away from the tear in case the owner spots it and peeks inside."

They lay in a tangled mess, crushed against the side, breath-ing the same air. Their lips were inches apart, their noses brushing. Byron wrapped his hand in his shirt to stop the bleeding. "I need to ask you something," he said in a hushed tone.

"Okay. Sounds serious."

"Jason messed with my head. He told me you're lying, and I'm being an idiot. I bought it."

Claire felt her nostrils flaring. "You what? How could you think I'm lying? After everything we've been through."

"You showed up one day and told me I was going to die. I had no choice but to believe it. Now you refuse to co-operate with anyone, and it made me think you're hiding something."

Another round of thunder sounded before drops of rain pattered against the outside of the car.

"Would you skydive?" she asked.

"Of course not."

"You're afraid of heights. You won't ever willingly put yourself in a situation where you have to face that fear. Well, my parents have schooled the fear of someone knowing my secret into me as long as I can remember." Claire closed her eyes, moved closer, and placed a hand on his cheek. "Your heart's racing, right? You're feeling hotter than usual. That's how I feel at the idea of sharing my gift. I trust six people in this world, and that's it."

"Claire," he breathed. "You do realize you're trying to convince me with seduction. That's conniving."

"Is it working?" she teased.

"Yes."

Nearing footsteps heckled their intimate moment. Both of them played dead. The intruder moved closer and Claire was certain their heartbeats were audible. Her nerves were quickly calmed when the driver's side opened, and the truck dipped slightly. The door slammed shut before the engine rumbled to life.

"Byron," she whispered once the car started to move. "I'm not lying."

"Only one of your visions have come true so far. The one about Ellie. All the others have changed because of the information you gave me. It's a little jarring." Claire could swear she heard a slight stagger in his voice.

"Why'd you still protect me, even if you doubted me?"

"I just knew."

It wasn't an answer, rather an evasion of an answer. She didn't want to push him, but she needed to. "Look at me." She held his chin in her palm. "I know it's dark, and you can't see, but use all of your senses. The closer we become, the richer and faster my dreams present. If you pull away, everything we've done will be for nothing. I need you as much as you need me."

33

Penn

The light drizzle evolved into a downpour, prompting Penn to bump her wipers up to full throttle. Her left elbow leaned against the car window while she bit on her thumbnail. She refused to believe it. The storm caused a momentary loss in transmission, awarding Byron and the girl another window of escape. She started to think fate was playing into their hands.

As she arrived at the stolen car, a few agents were studying the surroundings, shielded by black umbrellas. Empty and abandoned, the car stood neatly parked in the oak-sheltered lot. One small luck of thunder and GPS signal had been lost. Penn licked her lips, not accepting they had disappeared again. The UAV had searched the perimeter with no results. Well, no positive results. She fought the urge to drive into the darn car because they were right back at square one.

Almost completely discouraged, she remembered Byron's whisper in the shed: "I left you a note, be in touch." Hope surged, sending her back to the house on the river at once. The scene investigators should have found it by now. There was also the man they had found in the swamp, who was worth questioning. Penn didn't recognize him. Still, she had a strong suspicion that he was the abettor.

She was looking forward to arresting Jonathon Hoff for aiding a fugitive. *Revenge sure is sweet.* That was another sudden change in the man she thought she knew. Her partner had hated the guy, but the person she had fought in the woods was Hoff's BFF.

Investigating agents swarmed her as soon as she brought the car to a standstill in front of the house. Agent Langley opened the door as if she were royalty and handed her a plastic bag containing the letter. Penn leaned over to her glove compartment for a pair of rubber gloves and opened the folded piece of paper. In Byron's scribbly handwriting, she read:

Attack on 4 July. SD, DC, NY. Heading to...

The middle was smudged. She could only make out the word "alone" at the end.

"Where did you find this?" she asked, holding up the letter.

"On the desk in the room with the twin beds. There's a small leak in the roof that dripped onto the paper."

Penn poked at her eyes with one hand. Just when the facts were starting to make sense, Byron sent her a note about their whereabouts. Or it was a trap. Her head spun to the point where little black dots appeared before her eyes. For some mysterious reason, she leaned toward the double-agent theory. Byron was still on their side, extracting information from the girl who wasn't prone to providing it. He wasn't aware that they knew of Claire's supernatural abilities.

She pulled her phone from her pocket, snapped a photo of the note, and sent it to Trevor.

Penn: Black might still be with us.

His reply came instantly.

Trevor: Friends and family suggest she might be making things up in her head and believe it as the truth. She has coped over the years, but now they're considering mental illness. Brain scans show signs of epilepsy.

Penn: If that's true, why did they let her go out on her own? Pulling the wool over our eyes.

She left Trevor to deal with that side of the operation and contacted Agent Kaur, who answered in a single ring.
"Penn."
"What have you got for me?"
"We've taken him in for questioning, but he hasn't said a word."
"On my way. I'll get him to talk."

* * *

Penn looked at the man on the other side of the glass. Facing away from her, he lay on his arms. She stepped inside, pulled out the chair on the opposite side of the table, metal screeching against the floor. He paid her no mind.
"What were you doing in that swamp at that hour of the

morning?"

The door burst open and in came a tall, balding man, sporting an expensive charcoal suit. *Hate lawyers.*

"Ma'am, my client has nothing to say at this time. Do you have anything to charge him with?"

Her eyes bore into the attorney's pompous expression. "I would just like to ask him some questions."

"You've got the wrong guy." It was the first word the man had spoken since they arrested him. "I've never even used a gun."

The statement pushed Penn back into her chair. Kaur must have mentioned something about the shooting earlier on. She studied his face and noticed the dilated pupils, then left the room to locate her new partner. Referring to him as a partner didn't sit well with her.

"What's the background on this guy?"

Kaur held the tablet out to her. "Name's Charles Duffy. Twenty-four years old, born and raised in Plymouth. Still lives with his parents. Sketchy work record."

Penn clicked her cheek.

"Addict. He was in the wrong place at the wrong time. He's not our guy."

They needed another approach. *Think, what would you have done?* She hated referencing her old ways, although often needed it to get a tight grip on slippery situations.

Taking a breather to collect her thoughts, Penn sat down in one of the Roanoke office's consultation rooms. She wasn't sure what to make of the note. The location was blurred and even if it wasn't, it could be a ruse. She needed to lure them to her with a devilish offer. Hoff had a way of contacting him, and that would be her starting point. *Ugh.* She would have to face that prick again.

Penn rejoined Kaur in the temporary surveillance office. She opened her phone and dialed Hoff's number. It rang and rang without answer.

"He won't answer," said Kaur over her shoulder.

"I helped put his wife behind bars as much as Byron did. Why should he get all the credit? If I could convince him... "

"I've read the case reports. He hates women. No way he'll help you." Kaur squeezed her shoulder. "He won't admit guilt, either. He'll claim his mother often rents the place out, and that he mentioned it to Byron, or something. We have no proof that links him to aiding Agent Black and the girl."

Penn sagged back into her chair, unable to argue. She had considered contacting Doug Black, but they already had a hawk-eye on him. Should Byron be desperate enough to interact with him, they would know. She needed someone who had the means to get in touch with them. "We need some bait that'll bring them to us."

One of Kaur's eyebrows raised in thought. "Press release. It's time to make this public and offer a reward."

His sentence was hardly finished before she received an email from Doug's tail with a video attachment. Keen for some good news, she played the file.

Doug entered the restaurant. The waiters greeted him eagerly. He was probably a regular who tipped well. An extravagant place with contemporary chandeliers suspended from the ceiling and abstract flower decorations against the pillars. Round set tables, complete with five-course cutlery, wine glasses, and rose centerpieces filled the space.

The waiter showed him to a table where an emaciated, pale

woman was already seated. "Sorry, I'm late. My last meeting ran longer than expected," said Doug as he slid into his seat.

"Well, I see that hasn't changed," she said with the bare hint of a smile.

"Why am I here, Maryanne?"

The woman gave a single nod. "All right, I'll get right to the point. I have cancer, stage four, and I would like to see the kids again."

Doug scoffed with ridicule. "Now suddenly they're your kids, too? You resurface after 20 years and expect to see them?"

Penn felt like the wind had been knocked out of her. Maryanne was Byron's mother.

Her lips pulled into a tight line. "You made me leave. Don't pin that on me. But they are still my children, and I would like a chance to say goodbye. Will you help me, or should I find another way?"

"Erica has been looking for you. She'll be happy about this. Byron hasn't spoken to me in years. He's in some trouble." He shook his head. "But I'll let Erica know." He let out a deep breath. "I haven't had a drink in two years."

"You kept me away from my children for 20 years, don't expect a congratulation from me."

"You had an affair."

"Because I couldn't live with a man who constantly abused me, verbally and physically."

Doug looked down disconsolately. "I'm sorry, Maryanne. I'll call Erica and set it up. She has two beautiful little girls now, Cassandra and Ellie." He reached for his phone in his pocket.

Penn paused the video and looked to Kaur. "Well, whattaya know. Mama Black is dying." She couldn't imagine Byron's

247

reaction to the news. Inside, she felt a slight push against her heart. All these years he had spent hating her for leaving, were, in fact, his father's fault and now he wouldn't get the opportunity to reconnect. Then again, if one of her real parents ever reached out, she wouldn't give them the time of day. They had abandoned her; they didn't deserve a single minute of her time.

"The press release might be a bad idea."

"Why?"

"This case is very sensitive. If we share this news with the public, the attackers might retaliate, causing a public panic."

Kaur pushed out his lips, frowning. "Can't her parents do a missing person's press conference?"

Penn's phone rang before she could answer the question. The unknown number instilled a hope that it was Byron calling with an update, as his note had suggested.

"Penn."

"Hi, is this Taylor Penn?" a female voice asked.

"Yes, who's this?"

"My name is Erica Klein."

Penn almost dropped the phone. "Erica, how can I help you?"

"I can't get a hold of my brother. He gave me your number and said to call you should this ever happen."

Penn sighed. "I wish I could help you, but I have no idea where he is, either."

"Excuse me?" Erica's voice raised an octave in panic.

"Erica, Byron's gone missing, but I think you might be able to help us find him," she said with a diabolical smirk. It was so easy to tap into old habits.

34

Byron

Monday, 27 June 2022, 8 am

Byron stared at Claire as if he had gone mute, applying pressure to the wound in his right hand as a distraction. He felt more muddled than a patient waking up with amnesia. His feelings for Claire blinded his objectivity, and her proximity wasn't helping either. She was asking for another lie detector, like he had done when they first met, yet weeks of observation had suggested no untruths.

He closed his eyes and remembered Jason's words. Their impact had shaken him right back to the person he was pre-Claire. She spoke with an honest benevolence that was almost serpentine. Whether it was the truth or a manipulative way to keep him close, the damage had been done. He had already betrayed her. "I just knew," was all he could think of in that moment.

Truthfully, there was no point in handing her over to Penn. Claire would clam up in the presence of strangers. Unless it was her choice to join forces with them, she would be of no help. And if she was fabricating the dreams, he now had more time with her to figure it out. *Whatever, you're just trying to justify your foolish choice.* Either way, he would feed Penn the information if, and only if, she followed his instructions.

"Will you say something?" Claire asked.

"Let's just focus on getting out of this truck for now."

They had been driving for quite some time. No longer in the small town of Plymouth, for sure. The truck bumped, wobbled, and curved with the roads. Rain splattered into the opening in the fabric, spraying them as it landed on the bed.

Lady luck seemed to be on their side. No one was following them, and in his haste to avoid the rainstorm, the driver hadn't noticed the tear. Nevertheless, he held his gun close to bargain their way out, if needed. After what felt like an hour, maybe more, the truck stopped and the engine shut off. He heard the door open and close before hurried footfalls led away from them.

Claire stirred next to him. He placed a finger in front of his mouth to still her. He moved over to the opening and turned around to peek through the hole. Golden cornfields stretched for miles ahead of them. Nearby, a dog barked, and his nerves amplified. He readied the gun, then stuck his head out for a better view. The car was parked next to two others and a Jon Deere, in a carport adjacent to the house. There was a barn not too far away.

He didn't bother calling Claire, she would follow like a well-trained puppy. Squeezing his arms to his body, he crawled through. The coarse fabric tore a little more to make way for his broad shoulders. He kneeled behind the truck, waiting for Claire, who handed him the backpack and glided through with ease.

Heads ducked, they slipped past the house and down the

muddy pathway that led to the barn. Inside the house, he still heard dogs barking. Rainwater soaked them from the skies, though Byron didn't mind the soothing taste. He turned his injured palm upward, allowing the water to drain away the blood and sting. Moving through sludge during a downpour was no Sunday brunch. Then again, nothing in life worth fighting for was ever easy.

Gasping and panting, they made it to the wooden shelter. One side was stacked with corn and the other entrance led to a small stable. Byron looked around at the stalls that held only two horses. Claire's eyes lit up at the sight of them. She shied away from humans but apparently had no problem getting acquainted with horses.

There was a look in her eyes while water dripped from her skin: The same look of innocence she had given on the back of that getaway truck. His heart raced at its fastest pace yet. His mind bore no logicality when it came to Claire. Heck, he had abandoned everything he had spent his entire life building to journey into the unknown with her. If it had been anyone else, he wouldn't have believed them. No, he would have arrested them on the spot. For some reason, when Claire beckoned, he followed.

Even when he had the chance to spool back and mend fences with Penn, he'd chosen Claire. Because she held the key to saving his life? No, he tasted the answer on the tip of his tongue, but it refused clarification. He was an idiot, that's why. Thinking about it now changed nothing. He would make the same reckless mistake again, if it was a mistake at all.

"Wow, you are so beautiful." Claire stroked the horse's nose, prompting a delighted whinny from the muddy-brown steed.

"So are you," he let slip.

"You've told me that before." She blushed. "At your sister's house, remember?"

"Then it must be true."

"I wanna try something. I think it might help with my dreams." She moved closer.

He knew exactly what she was getting at. Claire was far from dumb she knew he couldn't resist her. Hell, when she had slapped him across the face, he'd comforted her. This girl had brought about a 180-degree change within him and he wasn't sure whether he liked it or not. If his last few days were spent in her arms, perhaps he wouldn't mind dying.

"This is awkward," she said.

"I betrayed you," he blurted, needing to come clean. "I told Penn where we're headed."

"So, that's what's been bugging you? I knew there was something."

"I didn't tell her about your visions, I swear. I was just so desperate for help and you were more reluctant than a donkey."

"I know I should be mad, but I can't blame you." She rose on her tiptoes and wrapped her arms around his neck. "We can't fight each other, we need each other. We'll figure something else out. In the dreams I've had of New York, we're calm. Maybe we find a way around her."

"Have you ever kissed someone, Claire?"

"Obviously not."

"You scared?" The excitement and fear surging through him were abruptly halted by her lips on his. Their slight connection conducted electricity from one to the other. At first, barely a touch, gentle and introductory. Soft and sensual quickly turned to fervent when the suppressed need flickered to life.

He evened his breathing and foul mind when they took a moment for air. For a few minutes, he just held her something he hadn't done much of in his life. He had never allowed himself to establish or feel any coherent connection.

"So," Claire looked up. "This rain won't stop soon, and we might die in a few days." She kissed him again and broke away just as soon as she started. "I'm, uh, feeling things that I'm not supposed to."

Yeah, those things are ransacking my brain right now. "You wanna stop?"

"No, I mean, yes. Ugh, I don't know." A loud sigh followed. "My mom, she taught me to wait till I'm married. I never thought it possible, and now we're here, about to die, and... "

Claire was different, special, worth the commitment of marriage. "Then wait." *Wow, what a hero you are. Like you don't want this more than anything.*

"But what if I never get the chance?" She pulled his hands from her waist and held them in her petite ones, an ebony and ivory contrast between their skin tones.

Byron kissed her forehead, moving his hands down her sides. "We can still kiss if you want," he whispered against her ear.

Goosebumps flared up on her pale skin. She looked to the ground, cheeks pink with an awkward giggle. "I guess. Okay, you win. Seduction isn't fair."

Every bit of doubt in Byron's mind disappeared as he knelt down in the pile of straw below, pulling her with him. He rubbed gentle patterns into her skin, attempting to soothe her anxious heart. Inside, he kicked himself for not believing her. She was fragile and terrified. Any person had to be blind not to see it.

At once he was a teenager again, making out for hours in the shadows of some party, wildly stretching the limits of decency. Except, he would remember this girl afterward. He would continue to kiss her when the sun overpowered the dark clouds that surrounded them, until he couldn't anymore. That day may arrive way too soon.

Transfixed by the experience, he never realized when soaking clothes dropped to the floor. Somewhere in their heated chimera, intentions had shifted. "You okay?"

"Yeah."

He eased her into what he considered to be unparalleled ecstasy, especially with Claire. Love, the word that had earlier eluded him. The reason he would protect her at all cost. They moved as one, in perfect sync and rhythm. Everything was ideal until Claire drew back.

"What's wrong? Did I hurt you?"

"No, but something did." She turned around, searched through the heap of hay until she spotted a brown paper bag, and opened it.

Byron blinked twice, to ensure he wasn't still daydreaming. The package contained at least a pound of white powder. Probably cocaine.

"Is this... ?"

"Yes."

Claire reburied it. They sat in silence, because of the act or the drugs, he wasn't sure.

She propped her head up. "Was that good? I mean I know... "

Byron couldn't hold back the chuckle. "Perfect." He pulled her into him, resting her head on his chest. While the rain battered the building outside, he pretended there was no tomorrow.

"Byron, you're with me, right?"

"I was so stupid. I'm sorry."

Claire snickered. "If sex was all it took to convince you, I would've suggested it a long time ago."

"It's not the sex, Claire, that's an animalistic act. I've had sex before. It's you."

"Shut up, you're starting to sound cheesy, and I don't like cheesy, Byron. Come on, old man, time to get dressed." Claire playfully slapped him.

He coughed. "Old man?"

"Well, yeah, you're ancient compared to me."

Her thigh muscles pulled as she started to stand. She was too strong for her own good, masking the pain with silly jokes.

"Did it hurt?"

"At first, but the pain subsided after a while."

"Claire," Byron pulled her back down, "that wasn't the last time for me."

"I know," she affirmed with a wink.

"Am I missing something here?" He tilted his head in confusion.

"I may have dreamt it." Claire coyly scrunched up her nose, as if caught stealing sugar.

"I really am sorry for doubting you."

"You're forgiven, we've established that."

He didn't deserve her forgiveness yet couldn't refuse a generous Santa nowhere close to Christmas. Truth be told, the spy in his head warned of lies, though his heart refused to believe it. The one organ in his body that had never worked before had now taken the reins. Sure, they still had tons of work and dangerous encounters to overcome, but an altered vibration filled the air. Claire had already experienced the difference in her vision, which is how she knew what they required to succeed.

They redressed in their damp clothes and sat crossed-legged on the wooden floor to plan their escape. "Penn will expect me to go to my father."

The storm outside started to calm. "Okay, so let's stay here. For now. My dreams will guide us until we have enough info to meet up with Penn."

"In this barn?" The left side of his face pulled into tight lines. "We need food and internet to research. We can't rely on your dreams alone."

"No, with these people. We have a silver-platter bargaining chip." She patted the spot where she had hidden the powder.

Those words were hazardous sounds. Any involvement with drugs was dangerous. Byron heard footsteps outside. He grabbed the gun next to him and aimed it at the entrance, shielding Claire with his body. He motioned with his hands for her to get the 'merch' and follow him. Squatting, they hid behind a horse in a different stable. The footfalls grew louder and entered the barn, then the owner passed them towards the back. A few low noises followed before the room turned silent once more.

He attuned his ears to the frequency of the muffled screeching. Byron assumed that the person should be tending to farm duties, although their stealthiness seemed secretive. He instructed Claire to stay put while he investigated. Two tiptoed steps later, he heard the snort and knew exactly what the person was doing.

With that info, he walked straight to the empty stall. He

expected a man but found a girl around Claire's age, maybe younger. "Does your family know about this?"

The brunette flipped around and almost collapsed to the ground in fright. Her eyes bulged at the sight of the gun and she hesitantly lifted her hands to the air. "Take whatever you need, just please don't shoot." Her lips trembled.

"It's okay, I'm not here to hurt you. We need your help."

"Who's 'we'?"

Claire made her way over and he pulled her to his side. "We."

"If this is about the package, we have it covered. We'll get your money, I swear," the girl said.

"Maybe you should sit down." Claire must have noticed the woman's shivering. "We're not here about that, but we do need your help."

"And you will help us if you want this back." Byron took the bag Claire had hidden behind her back and waved it in the air.

"No!" Fear claimed the girl's facial features. Her head slowly dipped and lifted. "What do you want?"

Claire took the lead. "You don't have to be afraid of us. We don't wanna hurt you, all we need is a place to sleep and internet access."

She swallowed and moved back an inch. "Who are you?"

"It doesn't matter," Byron tried for decent, but failed.

The girl closed her eyes. He could only imagine the mechanical strain of the gears in her head. Her gaze floated to the package in his hand. "You give that back and I'll help you."

"Sorry, no can do. I think I'll hold on to it for insurance until we leave."

Her face remained burdened, her pupils darting around in deep thought. "You can't stay here, but my boyfriend has a cottage in the backyard. I can take you there?"

"Anywhere with wi-fi's good."

Claire stepped forward. She aimed to touch the girl's shoulders, but stopped short and settled for a smile. "We're good people, I swear. You can relax. What's your name?"

"Alina. Alina Thompson."

"Alina Thompson, you'll soon realize the magnitude of helping us."

Unconvinced, she nodded and dropped to the floor. "I just need to get the keys."

Uncertainty crossed Claire's face, but Byron squeezed her hand for reassurance. No doubt Alina would do anything and more to get her drugs back. That bag was most likely a life-or-death scenario. She left the barn. While waiting, Claire tapped her feet, shuffling from one to the other. Byron hid the gun in the back of his pants and pulled her into his arms. "She'll be back, trust me."

"How can you be sure?"

"I have some experience with girls who have secrets to hide."

"Psst," Alina whispered, "let's go." She tipped her head for them to follow. They crept their way through the drizzle to the carport. Byron took the front seat of the oldish, red Jeep. Claire sat in the back. "I'll just say you're friends, if my dad asks." She started the engine and some rocking guitars blared to life.

"I love this song," Claire all but shouted.

"You like System?"

"How can someone not like System?"

Byron observed their surroundings while the girls chatted away as if they had been friends for years. Poor Claire had to be starved for simpler conversations. After all, she was still a young girl with a lifetime of prospects to explore.

He used the opportunity to align his more demanding thoughts. The research he had conducted suggested that al Qaeda, who did not die easily, and North Korea were at the top of his suspect list. The former continued with their under-handed movement of assets and strengths across Islamist and non-Islamist affiliates, while the latter was strong in their construction of ballistic submarines, constantly taunting the US with missile testing.

The current evidence was far from damning, though. It would be so much easier to put together a full picture had Trevor taken the bait. Byron could have been working side by side with those who had the facts at their fingertips, feeding them more and more info until they cracked the code. Bygones and no time left to dwell on them.

35

Claire

When the song ended, Alina switched to the Bluetooth headset and called a person named Vince.

There was only a millisecond of a ring before he answered, "Babe."

"We have a problem."

"What problem?"

Claire couldn't see Alina's face, but she imagined it wasn't an easy conversation to have. "Some people found the stock. They're blackmailin' me for a place to sleep and internet. We're on our way."

The guy's response was one profanity after the other.

"Vince," she tried to calm him down, "they're armed. We have no other choice. The chick seems cool."

"Why would you hide the stuff in the barn. Are you fucking crazy?" he yelled.

She ended the call and turned quiet. Silence persisted until they pulled into a driveway. The white color, detailed moldings, and 19th-century style of the house seemed to have jumped straight out of Victorian historical fiction. Beautiful. No other words to describe it. If Claire was unsuccessful in her quest to save thousands of lives, she wouldn't bring herself to regret the decision to embark on this journey.

She had only one regret: The longing she felt for her family and friends left a deep ache in its wake. Byron had forbidden her from making any contact, since he knew they would be monitored. He refused to involve them or Erica as accessories to any crime. If they didn't make it, she might not be able to say goodbye.

Claire sighed and followed Alina to the backyard where the boyfriend met them.

With a deep look of disapproval, he unlocked the double white doors of the cottage. Byron paused behind her and extended his hand to the skinny guy with a slumped posture and dark ruffled hair. "Dean Matthews."

"Vince Larson," he accepted.

Vince gave them a quick tour of the place, which had original wooden architecture still intact. Although modern, the furniture and decor added to the antique feel.

"So, my folks will be back at around 6 pm. I suggest you lie low after that."

"Sure, but for now, can I please borrow a laptop?" Byron asked. "I have a lot of research to do."

"Who are you people anyway?" asked Vince.

Claire pulled her mouth, attempting to formulate a believable response.

"Former FBI," Byron answered. "Long story short, we found a mole and we're trying to rectify a situation that will spare thousands of lives. Right now, we're laying low until we receive more info from our source."

Vince chuckled while Alina's eyes grew to twice their size.

"You sure don't look like FBI," Vince noted.

"What does the FBI look like?" Byron fired back. "People have the wrong idea about us. We're just normal human beings with 70-hour workweeks."

Vince's lips moved, but nothing came out. Claire couldn't interpret whether his sudden reticence was because he was intimidated or scared.

"Hey, do y'all want somethin' to eat?" Alina asked, changing the subject.

"That would be great, thanks. Need any help?" Claire offered.

"Sure."

She joined Alina and Vince on their way to the main house. Vince left the two of them in the kitchen to prep some sandwiches while he fetched his laptop. Alina's vibrancy overpowered her, and Claire had to duck and dive her simple touches, as the girl spoke with her hands. But Alina was too high to notice and her hands trembled as she broke off pieces of lettuce. Her auburn waves bounced with her hurried movements, and dark pupils claimed the brown in her irises. She was as skinny as Claire, although it could have been a side effect of the drugs and not the result of an overactive metabolism.

The need to rescue the girl from the downward spiral of abuse nagged at her. Despite their difficult introduction, Claire liked her a lot. If she didn't rid herself of her addiction, her natural beauty would soon nose-dive.

"Your boyfriend." Alina suddenly stopped her incessant chatter. "He won't say anything, right? To my dad, or your contacts, or whatever?"

"Nah, he's harmless. We were just desperate for your help."

"You seem so different. I don't get it."

They were spectrums apart and yet God or the universe had pushed them together. "There's a lot in the world I don't understand."

Alina gave her a you-just-spoke-Spanish look and continued chopping tomatoes.

Byron barely ate before losing himself in the web. He had told her that North Korea was his prime contender because of their secrecy and unwillingness to co-operate with the rest of the world. Several sanctions weren't enough to push them toward conformity.

He read one article after the other by investigative journalists and reports on negotiations between the US and the hostile eastern country. Claire followed as far as she could, asking questions on their nuclear operations and war with the US.

"The North Korean dictator president doesn't appreciate any country in alignment with their southern rivals. He's made several threats to strike both countries," Byron explained. "You see, in the wake of the Korean War, we've made the mistake of disregarding them as a nation."

"Isn't that proof enough?"

"I don't know, the feds should have all of this info. If only I had some spies on the inside that could seek the confirmation we need." Byron sighed, running a hand over his face. "Two days, Claire. That's it."

"Pressure much?" They turned back to the screen and Byron opened Twitter. Claire assumed it was for information, but instead he scanned Vince's logged-in profile. "What are you doing?"

"Trying to get a read on Vince. I don't trust him." Byron delved into his search history. The top item on the list was for the fake name Byron had given them. There were some job searches, music downloads, odd YouTube videos. Funny and disturbing stuff. A lot of Netflix and social media. Clearly nothing that interested or surprised Byron as he turned back to news articles.

The shrinking of US household sizes may be coming to an end

Nothing of interest.

Tech exec Edward Tomb has a new nemesis

The guy was always in the news.

FBI agent's sister critical after attempting to locate him

Immediately, Byron clicked on the link.

Moments before FBI Agent Byron Black's sister was to appear at a press conference, an unknown vehicle rammed into the driver's side of her rental car and sped away. Mrs. Erica Klein discovered that her brother was missing earlier today and arranged for a press conference to raise awareness and plead for public information on his whereabouts.

The NYPD has no lead on the driver as yet and can't link the two incidents without such information.

Without reading further, she turned to look at Byron, who sneered at the screen. Claire frowned. *Is he in denial?*

He pecked her on the cheek. "Relax, she's fine. This is

Penn's way of getting my attention."

"I thought you said Penn knows where we're headed?"

"Either she didn't get my note, or she doesn't believe me." He wiped a thumb over his snarky smirk. "Act normal. Don't give anything away."

"Byron." Claire tugged at his arm. "What if you're wrong?"

"Then it wouldn't have been this big. I'm a nobody. No one cares what happens to me or my sister."

When the clock raced to 6 pm, Alina showed up with beers and a bottle of vodka. Claire cringed as her previous non-pleasant experience with liquor returned. The girl directed them into the small living room, where all three plopped down on the couch after the long, eventful day. Their hosts were only hospitable for one reason.

Vince entered and Byron eyed him like a sly vulture. He walked around the wooden coffee table and sat down next to his girlfriend. His stare kept drifting to Byron. Claire imagined they were instinctively searching for the "stock", as they referred to it.

The night wore on, broomstick-stiff. However, Byron seemed way too relaxed about a situation Claire couldn't exile from her mind. If something had happened to Erica, she was to blame. She forced a smile when conversation called for it, but couldn't bring herself to fully participate.

At some point, she rested her head on Byron's shoulder and only awoke when he scooped her into his arms. Bridal style, he carried her to the bedroom. "Erica is not the kind for press conferences. She's fine," he whispered.

"Okay." Claire closed her eyes and fell back to sleep within seconds.

"No!" Claire yelled, wriggling her arm from the tight grip. "Let go of me. My boyfriend is up there."

The man ignored her and continued pulling her down the steps. He ripped the door open, pushed her inside, and locked it. She noticed the cars around her and realized they were in the basement parking. Before she could process anything, he yanked at her arm, dragging her down another set of steps and into a room that appeared to be a workshop or a laboratory: Sophisticated, sterile, and downright spectacular.

"We have to go back up for my boyfriend," she demanded, stomping her foot.

"If we do, we'll die," he said with a heavy British accent. "Miss, your boyfriend's gone. I'm sorry."

"No," she shook her head. "No, you're wrong." She turned back to the door and jiggled it. "Unlock it!"

He pulled her away, pressing her arms to her sides. Claire dropped to the floor, tears spilling out. "No!" she cried, squeezing herself with her own arms, trying and failing to rid herself of the sharp pain in her chest. "No!" she sobbed, rocking back and forth as the agony spread through her veins.

The man squeezed her shoulder from above. "I'm so sorry."

"Who did this?" she asked in a voice laced with fury.

"I have an idea, but let's find out." He walked over to a laptop on the workbench against the wall and switched it on. For the first time Claire got a good look at the man: Reddish spiky hair atop an oblong face, not unlike her own, with a few tender lines and freckles around his cobalt eyes.

III

Deaths

36

Penn

Penn paused in front of the hospital room door and let out a deep breath. She stepped inside and examined all of the monitors and beeping machines connected to the woman. Her eyes were sealed and her body covered with white, sterile bandages. Her face was peaceful, almost smiling. Lifeless but still alive.

The aim was a few scrapes and bruises, just enough to scare Byron out of hiding, not a damn coma. With a mournful nod, she left the room and met Kaur outside the building.

"And?" he asked.

"Critical. Have you heard anything?"

"Nope, nothing so far. A few phony call-ins desperate for the reward money."

The traffic back to the New York surveillance office was worse than any romantic comedy Penn had ever been forced to endure. This damn city sure never slept nothing now seemed appealing about her old home. Not the honking or the bustling or the funky billboards. Jeez, she could even smell the stale beer from surrounding bars.

The fourth of July crept towards them and she had no lead on Byron and Claire. If they were in the middle of nowhere without technology, he wouldn't even know his twin was in a hospital bed. If he did, no scenario would see him abandoning Erica in her state. Not even for the intel Claire had to offer. His sister was the most important thing in his life.

The last few days had been a sprint from one city to the next, and now all she could do was wait for him to return to the vile place where dreams were supposedly made. Penn still actively searched every other platform she had, but thus far all roads led to dead ends. No doubt they had hitched a ride with someone, and that ride could be well on its way to Texas by now. Since their escape, there had been no responses on social media, and no inklings or bites on any other lines.

Back in the office, she stared at the whiteboard filled with photos of them; lines drawn to family members and other persons of interest; places they had been spotted; cars they had driven; and anything else that caught their attention. But the final piece of the puzzle was missing.

"Ma'am!" Agent Bisset came bolting toward her. "You wanna take this call."

Eyes narrowed, she reached for the phone. "Agent Penn."

"Hi, uh…" The man on the line cleared his throat. "I need to speak to the person looking for Byron Black."

"This is she."

"Good, I know exactly where your missing person is."

The sentence did nothing to enthuse her. Every person who wanted in on the generous reward knew exactly where he was. "And where might that be?"

"I want some proof of the reward before I offer any more

information. In the meantime, I can tell you some things that might interest you. He's with his girlfriend, Claire Baxter, wearing blue Nike shorts and a plain gray T-shirt."

Penn mouthed, "Trace the call!" to Bisset, who responded with a short nod, indicating they were already on it. She closed her eyes, trying to recall what Byron wore earlier that day. "You have my attention."

"I want the reward money wired to my account before I give up their location," he said with a laughable amount of cockiness.

"That's not really how it works. How do I know you're not lying?"

"I can send you a picture I took of him an hour ago."

Bisset gave her a thumbs up they had the caller's location. Nonetheless, she humored the boastful guy on the other end of the line. "Okay, send a Google Drive link to my Gmail account." Penn had a trash email set up for occasions like these. "Penny.wize@gmail.com. Wize with a z."

"Sending it right now."

Penn moved the phone away from her ear and covered the mouthpiece. "Get a team ready. I'm on my way," she whispered to Bisset, who saluted the order. Penn checked her email. She refreshed the screen until the link appeared, which opened to a photo of Byron sitting on a couch. He had a beer in his hand while Claire leaned on his shoulder. Their positions seemed much calmer than the status quo beckoned.

"Where are they now?" she asked the informer.

"No, money first, then we talk."

Ignoring his plea, she ended the call and hurried to Bisset. "Tell me about the caller."

"The call came from a payphone in East Raleigh, North

Carolina."

"Damn, the SOB was smart enough to hide his exact location. It must be someone they know who's desperate for cash." Penn stared blankly ahead as the phone rang once more.

"Ma'am, what do you want us to do?"

"Just wait, I'll convince him." She winked, answering the phone. "Listen up, here's how this'll work. You either give me their location and get your reward money or I find it anyway and you get nothing."

"I have no guarantees."

"I'm pretty sure the dogs I'm bringing with me can easily sniff out the drugs you're using. Do you know what the sentence for possession is? It's a Class 1 felony with up to a year in prison."

Penn heard heavy breathing on the line, followed by the phone clanking against metal. "I'd better get my payment, or I'm suing."

"Relax, drop me an email with the address and your PayPal account. If it checks out, you'll get your money." She ended the call and looked up to her team member. "Swaggering attitude and desperate for cash. Had to be drugs." She shrugged. Her parents had ensured she knew every telltale sign.

Penn opened the previous e-mail, sent from vincelarson72@yahoo.com. Nothing new had arrived. "Find the address for a Vince Larson in East Raleigh."

"What's the status?" Kaur joined them from behind.

"Someone's responded to the article. He wants the reward money before he co-operates. But, he's an idiot."

Her newfound partner shook his head, scoffing at her comment. "Most hotshots are."

"Bisset, get a SWAT team on standby," Penn instructed. "Guess we're heading back to North Carolina. At least it's better than this hellhole of a city."

37

Byron

Monday, 21 June 2022, 11:30 pm

Byron squeezed himself out of the narrow gap between the front and backseat of Alina's Jeep. He aimed the pistol at the driver's seat, waiting for Vince to return. Overconfidence fizzled through his veins, ascribed to outsmarting an entire organization time and again. He had to shake it before he made a millimeter of a mistake. Outside, hands and feet banged against the car door and it opened.

"Hello, Vince."

The young guy jumped into the air and his breathing amplified when he noticed the 9mm in Byron's hand.

"Now do I look like the FBI? Tell me, how is Penn? She on her way here?"

Vince shook his head.

"Trust me, she is. Now, you're gonna drive us to New York." Baby noises slipped from Vince's lips as he tried to find his voice. "Start the car." Byron ripped the kid's phone from his baggy jean pocket and threw it into the street.

Shivering, he did as told, then turned the earsplitting metal music down. They exited the diner's parking lot and pulled into the road.

"Don't even think about the highway. We drive back roads that take twice as long. Before that, you need to stop at a Trademart." Byron refused to play nice any longer. From now on, he would do whatever necessary to solve the problem. The limited time left called for his intervention.

Since Trademart claimed those parts of the US like a deadly disease, they reached one within minutes. Byron never did much like the mall-like chain store he preferred exclusive quality when he did buy something once every shipwreck but right now, he needed the 24-hour convenience.

The doors slid open. The store didn't throng with its usual daytime buzz, only low background music, and the occasional beeping scanner. They beelined for the pharmacy section while he clutched Vince's arm tighter.

"If they don't have wigs, get spray dye," he whispered to Claire, "and a battery-operated shaver." While Claire tended to the hair-masking, he searched for clothes and over-the-counter reading glasses the kind big enough to cover their eyes and noses. Their faces were now all over the news and social media. Anyone could recognize them.

As if they had entered a fastest-shopper competition, they grabbed the necessities and marched to the check-out counter. Byron had instructed Claire not to look up at all. Any camera to which the chasers had access would perform an automatic facial recognition procedure.

Byron loosened his grip on Vince's arm as they approached the cashiers, but ensured he was sandwiched between him and Claire without hope of escape. The guy was too much of a coward to fight back.

Head down, he glanced at the transaction. Claire focused on her goods, moving it through the counter from unpaid to paid. Luckily, owing to the time of night, the cashier appeared to be half asleep. She didn't pay much attention to the suspicious items Claire was buying. Absently, she moved the objects through the scanner; the machine beeping as it recognized the barcodes.

Byron noticed Claire stifling a laugh while handing the lady money. Nothing about their current situation offered any humor. Ridicule perhaps, but not comedy. She motioned for him to move. He was dying to know about her dream. She hadn't had a chance to tell him. There was no time for a chat, only to get up and go.

> "Claire, wake up," he whispered, shaking the hungry lioness. "We have to go."
>
> "Go where?" she groaned.
>
> "There's a reward for any person with information on my whereabouts. Vince must think I'm dumb or blind, he's gonna rat us out."
>
> Before he could blink, she was up. "What's the plan?"
>
> "We hide in the car. He'll lure Penn here while he takes us to New York. It's the perfect distraction, but it won't last long."
>
> "How do we get in the car?"
>
> "I unlocked it earlier before they left. We'll hide in the back."

In the car, Claire rifled through the bags behind him until she found her black-haired wig. "How do I look?" She turned from side to side, showcasing her new image.

Byron gave her a brief look, with half an eye on the road. "Half Chinese." And jalapeno pepper-hot. *Calm your thoughts. Now's not the time.* Claire's girlish blonde curls gave her an innocent, naïve guise. In the wig, she could pass as a North-Korean spy, even if her face was a tad long.

"Good, that's what I was going for."

He shifted his attention back to the road, but could still hear her rummaging through the paper bag. A shallow drilling noise started behind him the hair clipper. As he looked over, she dragged the shaver through Vince's hair.

"What the... ?" Vince ran a hand through the shaven patch. "Are you out of your mind?"

"It suits you," Byron chuckled. "You should be unrecognizable, too. Penn probably knows what you look like by now."

Claire continued shaving until little hair remained. Uneven blotches and holes poked out. It looked terrible, but Vince wasn't going to object with a gun pointed at him.

Instead of shaving Byron's hair, she cropped it short before spraying it with silver an extra precaution beneath his new baseball cap. Afterward, they changed into fresh clothes and donned their reading glasses.

Byron reached into the back and squeezed Claire's knee in thanks. Then he faced Vince. "Keep your eyes open for flashing lights and other warnings of checkpoints. We'd want to avoid those, unless you have a fake driver's license?"

"No. Will you shut up already?"

Byron clenched his jaw at Vince's attitude. "Where's your girlfriend?"

"At home, asleep. She had nothing to do with this. Even tried to talk me out of it. She likes her," he said, tilting his head back and gesturing to Claire. "I told her we'd be idiots not to go for it."

Byron slammed the dashboard. "That means they'll be able to trace the car." He looked around as if the answer to their problem would jump out at him.

"Crash it," Claire said.

"What?" He whirled his head around.

Claire moved toward him. "I bumped into a car on my way to Williamsville. If we crash the car into another, the other driver will be sure to step out, right? Then we steal that car."

"What have I done to you?" Byron wasn't joking he was growing increasingly concerned about her criminal mind.

Claire flipped her new Chinese bob as if he'd given her a compliment. "I'm a fast learner."

"I hope you can forget about it once this is over. If it ever is... Okay, let's get it over with so you can tell me about the... you know." He circumvented any word relating to clairvoyance and turned to face the front.

"Look for a car with one guy, preferably not too old."

He waited until they were on the open road, to avoid spectators. While scrutinizing the cars that passed them, a booming strike of lighting announced another storm. Good. They could use the distraction to their advantage. Byron profiled each fellow driver as if compiling a possible suspect list. Trucks dominated the road and cars were few and far between. If the men who fitted the bill looked too dangerous, he scratched them, too.

As the rain fell, so did the drivers' IQs. He could never understand how people degenerated into panic states along with a small change in weather conditions. Unfortunately, it meant that the traffic clogged up, increasing the number of witnesses to their impending crime. To hell with them. They needed a car to get away, and this was their only opportunity. He considered hitchhiking, but nowadays people were too cautious to invite strangers into their cars.

His desperation amplified with the intensity of the rain-drops, which obscured his view. Once he spotted the blue Toyota Prius they had passed earlier, he decided it was time for action. "That guy," he said to Vince, pointing diagonally to the right. "He should work."

"Alina will kill me for dinging her car."

"Well, if you don't co-operate, you'll be dead anyway. Get in front of him." He had no intention of shooting the guy, but he needed Vince to believe that he would do it. Face vacant, Vince flipped on his right indicator, although none of the trucks allowed him a gap.

"Stay on it."

He moved forward to keep up with the Prius, but Vince wasn't great at hiding the obvious. They trailed him for a couple of minutes until the car veered into their lane. "Should I just crash into him?"

"No, that'll give him a chance to drive away. Get in front of him, then hit the brakes when his momentum is enough to ram into us." Still blatantly obvious, Vince half-circled the car to the front. It took another few miles before a downhill opportunity presented itself. "Claire, buckle up." Byron didn't wait for Vince to mess up their operation. The impact had to be enough for a minor bump and not complete destruction of the car. He did a quick Newton calculation and pulled the handbrake at the perfect moment.

Both cars squealed to a stop, scorching tires was becoming a familiar smell. The impact was more intense than the sound of the crash. It jolted him forward, then rocked him back into the seat, causing the airbags to inflate. Byron scrambled out of the car. Hiding the gun in the front of his shorts, he stomped his way to their victim, hands balled into fists with pretend rage.

The driver's door opened, followed by a black umbrella, and out stepped a guy who was the splitting image of Eddie Murphy.

"What the hell, man?" said the driver. The man's response came out way too evenly to be considered aggressive.

Byron moved closer, cursing himself for his next move, given that their victim appeared to be a husband and father. He meant the man no harm. Waiting for Vince and Claire, he inspected the fender. The bump was too light to cause any real damage. A few cracks and crushed lights on both cars, but nothing major. Not according to script, the Jeep's engine sounded and sped away. And there it was, the millimeter mistake caused by overconfidence.

At once, Byron grabbed the gun and slyly poked it into the gentleman's stomach. "Get in."

With rubber-ball-sized eyes, he nodded. The man back-tracked into his seat and Byron removed the key from the ignition. He jogged around and slid into the other side before handing the keys back to him.

"Go! My girl is in that car. Your life depends on hers."

The car started and took off with only one functioning headlight. The wipers worked overtime while their heavy breaths steamed up the windows. Byron kept wiping it away with his hands until the airconditioner cleared the haze. He found Claire looking at him through the back window. The vapor obscured her face, but he imagined those arctic eyes pleading.

"Please," he whispered, vulnerably, "I can't lose her."

Without a word, the man sped up, narrowing the distance between the two cars. Vince wasn't easily discouraged. He used the intervening trucks to play hide-and-seek.

"I recognize you," said the man beside him. "You were all over social media today."

"Yeah, so I've heard. Don't believe everything you read."

"Why?"

"Because my sister's fine," he shouted, needing it to be true. Hope was the only thing he could hold on to. "Just keep your eyes on the road."

They held a steady distance. Vince had no opportunity to escape, although the Jeep could very well serve as a strong smoke signal and lead Penn and her pitbulls right to them. That appeared to be the boy's tactic: He was playing for time until the FBI showed up.

38

Claire

Tuesday, 28 June 2022, 2 am

The heavens seemed to have an unresolved quarrel with the earth, flooding it with liquid power and static force. Outside, truckloads rattled as the wind countered its potency. With a strong grip on the knife in the bag, Claire turned back to look at Byron. Her window was too foggy to distinguish much of anything, although she could feel his eyes on her. *Dear God, please forgive me for what I'm about to do.*

Claire and Vince hadn't spoken a word to each other. The small space between them was filled by silence and the stench of overwhelming humidity. Slowly, Claire pulled back her right hand until the sharp blade became visible. Hiding it from Vince's view, she moved an inch to the right. His attention flicked straight to the rearview mirror, yet he said nothing as she resumed her rigid position.

Breathing became a testing task and sensation faded from her fingertips. Claire couldn't risk threatening him with the knife to his throat, as Byron had done to Penn. Touch presented an opportunity for a vision that would enable him to rip the dagger from her hand and stab her instead. She garnered all the courage she held inside and jabbed the dagger into his right bicep. Vince groaned as his left hand flew to the wound, but before he reached the cut, Claire pulled with all her might and plunged it into his side. She squeezed her eyes shut, unable to stomach the blood dripping from him, like a severed oil pipe.

His body went limp and his eyes rolled back, hopefully owing to the sight of blood. The Jeep swerved left. In one swift movement, she caught the wheel and centered it back into the lane. She climbed onto his lap, pulled off the road, and brought the car to a standstill. Only then did she realize the tears streaming down her face. She barely had time to process anything before Byron knocked on the window. Her shaking hands struggled to unlock the door, but as soon as she did, he ripped it open and pulled her into his chest. "You're okay. You did so well." He kissed her forehead, although Claire sensed his quivering, too.

"I didn't... " she sniffed, " ... mean... to hurt him."

"It's fine, sweetheart. We'll help him."

Another guy, whom she assumed to be the driver, ran to meet them with an umbrella in one hand and a first-aid kit in the other. "He might be okay," said the man, dressing the wounds with bandages.

"Come on." Byron dragged her toward the Prius behind them. "It looks like he knows what he's doing." He opened the car door and inched her into the back before returning to the Jeep. Moments later, the two men carried an unconscious Vince to the passenger seat. Carrying their possessions on his shoulder, Byron slid in next to her. Both of their bodies were soaking wet and cold against the synthetic leather. He buried her head in the crook of his neck, resting his chin on top of her hair. Languid strokes on her arms chased the goosebumps away.

They sat alone for a few minutes, both occupied with the demons in their minds, until the car door opening interrupted their internal battles. "He's alive for now." The unknown man fell into his seat.

"Shouldn't we call 911?" Claire sat up, alarmed.

"No! Too dangerous." Byron pulled her back. "Let's go," he said, handing the car key to the driver.

"How did you know how to do all that?" Claire asked the nameless man.

"First aid training. My partner and I both did it before applying to adopt."

Once his words registered, the guilt caused Claire to swallow hard. "You have kids?"

"Only one, but we've applied for another." Shockingly, he smiled at her in the rearview mirror.

"Why are you helping us?"

"I'm forcing him." Byron lifted his shirt to reveal the gun.

"That's not the only reason," he said with the smile still fixed. "I'm a spiritual guide and leader of holistic energy. I read auras and yours are loud and clear."

"Yeah?" Claire moved forward, pricking her ears. "What do they say?"

"His," the man pointed his thumb in Byron's direction, "sorry what are y'all's names? I'm Leslie."

"I'm Claire, this is Byron," she half-smiled.

"Well okay, Byron's aura was charcoal when we first met. His energy was strong but misplaced. I sensed goodness buried deep within him."

"What does charcoal mean?"

"I consider it a veil of protection. He doesn't want others to see him, but when he spoke about you, flashes of red flew in. And together you wear a deep-red aura."

Byron gave a slight shake of his head. He didn't believe the mumbo-jumbo, but his face held an I'm-humoring-you grin. Claire linked her right hand with his left and turned back to Leslie. "So, what does red mean?"

"It's the color of passion. Can be good or bad; the need to show strength; or the deep desire to act aggressively." Their eyes met in the mirror.

"Maybe he does know how to read auras," Byron murmured.

"Sure seems like it." Claire watched Leslie. She didn't have to be a psychic or a spiritual energy reader to know he was happy. His lips were curved into constant content and no situation seemed to trip him up. "Do you think we'll go back to our normal lives like nothing happened?" she asked Byron, longing for simpler times.

"I don't know. Tell me about your dream."

She closed her eyes, rubbing her temples.

"Drain your negative energy," Leslie shouted from the front.

Claire looked up. "What do you mean?"

"You have a negative energy about the task you're trying to perform. Let go and the struggle should dissipate. Take a deep breath." He swerved his free hand in an elegant 'breathe in' gesture. "Now, focus on the air you're breathing. What does it feel and taste like?"

Claire did as instructed, assuming he was a meditation expert. She inhaled, allowing the musty air to fill her lungs. It didn't taste like much, but the exercise itself was freeing. She surrendered to her surroundings and focused her mind on the breaths. Deep in and deep out, as the YouTube yoga instructor had explained. She repeated the action until she found some peace, restoring bits and pieces of the dream.

"The guy that saved me, he's the one that can help us," she said, as if the event had occurred in the past and not the future.

Byron caught on to her evasiveness. "Do you know who he is?"

"I assume he lives in your father's building. He's British. Has a lab in the basement."

"Good. Then he won't be too hard to find. For now, there's not much we can do." Byron stared at her as if she were made of porcelain. For a whole minute, his eyes didn't waver to the point of discomfort.

"Move in with me?"

The words shocked, jolting her away from him. "What?"

"Sorry." He realized his mistake and poked a middle finger and thumb into his eyes. "No, I'm not. You know it takes everything out of me to trust someone, to let them in. I don't want you to leave if we survive."

"I have family and friends. Grad school."

"I see," he said, and Claire could feel him crawling back into his shell. Not that she didn't want to be with him, but the future looked bleak and before all of this, she had a life a life she couldn't just give up to play house with him.

Certain topics should be avoided on the brink of a nuclear war. They needed their heads in one hat to succeed with this impossible task. Now one little sentence had ruined their dynamic. Pretending not to be worried, Claire held his hand and stared out the window at the dark skies that represented their current reality with impeccable accuracy.

Byron pulled out a phone and tapped on the screen

Claire turned to face him. "Where did you get that?"

"It's his." He motioned to Leslie. "We need to arrange with my dad. We can't just show up there. I'm pretty sure they have him on 24/7 surveillance."

Her internal heat rose. According to her dreams, they would arrive safely, but as Byron had crudely pointed out, they hadn't vested since she had altered their paths. "So how will you contact him?"

"I'm bargaining on the fact that my mom still has the same number. I called it a few years ago and it rang with no answer." He let out a dejected sigh. "She drilled her number into me from kindergarten. I'll never forget it."

"Were cellphones around back then?"

"They looked like bricks, but they were around."

"I hope it works. From what I've gathered, the two of you are fighting an important battle," Leslie said.

"That's putting it mildly." She smiled at the man who had so far been nothing but kind and helpful. After Vince's blindside, she knew not to trust it, although Leslie seemed more sincere than anyone else they had encountered. Still, he could be a salesman.

Byron's face shuffled between a bizarre mix of emotions as he dialed the number: From hopeful to distressed, to horrified. The storm had calmed slightly, bringing a deafening silence to the car. Like a spectator, she sat back in her seat, watching the game play out.

Claire yawned. She had slept little these past few days. Her body had been functioning on adrenaline alone. Waiting for Byron's mom to answer was like adding the final touch to her office building project at 2 am and hoping it didn't tumble to the ground.

"Mom," Byron said. "Oh, thank god."

She leaned in to listen to the other end of the line, but his mother's voice was too weak.

"I need to speak to Dad urgently. Are you with him? Can you put him on the line?" A slight pause. "It doesn't matter, it's urgent." Byron pulled the phone away from his ear and whispered, "You were right, she's there with him." Several seconds passed before he spoke again. "Dad, I need your help, it's life or death."

Claire pushed her ear against the other side. "Don't think I can. The cops are tracking my every move."

"Not to worry. I know how to slip in and out of the building unseen. We're on our way. We should be there by tomorrow afternoon."

"What's going on?" Doug's voice was lathered with concern.

"Can't explain, but keep the obvious curtains closed and stay home until we get there. Like I said, it's life or death." He hung up without saying goodbye. Before she could question him, Claire's eyes fell shut. She tried to keep them functioning, but couldn't. The car's motion and lack of sleep lulled her into slumber.

39

Byron

The cut-throat stage was upon them. The stakes were high now. He couldn't take Vince and Leslie with him to his father's place. Even though he hated gambling, he had no option but to call Leslie's bluff about believing in their plan. They would only stay with his father for a few minutes until they located the Brit in the building, anyway. His original plan was to leave them in the middle of nowhere with nothing, but the man had a family to get back to.

Byron could handle immense pressure, although this burden was an Everest compared to the mine dumps he was used to. Never did he have any suicidal notions, but now he considered jumping from the moving car especially after Claire's blindsiding declination. At least it opened his eyes to her perspective. Claire considered it a holiday romance on their quest to triumph, while he was about ready to marry her. Typical. He was falling into the one trap he had sworn to avoid.

"Leslie," he patted the man's shoulder, "all this talk of spirituality, is it true?"

"Of course, it is. You wanna know if you can trust me?"

"No, I have no choice but to trust you." Byron used his thumb to wipe the sweat from his brows. "I need you to understand the consequences if you betray us. Your family might die. Simply put, war is upon us and only Claire can end it."

"Because of her gifts, I presume," Leslie spoke with his hands for dramatic effect. "You can count on me as long as I can count on you."

"We'll try our best, but I can't make any promises." He said nothing about the gift. Leslie seemed to have a sixth sense, too, and Byron left him to believe whatever he chose.

The man nodded, his usual smile somewhat broken. Byron drew his burning eyes to Claire. Soon he wouldn't be able to keep them open. He could only hope Lady Luck pulled through. Well, her and the gun next to him. The harder he fought, the stronger the desire for sleep became, until he finally gave in.

* * *

Tuesday, 28 June 2022, 7 am

The sun's perky glimmer and an urgency to pee brought him to consciousness.

"I need to pee!"

"Me too," said Claire next to him. Her eyes were puffy and her hair worse than a bird's nest.

"You'll have to go in the bushes," Leslie said. "We're nowhere near a gas station."

When Byron sat up, he noticed Vince was awake, fiddling with the seatbelt while his knees bounced rapidly. Perhaps the guy's addiction was worse than he had thought. Byron clutched the gun when Leslie pulled on to the shoulder of the road. He asked Claire and Leslie to go first. When they returned, he hopped out and dragged Vince with him into the trees.

Defeated, Vince limped along. Byron gave him a once-over and knew the wound was infected. His arm was swollen and his face pale and glistening with sweat. He wanted to ask whether Vince was okay, but there was no point. He wasn't. They went along with their business in silent hatred for the other.

Byron aimed the gun at him. "I'm sorry about this, but you'll have to stay here."

Slowly, the boy lifted his arms. He said nothing. What was there to say? Holding the gun in place, Byron backtracked until he was out of the trees and ran to the car. He yelled, "Go!" as he jumped into the passenger side.

Leslie stomped on the pedal. Claire asked, "You're just gonna leave him here?"

"What other choice do I have?"

She bit her lip and said nothing as the journey continued: The long, battered road that led back home. Byron see-sawed in and out of naps. They had been on the road for so long that the color green had become nauseating, a glaring reminder that a serpent of danger and betrayal lurked behind every bush. The closer to New York they grew, the more his arm hair bristled and his stomach tightened. He didn't know what was worse: Mom and Dad or the possibility of failure. It was a possibility that sprouted to harvesting quality with each passing day.

Increased traffic, hooting, and polluted air revealed the city. Home sweet home. The narrow back roads they had used grew into large double lanes when they entered the city. Yup, good old New York. He looked out the window.

"Take a right up front!"

"What's the plan here?" Leslie asked.

"You can drop us and get a motel." Byron rummaged through the bag and grabbed the last few hundred-dollar bills they had left. "Here." He handed it to Leslie. "You need rest." Everything hurt as he said the words. Leslie's spirituality made him a strong contender for their cause. The excursion would have been so much easier with someone like him along.

"Left at the second street." He pointed with his finger, then turned to Claire. "You see that apartment building on the corner, that's where I lived."

She moved in closer and grinned. "I hope you'll show me someday." They hadn't been all that affectionate after the incident, something she wanted to remedy by the looks of it. He couldn't. He was no one's toy, not even hers. Never again did he want to find himself in someone else's power. *You already are, you fool!*

Byron directed Leslie toward the Upper East Side of Manhattan. At the park where his mother had taken them to play as kids, he said, "Park there, we'll walk from here."

Leslie stopped, turned around, and made to grab Claire's hand. Byron went stiff as she pulled her arm away. The man didn't seem to take offense and said, "I wish you the best of luck, my dear. Believe in yourself and your talents and you'll succeed."

Claire opened the door and nodded. "People like you are the reason we'll do whatever it takes. Your family is lucky to have you."

"Thank you." Byron shook his hand. "You are the small

miracle we'd been hoping for. If you're sincere."

"I can assure you, I am. If you need anything, you call me."

They escaped the car and took to the pathway along the sidewalk. It wasn't far. Byron didn't want them to be visible for too long, even in their disguises.

Claire reached for his hand as they strolled and he took it, needing the strength she provided. "Can you give me those hairpins you bought?"

"Sure." She unzipped the bag on his shoulder and searched with her hand. "Here you go."

"Thanks." Byron wanted to pick up the pace, but blending in was more important. The building he had known for a long time had been painted and modernized, but the bricks still held an outdated charm. In front, a small fountain bubbled among luscious gardens in the center of a newly paved circle that led to the entrance. The doorman still wore the same maroon uniform, matching the pillars in front of the immaculate glass sliding doors.

Pretending to pass by, they rounded the corner to the side entrance, which led to the recreational parlor, which was available for private parties. Byron paused in front of the neatly trimmed shrub fence.

"Pretend you're telling me a joke."

"How do you make holy water?"

"I just know this will be bad."

"You boil the hell out of it."

"Yup, terrible." He discreetly searched for anyone out of place. His eye caught a guy sitting in a blue Fiat with the seat slightly reclined. The man seemed to guard the entrance. Since Claire wore a better disguise, he hid behind her, pulling her toward the narrow pathway that led to the side door.

Shaded by a big leafy tree, he reached for the hairpins, as if removing his key. "Just continue to talk and laugh."

"You know, I've always wondered what it'll be like when you meet my mom," Claire chatted away.

He bent one pin into a ninety-degree angle. It wasn't all that easy with the cut in his hand still aching but he managed to insert it into the lock.

Claire didn't seem to notice. "She's a little crazy, you know. She'll get all up into your business while showering you with her famous cakes and tea." He held the bottom pin down, inserted another, and started turning.

"She never stops talking while my dad hardly ever says a word, but they're kinda perfect for each other, you know." As the pins turned, he heard the lock barrels clicking into place. Within seconds, the door was unlocked, and they slipped inside, where the interior smelled like money.

A resident who was reading a newspaper in one of the chairs, looked up. A numbness spread through his limbs. He grabbed Claire and pecked her lips as a distraction. At that, the man shook his head and continued reading. Pretending to fit in, they ambled through the room and ascended the stairs.

Climbing nine sets of stairs was no stroll in the park, not even for his fit physique. Both of them puffed their way to his father's floor. On the last two flights, he could feel a slight burn in his thighs. Claire seemed to struggle with the climb. He looked over his shoulder and whispered, "There's a camera in the hallway as you exit the steps. You should stand on that side with your back to it. We keep kissing to hide our faces all the way to the door."

"I won't object to that."

Byron grinned because kissing her wasn't torture for him

either. Only, it meant something different to him. His heart heaved in his chest on the final incline, engulfed by nerves at setting foot in the past.

"I'm right here." Claire sensed his hesitance and took the lead. Just as he had explained, they wrapped themselves in each other when they exited the steps. It was only a precaution. He was almost certain the bulldogs were guarding the front and basement entrances they had bypassed. Lips locked, they stumbled down the hardwood passages until the door came into view. The dreaded door: The place where childhood nightmares had been bred. Before he knocked, it swung open.

40

Penn

Tuesday, 28 June 2022, 11 am

With her tail between her legs, Penn slinked back into the New York office. She was on the verge of admitting that Byron was too smart to outplay. He was borderline genius and his accomplice could see into the damn future. It was a dangerous combination nearly impossible to defeat.

She had no more moves left on the chessboard. She had tried safe, invasive, and dirty all to no avail. Her cheating tricks had almost caused Erica's death. She never meant the harm to be severe, but apparently, they only trained assassins to kill.

They had found the girlfriend's Jeep abandoned on the road, soiled with blood, yet no trace of the escapees. Byron's diversions also shattered her hopes that he was playing both sides.

"Afternoon, Agent Penn," said the last voice she wanted to hear.

Penn looked up. She had no idea what he was doing there. If he wanted to fire her, he should go ahead and do it. "Sir, shouldn't you be in Washington with the director and other agencies trying to solve the bigger crisis?"

"They've sent me here to find the girl. I'm taking your place in this operation since you seem incapable of carrying out a simple task. Brief me."

She walked over to the board that held the specifics of the case. "I tried to lure him here by putting his sister in the hospital." She pointed to the photo of Erica. "We've also gained the public's help by flooding social media with the offer of a reward."

"See, that was your first mistake. The moment he learned that, he flew even lower below the radar. Now all you have is an innocent person fighting for her life." Trevor flashed her a condescending glare.

"I thought the news would bring him to us. His sister is the most important person in his life."

The boss stood from his seat. "You might not want to believe this, but that girl seems to be more important than anything, and this cause they are fighting for is bigger than any of us."

"Then why aren't they fighting with us?"

"Perhaps there are people among us they don't trust?" he suggested, his lips tightening to a pout.

"A mole?" Her brows pulled together. "Any ideas?"

"No, but now you have a new assignment. Find out who it is. But first, continue with the update."

Penn nodded and focused her attention back on the board. "We got a hit on Vince Larson who claimed to know where they were. We tracked him down, sent a SWAT team in to find him, but they found his parents and girlfriend asleep with no idea of his whereabouts."

"And then?"

"We flew in and questioned them." Penn opened her laptop

to a photo of Alina Pierce. "This girl explained that Black and Baxter had forced her with a gun to provide them with shelter. She said they seemed like good people who had lost their way."

"Odd." Trevor frowned. "Why were they hiding with strangers while trying to prevent a disaster? And why did this girl trust them?"

"I don't know, but remember that Claire can see the future."

"Mmm." He rubbed at his forehead with one hand. "I'm still not too sure about that."

Penn found it strange that Trevor didn't buy into something that came straight from the girl's mouth. "I assume Vince planned to use them for money all along. He's an addict. Anyway, he never returned home, and we found the car he was driving abandoned on College Street in Oxford, North Carolina." She turned her laptop around to show him images of the Jeep.

"No sign of them after that?"

She shook her head. "Nothing."

"Why wasn't the loggerhead this smart while working for me?"

"Sir," Penn found an inner vulnerability, "what's the status on the bombs?"

"All the ambassadors have set up meetings with possible suspect countries: North Korea, Russia, China, Iraq, and so on. The military and undercover CIA agents have been briefed to constrict their hold on information, and several spy crafts have been deployed, too."

She looked down at her feet. "Have they found anything?"

"No, none of them seemed to have moved their women and children to safety. Normal operations of nuclear vessels continue in North Korea, but their plans are unclear."

With a tight-lipped smile, he wiped some sweat from his forehead. "Thank you, Agent Penn. I want a daily update on the mole. Is that clear?"

"Yes, Sir."

41

Byron

Tuesday, 28 June 2022, 3 pm

Except for a few extra gray hairs and forehead creases, Doug looked exactly the same. He beckoned them inside and shut the door.

"Dad," Byron nodded, then pointed to Claire. "This is Claire. And this is my dad, Douglas Black."

"Well, you are ravishing, my dear." His father hugged her, sending a shiver of uneasiness down his spine. He grimaced. "Your mother's upstairs, resting. She's ill and getting weaker by the day."

Instead of responding or glancing at the place he once called home, Byron headed straight to his old bedroom. He paused in front of the door as memories good and bad suddenly flooded his mind. The door creaked with age as he opened it. His father seemed to have kept the room more or less the same, as if a reminder that he once had a son.

"It's not as fascinating now that I've already seen it." Claire squeezed past him. "By the way, this is almost exactly how it went in my dream. And those stairs we used are definitely where I... where you..."

"Die? I hope not everything you envision becomes a reality."

A weary expression crossed her face. "If all else fails, we hide in the scientist's lab before the 4th of July, but we have to try. My family and friends are out there. Who knows what might happen to them?"

"Yeah, of course. We'll try everything we possibly can." He pulled her against his chest. "We'll find a way, I promise."

The door pushed open. He expected to see his mother or father, but the doorway revealed the girl he had dated on and off through college. She held a tray in her hands. "You must be starving, I brought you some juice and snacks."

Byron felt all the wrinkles in his face contort in bafflement. "Stacey? What are you doing here?"

She blinked. "Your dad didn't tell you? Oh, now this is awkward."

"Context?" Claire looked at him quizzically.

"We used to date," Stacey explained on her way to the desk to sit the tray down. "But Byron is totally incapable of commitment. Luckily, his dad is the complete opposite."

Byron barked out a laugh in ridicule. "You're dating my dad? After everything I told you, you sleep in his bed?"

"Well, you were always a little melodramatic. Besides," she shrugged, "he's changed."

Thinking about it, their relationship made perfect sense. Stacey had always loved money and his father used to stare at her ass for a few seconds too long when she wasn't looking.

"Guess that explains my mother's presence. As far as I know, they're still married."

Stacey waved her hand. "Heavens no, your mother wanted to see you and your sister, and he thought helping her out may right the wrongs of the past."

"Great, Stace, go ahead and believe the bullshit he spews your way, but don't come crying to me when he starts hitting you for looking at other men," Byron snarled out of genuine concern. His father charmed his way into women's lives and only revealed his true self once it was too late.

"Uh, Byron," Claire interjected as Stacey's face fell. "Perhaps now is not the time. I'm Claire, by the way." She waved hello.

"Be careful, Claire, or you'll find yourself in more tears than you can cry over this one." Stacey's eyes bore into him. He regretted breaking her heart. In his defense, he had tried, but the accusation wasn't unfounded. He used to be incapable of commitment.

"Appreciate the concern," Claire said.

Stacey's arms folded and she stomped off into the hall.

"What is wrong with you?" Claire shut the door. "She was trying to be polite and you just had to burst her happy bubble. We need allies right now, not enemies."

"Don't worry, my father is many things, but he won't let anyone get to us. Only he has the right to hurt his family." He rolled his eyes. "In high school there was this jealous girl who spread rumors about me and Erica, and my dad sued her father for thousands."

Claire shivered. "I'm sorry you had to grow up in constant fear of being mistreated."

"Nah, I'm okay. I refused to let him break me. I bet your childhood wasn't all that great either."

She scrunched up her nose with a little pout that brought her youth to the fore. "No, but both my parents loved and protected me. Too damn much." She buried her head into his chest. "I guess we should go downstairs."

"Not yet, I can't face it right now." He leaned in to kiss her and walked her backward to the bed. Her knees dipped when they hit the mattress and she fell into it, pulling her with him. And boy did they kiss, the window-steaming, I-can't-get-enough-of-you kind of kissing.

"Wait, wait, wait..." Claire pulled her face away, her lips red and swollen. "We can't do this now."

"Why not?" He kissed his way down her throat with no intention of stopping. These few moments alone were all they had, and he planned to make the most of them.

"Um, I can think of like 10 reasons. We have a person to find and your family is waiting for us. Time is running out."

"And half an hour won't change that."

"You're the worst," she groaned, yet pulled him back down to her.

"How would you know? You have no one to compare... " A desperate knock interrupted his teasing. Before they could answer, the door fluttered open. The moment he saw his face, Byron knew he had lied to himself because the truth was too big a burden to bear.

"No." Byron shook his head. "Tell me it's not true?"

Dan grabbed him by the shirt and pulled his arm back. Byron didn't even dodge the blow. He deserved it. A cracking sound rang through his ears as Dan's fist connected with his cheekbone, and he felt the coppery taste of blood on his tongue.

"Woah, woah, wait!" his father intervened, stepping between them. "Violence isn't necessary."

"Erica's fighting for her life because of him while he's making out with his girlfriend!" Dan glared, ready to pounce again. At once, the guilt became a flesh-eating bacterium that chewed its way from the inside out.

"What?" Claire shouted. "No, no, no. This is all my fault! Don't blame him, blame me!"

"Is she okay?" Byron asked with large, imploring eyes. "Tell me she's okay!" he demanded, feeling his heart splinter in two. She had to be okay. He almost sank to the ground.

"What do you think?" Dan hissed. "She's badly injured and in a coma."

"Let's be rational about this." Doug waved his hands, trying to calm them. "Byron had nothing to do with hurting Erica. We should stand together during this time."

The man who occupied his father's body sounded like an imposter.

"To hell with all of you." Dan turned around and ripped at the door. "The girls and I will get a hotel."

"Uncle By!" Ellie flew into his arms when the wooden barrier between them opened.

"Hey, munchkin."

Dan pulled the girl from Byron and stomped to the next room. He could hear Ellie squealing and screaming, wanting to return, while his father protested the rash action. The sharp pain in his chest erupted: Heartache. Even if they saved the country, Erica might never recover, and those girls would have to grow up without a mother. And he was responsible.

While the guilt paralyzed him, a pair of soft hands pushed a Kleenex against his bleeding nose. "Look at me!" Claire said, steadying his chin. "You can't let this get to you. We still have a job to do. All we can do for Erica is pray, but we can save many other people, including those girls."

Like always, Claire was the glue holding him together.

Without her, he would've shattered many times. Blaming her would be so much easier, but they had made decisions together. If it was a mistake, they would sink as one. Thanks to her vulnerable we-need-each-other speech the other day, he had pulled himself out of the downward spiral before the ice had melted. He felt it warming up again. They were sliding on a paper-thin fragment that could give way at any moment.

"Are you mad at me?" she asked.

"No."

"Why not?"

"Because it was my decision to trust you and to help you. You never held a gun to my head."

A semblance of a smile crossed her lips. "Say goodbye to your mother. I think we should go."

"No." He shook his head. "I'll come back for that. Dan might be in contact with Penn. We have to get out now."

"Okay." Claire straightened the bed. He looked around the room for any other sign of their presence. A small drop of his blood had spilled on the floor. Byron used the Kleenex to wipe it away, although their DNA was all over the room. At least it wasn't a murder case in which every inch of fiber would be tested if they came at all. With Penn's desperation, anything was possible.

He marched to Erica's old room next door and entered without knocking. "Dan, look, I know it doesn't mean much, but I am sorry. We have to trust that she'll be okay. You guys should stay. We're leaving."

Dan, seemingly much calmer, paused his packing and looked up. "Do you have any idea how worried we were? And here you are, alive and kicking. What's going on?"

"I can't explain, but I assure you this is more important

than you and I can comprehend."

"Yeah," he scoffed. "Sure looked like it with the way you and Claire were kissing earlier. Is it her? Is she in trouble?"

"No, it's way worse. We only took a moment for ourselves. We don't get such a luxury often."

Dan gave an I-don't-believe-you nod and carried on roughly bundling clothes into a suitcase. There was so much more Byron wanted to say, but it would likely be in vain. No apology could change Erica's condition. Nothing he said would undo the accident. He wanted to ask about the severity of the damage, except it wouldn't do either of them any good. All he had left was a belief in the greater good of their battle. He had to keep his eyes firmly on the desired outcome for which they strived.

42

Claire

Tuesday, 28 June 2022, 4 pm

Claire stretched her back and shoulders, readying herself for the next and hopefully final assignment. She slung the backpack over her shoulder. The metal of the weapons clinked inside, responding to the swift movement. She peeked her head into the hallway. Dan and Byron were next door. Doug and Stacey were in the living room.

The urgent knock on the front door sent her backward with a start. Living on the edge did that to a person. Each unidentified sight or sound was a threat. She reversed further into the room, hoping beyond all hopes that Byron would return soon. A cold tremor overcame her when footsteps thumped down the hall.

Her first instinct was the window, but when she pulled the blinds away, there was no escape for a non-athletic person. Claire opened the closet. It was mostly empty, save for a few boxes, sheets, and a travel suitcase on the floor. It would have to do. She stepped inside and gently tugged the doors closed. Forcing all of her limbs into a tiny ball, she hid inside the case.

Once covered, she reached for the zipper on the outside and pulled it up as far as her reach allowed. Her bag got stuck in its path. She tried to wriggle it loose, but was too scared to make any sound.

All of the barriers obstructed her hearing, but her fear would not subside. When the bedroom door opened, she knew her panic wasn't unjustified. Two sets of footsteps came in, wanton and serious. Someone inside that house had ratted them out, and for some reason Claire didn't suspect Dan, as Byron had. The tracks grew closer, prompting Claire to hold her breath. *God, I know I haven't been all that good lately, but You know I have everyone's best interest at heart.*

The closet doors swung open. She squeezed her eyes shut, even though it was already pitch black inside her cocoon. Her body ached with the tight squeeze and her lungs burnt from the lack of air. In the distance, someone shouted a name that she couldn't make out. The presence in front of her disappeared. A commotion sounded from the hall, screeching and banging against something. They had Byron; she knew it.

Tears threatened her eyes, but she pushed them back in. She was now all alone. With Byron at her side, the possibility of success was needle-thin, but without him, it was a Bigfoot hunt. She thought of everyone she loved, and everyone she was fighting for: Her mother, her father, her friends, Byron, and his family. Their faces appeared so real in her mind, she couldn't give up. Claire would find the scientist without him and when she succeeded, she would save Byron. *Think, Claire, think.*

The balconies on the east side of the building inspired her escape plan. She trained her ears on the commotion outside, following its path until she heard nothing more. She removed the knife from the bag and held it steady before unzipping the suitcase. Her hand shivered as she lifted the flap an inch and peered through the tiny gap. With the coast clear, Claire climbed out and tiptoed across the room.

When she peeked down the passage, she spotted them rounding the corner into the living room. Byron was in cuffs, his hair disheveled and his shirt dark with sweat. Three people were holding him down. Yup. Even after being caught, Byron wouldn't go down without a fight. He shook his head and for the briefest second, their eyes met. She stepped back out of sight. There was further banging and clanging, and she knew he was creating a diversion.

While Byron fought all three cops, Claire used her minuscule crack of a chance. She placed the knife back and hid the bag. Using every shadow to conceal herself, she sneaked down the hall to what she assumed was the master bedroom. Muffled cries came from the room next to Byron's, and it pulled at her heart, but she ignored it and kept forward. She didn't bother switching the light on, snaked across the floor, through the sliding doors, and on to the balcony. *Okay, I'm outside. Now what?* She was on the ninth floor, railed by tempered glass balustrades.

Claire looked down, her stomach churning from the height. There was no other way out but to climb down on to the identical balcony below her. She took a deep breath, then carefully hauled herself over the rail next to the wall, anchoring her toes in the tiny gap between the glass panel and the tiled floor. Several times she bent down to attempt the climb, but fear stole her courage. It would have been 10 times worse for Byron, given his fear of heights. Her breaths became scratchy and ragged. It was now or never.

Her heart beating like crazy, she bent her knees and dangled one leg down to the balcony below. Thank heavens she was tall and New York City apartments clustered together to save space. Using all of her might, she held on to the floor and lowered the other leg until her tiptoes touched the glass below. Without another thought, she pushed herself forward, scraping her knees as she landed on the tiles with a thud.

While Claire tried to regain her composure, the sliding door opened and an elderly woman in bowling attire stared at her. She hadn't thought that far ahead. Moisture rushed to her eyes, causing her to sniffle. "I'm so sorry," she tried to muster through the tears.

"What on earth happened to you, child?"

Think, Claire, she told herself, but no lie came to mind. Instead, she just cried.

"Come on in. Let me make you some tea. Should I call 911?"

"No, it's uh... You see..." And then she stumbled upon a lame idea while the woman steered her through the house. Claire shivered at the touch, hoping it wouldn't prompt any visions. "I started seeing the guy that lives upstairs." She wiped the wetness from her eyes.

The lady ruffled the teal cushions on the couch and gestured for her to sit. "Did he hurt you?"

"No, no." Claire waved dismissively. "Not physically, but emotionally, yes."

"What's going on?" A deep male voice asked, and when Claire turned her head, she saw the woman's husband.

"Another one of his victims." The woman tilted her head to the roof.

"What?" Claire asked. "I'm not the first?"

"Afraid not. A few years ago, we saved another one of

his women. I wonder whatever happened to her," she said, disappearing into the kitchen.

"I don't know him personally," the husband came to sit across from her, "but I do know he's bad news. You need to stay away from him."

Claire nodded.

"There you go, my dear." The woman brought out a tray with tea and biscuits. "I made it nice and strong."

"Thank you."

"Are you sure you don't want me to call an ambulance? You look very shaken up."

Her knees burnt from the scrapes, but it was nothing she couldn't handle. "No, I'm fine. I just need a bath and some rest." Claire added sugar and milk to her cup and brought it to her chest. "Do you know a British man with reddish hair that lives in the building? He was also of some assistance and I would like to thank him."

"Are you referring to Edward Tomb, the billionaire?" the man asked. "He lives in the penthouse at the top."

"The Edward Tomb, the tech genius?" Claire's mouth hung agape. The man in her dreams was famous.

"Yes," the woman smiled. "Lovely young man, but I doubt you'll find him. He's hardly ever home."

"Oh, that's a pity." Claire tried to mask her sharp dis-appointment with a sip of tea. She stretched out her visit, thinking she might be safe there. She asked about the couple's family and their life, and they were more than willing to answer.

"Thank you very much for this," she said after her second cup and half a dozen cookies, but if you don't mind, I'd like to get home.

"Of course, let me walk you out." Both of them walked her to the door and warned her against Doug Black for a final time. She politely agreed and hurried to the staircase with her head bowed when she realized her wig had fallen off somewhere in the struggle. As she made it to the top floor, the elevator bell dinged, turning her insides cold.

She stared at the ground. The man from her dream stepped out. Claire lifted her gaze and looked him straight in the eyes.

"Can I help you?" he asked with a broad-shouldered confidence she wasn't expecting.

"Yes," she blurted out, remaining on the top step, out of the camera's view. "And I can also help you."

"Is that so?" he responded with an I-doubt-that skepticism.

"Look, I'm gonna be frank and forward, and you might not believe me. I get visions of the future. I had one of a nuclear blast. You saved me and took me to your lab downstairs. Now, I need your help to stop it."

"Come in." He hurried to the door, which unlocked with the click of a button.

"What? Just like that? I could be a serial killer, you know."

"Miss, you look like you've been run over by a truck. Come inside."

The lights switched on and the temperature dropped when she followed him into the most beautiful home she had ever seen. Everything was fresh and techy. Even the adorning plants grew so beautifully that they had to be genetically manipulated. There were so much space and windows, abruptly clothed with cream curtains when Mr. Billionaire pressed a button on a remote.

All of the furniture was oddly shaped in different shades of white and glass, apart from a black piano in the corner. He had to be married, judging by the feminine touch. *You're being sexist, men have good taste too.*

"Can I offer you something to drink?"

"No, thanks."

"How about something to eat?"

"Actually, yes, I'm starving."

He looked her up and down. "Yes, you need some flesh on those bones." He waved to Claire to follow him to the kitchen: A long, narrow room with a large island in the middle; all oak cabinets, marble tops, and metallic appliances.

"My assistant usually brings my dinner to the office, so I've already eaten, but I can whip something up for you."

"You cook?"

"Sort of, mum taught me back in England but I'm no Gordon Ramsay." He pressed some button on the fridge and the screen revealed its contents. Claire was ridiculously wowed by the marvel.

"How about a ham sandwich?"

"Perfect." Almost like a pregnant woman with raging hormones, she started crying again.

Edward didn't seem to notice while pulling the ingredients from the fridge. "What's your name, love?"

Being referred to as "love" should have bothered her, but the way he said it made it seem like part of his British vocabulary.

"Claire Baxter."

"I'm Edward Tomb. Let me be honest. There are two people in this world who know about my lab in the basement and you're not one of them. I've been obsessed with trying to find ways to save humanity from an apocalypse and here you walk in, mentioning both. I couldn't ignore it."

Claire looked down at her feet. "The FBI are after me. I don't know if they'll be able to track me here, but they want to know what I know, and I don't trust them."

"Good call." He puckered his lips. "You can explain everything once you've eaten."

They sat down at the long, glass dining table with fluffy, ivory chairs. Claire fell into her story, telling him everything, from the start of her gift to how she ended up in front of his apartment. He frowned and nodded, absorbing every small detail, as if he would write an exam on it. He never questioned her and the expression he wore suggested he believed every word she told him.

"Okay, any theories?" Edward asked.

"Byron researched every article he could find, and his theory was North Korea."

"It's a possibility. Get some rest tonight. We'll start working first thing tomorrow. I hope you have more dreams without him."

If it was possible. She could feel her heart cracking. "Yeah, me too."

"I have to hand it to you, you are one brave woman."

"I suppose." She shrugged.

He showed her to the guest bedroom, outfitted with elegant wooden furniture, and clad with white-and-copper bedding. A modern fireplace stood out against the soft brown of the walls. The bathroom was carved from pale-gray marble and a shower bigger than her entire bathroom at home. Claire scrubbed the last few horrific days from her skin, reveled in the soft fiber of the towels, and found a clean T-shirt on the bed. Fresh tears sprang to her eyes once she settled into the

Egyptian cotton sheets. Byron was gone and she might never see him again.

Images of his face flashed through her mind. Although their love was short-lived, it ran deep and strong, as did the ache of his absence. She had grown so used to him that she struggled to fall asleep despite being over-tired. Eventually, she had to resort to her newfound meditation methods to relax into unconsciousness.

43

Byron

Tuesday, 28 June 2022, 5 pm

Trees rustled in the wind outside the car. The ride was jerky: Stop, go, stop, go, curving its path through traffic, the whiff of masculine defeat in the air. How could he have been so careless and naïve? They shouldn't have gone to his father's place at all. They should have searched for the owner of the lab as soon as they reached the building. He didn't know who had revealed their location. Leslie, Vince, Dan, Stacey?

He knew trusting Leslie was a gamble that he couldn't afford to take, but in the end, his heart had won out that small organ in his body he had only recently discovered. When Byron looked up from his bound hands, the car entered a building and the outsides darkened even more as they crossed into the basement parking. Cuffed and humiliated, an unknown agent dragged him inside, through the fluorescent-lit corridors to a six-by-eight cell with nothing but a toilet/sink and a bed. It looked so different from the other side.

How would they conquer this evil from inside a prison? Even if Claire had hidden somewhere, the remaining two agents would have found her after they had taken him away. They would have left no stone unturned. Why, though? Was the 'false' statement such a big deal for them, or did they suspect more?

He wasn't alone with his thoughts for too long. The door scrambled open and in walked his father. "Don't worry, we'll sort this out."

"I need to know if Claire's all right."

"I don't know. I left straight after they took you."

"Dad," he grabbed Doug by the shoulders, "you have to find out what's going on with her."

"I'm here to defend you. Your arraignment will be tomorrow, and you need to tell me everything so I can prepare."

"Listen to me." Byron shook with desperation. "I don't care about me. If you wanna help me, then help her."

"Okay, calm down." He eased Byron on to the bed. "I'll try to find out what's going on with her if you let me help you."

"I can't."

"Byron." His father turned serious. "You are being charged with several crimes that could land you in here for years. I can only make it go away if you explain what the hell is going on with you."

"Even if I do tell you, you'll think I'm crazy."

"Good to know I can use a temporary insanity defense."

"It's not a joke." Byron felt so confused, he couldn't think straight. Should he tell his father the story or not? What would he even plead before a judge? He was sure as hell guilty of most of the crimes: Evading the police, assaulting a federal officer, and withholding information. It didn't matter in the grand scheme of things. They would be dead in a few days if he couldn't find a way out. He looked up. "Get me Penn."

"I was told she no longer works your case."

"What? Since when? I don't care, tell them I'll only talk to her. Privately."

Doug's lips moved as if to say something, but he turned around and nodded for the guard to let him out. The door buzzed and his father blurred into the light, like a star dissolving behind a cloud. His confession to Penn would be an act of desperation. If he could convince her, she had the means to help them escape. With one arm behind his head, he lay down on the cot, revising his speech. He wouldn't give her any more than necessary, only enough to spark panic and guilt. Fear had brimmed in her eyes when she had read that letter the first time. All he had to do was add a reagent to activate it once more.

He waited and waited until he was drowning in a sea of uncertainty. He thought about Claire, scared of any touch, being dragged to a cell like this. He thought of any visions she might have had. And then the thought of never seeing her again produced a single tear. The last time he'd cried was when his mother had left them, when he had realized she wasn't coming back. After that night, he'd never allowed himself to love or trust, or any tears ever again. Until now. Finally, the agony drowned him in a fitful sleep.

Wednesday, 29 June 2022, 7 am

Somewhere in the distance, Byron heard a droning sound and a click. He knew it was trying to rip him from this perfect moment, from the smiling faces of his family. A strong hand pulled at his arm.

"Time to get up."

He let go of the dream and opened his eyes. The small room

318

had no windows, so he had no idea of the time. The guard cuffed him, then dragged him down the hallway and into a room not much bigger than his cell. Penn was seated at the small table in the center, propped up on her elbows. She didn't look up, as if she hadn't heard them enter. Last night his whole speech had been prepared, but now he couldn't even form a greeting.

"I'm told you'll only talk to me," she said without looking at him.

"Look, Taylor, I'm sorry."

"I'm not here for that. Either you tell me what you know or I'm leaving."

"No, not here. I said I'll talk to you privately. In my cell, take it or leave it."

Penn stood and pushed her chair back, as if their conversation was already over. "You know that's not allowed. I'll forward everything you say anyway, so what's the point?"

"That's the deal." Once again, he placed all of his chips on one bet. They wanted information and Claire would be mute, so he bargained on their desperation to give in to his demands.

Penn sent him a knowing look before she left the room and the guard escorted him back to the cell. He knew his arraignment would be soon. No way would the judge award him bail, not with him being a flight risk. No matter how many devils his father could save from prison, Byron's only option was Taylor Penn. With nothing else to do, he lay down on the bed and remained patient. She would come. She had to.

Not half an hour later, he heard brisk footsteps squeaking down the linoleum. Byron grinned. Her profile appeared in the glass panel next to the door before the guard unlocked it.

"Fine, you win." Penn walked in and closed the door. "Now,

you talk."

He sat up, moved to the edge of the bed. "You got a voice recorder?"

"Don't be ridiculous."

He noticed the quick blink after her answer. Not even his ex-partner could fool him. "Get rid of it before I say anything."

She eyed him warily, then removed the device from her pocket and handed it to him to ensure it was off.

"Happy?"

"No, I'd be happy when I'm no longer in here."

"That won't happen for a long time. First, tell me about the bombs."

Byron inhaled for some much-needed courage. "I need you to help me escape."

"Excuse me," she choked.

"Taylor, you don't understand what we're facing. I can't help anyone while I'm stuck in here."

She moved closer and looked him in the eye. "Then why are you working against us and not with us?"

"The FBI can't be trusted, but I swear to you we're trying to save everyone."

"Who? Tell me who can't be trusted?"

It wasn't one person; it was the uncertainty of their actions that posed a threat. "I don't know. We have more info than anyone, but not enough. As soon as we do, I'll let you know, and we can stop it."

"Byron, the 4th of July is around the corner. There's no time left."

Exactly why I have to get out of here as soon as possible. "I know, but there's still time and we can't stop fighting until it runs out."

"Why didn't you trust me from the start?"

"It wasn't my decision."

"Oh, it's the girl, huh? The one that's so important to you." Jealousy or condescension oozed from her words. "The one who let you go to prison to save herself."

"Save herself" sounded like rain on a lazy Sunday morning. They hadn't found her. *How?* Claire was smart and resourceful, but he knew the agents would have scoured every inch of his father's apartment and the building for her. The relief brought more questions with it. *Had she found the lab owner? Had she told him anything? Did she still need him if she was safe?*

"Did I hit a nerve?" Penn asked with a mischievous glint in her eyes.

"I made sure she was safe."

"Then I assume you won't tell us where she is?"

"I don't know." He shrugged, feeling a calm settle inside. "Back to the point, will you help me or not?"

"I'm sorry," was all she said before she left.

Byron sighed and stamped his foot on the ground. He surged to his feet and splashed water from the toilet sink onto his face. He should have kept his mouth shut about Claire. One mention of her and Penn turned into an enemy. Now she would probably blabber his request to Trevor, and they would allow him no visitors except his father.

While wiping the drops from his face, a guard came in and cuffed him. It was time to be charged. He steered him to a set of sliding doors at the end of the hall where the same black Dodge was waiting. Through the familiar bustle of traffic, it took them roughly 15 minutes to get to the courthouse. They took Byron to a room where his father was waiting, leaning against a small table.

"You're pleading not guilty to all charges." He handed him a suit.

"Whatever you say," he agreed, not in the mood to argue. Byron took the suit from him and started to undress.

"Good to see you still work out."

"Dad, would you mind?" He gestured to Doug to turn around. The guard kept his gaze planted.

The handle on the door leading inward to the offices squeaked and dipped. Doug and the guard turned toward the sound while Byron pulled the shirt over his shoulders.

"Gentlemen," a woman's voice said behind him. "There had been some misunderstanding. This case is getting thrown out." Byron swiveled to face her. She produced a piece of paper carrying the judge's signature, declaring Byron a free man.

"But I can't just... " the guard interjected.

"If you don't believe this, you're welcome to accompany me to Judge Fairchild's office."

Byron looked at the short, sturdy woman, trying and failing to figure out what was going on.

"No need." He waved his hand and left the room.

"Get dressed. We need to go."

"Please tell me that piece of paper is legit?" Doug said.

The dark-skinned woman nodded. "It is. It took a helluva lot of convincing. At least Judge Fairchild has vision. Mr. Black, you need to come with me." Her accent sounded foreign, Jamaican perhaps.

"Uh-huh."

Doug pulled him aside. "Byron, what's going on here?"

"Can't explain. Thanks for the suit. Send me a bill." Hiding his face, Byron followed his savior out of the courtroom to where a silver Lexus awaited. She slid into the backseat and shifted up to make space for him.

"I hope you're worth it." She pulled her nose up as if he were a bug that needed to be squashed.

"Who are you?"

"I'm Edward Tomb's assistant, and he just broke his neck to get you out of there."

"The tech revolutionist?"

"Do you know another Edward Tomb?" She looked away and silence ensued for the rest of the drive. The car pulled into the basement lot. "This is where I leave you. I'm sure you can find your way to the penthouse."

"Thank you." Byron nodded. "For everything." He took the stairs instead of the elevator to avoid cameras. Knowing what rested at the end, it almost didn't feel like exercise. On the top step, he hung his head forward and took a deep breath to wind down. When he looked up at the skillfully carved wooden door, his lips curved into a smile. He'd made it.

44

Claire

Wednesday, 29 June 2022, 12 pm

The floors clunked as Claire anxiously tapped her sneakered foot below the office's desk. She had lost the flashcards of her dreams, so she'd had to reconstruct them to give Edward a more refined picture of her visions. He regarded the matter as seriously as one of his multi-million-dollar investments.

"Hey, Claire," he called from somewhere in the house.

"Yes?"

"Can you come into the living room for a sec?"

"Ugh," she sighed. Claire didn't like being disturbed while in the middle of something. "Coming." She made her way down the hallway that led to the front room. When she found them, she had to blink, imagining that her eyes were misleading her. But when she opened them again, both men were still standing there. At once, she threw herself into Byron's arms. He caught her and held on, like a child who had found his favorite toy.

"How are you here?"

"Your new friend pulled some strings."

"Of course, he did."

"Well, I couldn't look into her moping face for another second," Edward joked next to them.

"Thank you so much." Claire let go of Byron and turned to their new partner. "You don't know how much this means."

"Oh, I think I do. Now, let's get down to business. I'll ask Drew to prepare some lunch."

Edward left and they took a seat on the couch. Claire kept staring at Byron's face as if he would evaporate at any moment.

"Any new dreams?"

"No, I couldn't really sleep last night. I suspect that's why Edward stepped in. But I'm recreating them to give him a clearer picture."

"You told him?"

His sudden apprehensive tone surprised her. "I had to."

"I've been wanting to tell people, to ask for their help all this time, but you refused. Here, you walk into a complete stranger's home and say: 'Hi, I can see the future.'"

She understood his anger, but Claire relied on her visions to clarify who she could trust. "In my dream he saved me, and I needed his help. What else was I supposed to do?"

"Am I interrupting?" Edward reappeared in the doorway.

"Uh, no, sorry." Claire waved him in. "We often bump heads."

"Mr. Black, I have to agree with Claire. You never know who you can trust in politics or any branch of government. That includes the FBI."

"I get that, but the two of us didn't have the resources to take this thing down on our own. The plan was to gain enough information before we approached them. We still don't have that."

Edward made himself comfortable in the seat across from them. "I do."

Claire had forgotten that Byron had given her two days to come up with the source. Those two days had now lapsed. "Byron," she took his hand in hers, "you didn't tell anyone, did you?"

"Of course not." He pulled her forehead to his lips, his overgrown beard tickling her skin. "So, what's first on the agenda?"

"I think we need a back-up plan in case we fail," Edward spoke up. "Or rather, I have a back-up plan. That's how I got the judge to discard the case."

Claire and Byron shared a look of confusion, then faced him. "Care to enlighten us," Byron said, and she could feel the way his muscles contorted, now that he was no longer in charge.

"I bought an abandoned military base, which I'm restoring as a doomsday bunker. I was planning to sell off the units. Well, too late now. It's not quite complete, but it's habitable."

"You want us to give up?" Byron asked; his skin turning to fire in her palm.

"No, I want us to get our loved ones to safety before it's too late. We can still work from there."

With the threat looming closer without resolve, she said, "It's not a bad idea." She squeezed Byron's shoulder to calm him down.

"What about Erica and the rest of the people? The moment we're safe, we won't work as hard to solve the problem and Erica will be left up here to die."

Claire hadn't considered that. He had a point. "Then we," she pointed to the three of them, "don't go until we've stopped it."

Byron brought his sullen face closer to hers. "It'll take days to get everyone to safety. It's time we don't have."

"We can do it in a day or two," said Edward. "I can fly the chopper. Since your family are all here, we'll take them first."

Claire felt a sudden unease swirling in her stomach. Someone in his family was against them. She didn't know who, but those agents had shown up right after they had arrived. It couldn't be a coincidence. And was Byron's father even worth saving? Could he be trusted? Byron seemed certain that they could trust him.

"How many people can this bunker house?" Byron asked.

"Fifty, more or less."

"Fine, but I'll only agree if we save everyone that helped us get here," Byron challenged.

Edward smiled, leaning back in his seat. "Mr. Black, I don't need your permission to take my family to safety. I was simply giving you the opportunity to save yours, too. But I agree, this wouldn't be possible without you or anyone that helped you, therefore the bunker is open to them."

"Okay," Byron agreed just as Drew called them into the dining room, which was laden with grilled fish, rice, and vegetables. They ate the best food Claire had tasted in weeks while discussing the logistics of the safety mission. They agreed that Hoff should be included, although the 'Leslie' subject was more somber. Claire insisted he was innocent, but Byron argued he could have been the FBI's informant. In the end, they decided he would be last on the list.

Drew, the butler, would deliver a letter to Byron's father in the morning. Edward gave him clear directions to hand it directly to Doug and no one else. The specifics instructed

Doug to vacate his home, along with his family, to the roof of the building at exactly 8 am the following morning.

Claire liked Edward. He was intelligent, easy-going, and straight to the point. Byron didn't. He didn't have to tell her that, she knew it. As she watched the billionaire (*trillionaire?*) curiosity budded within her. She found herself wanting to touch him for a personalized insight, but she wouldn't dare.

As soon as Byron's family had settled in, they would collect Claire's family in Oregon. Edward would arrange a travel bus to take his and the judge's people down, though that trip would take a while longer. He had agreed that if Hoff and Leslie made it to the bus's arrival point on time, they would receive a unit. Byron was sure to send an immediate text with the specifics to the burner phone that Hoff still carried. Claire asked Edward to get Leslie's number from Byron's mother and to send him the details, too. He agreed.

The abandoned base, next to the Pacific somewhere near Seattle, had apparently been used by the navy to defend enemy warships. It sounded rather creepy, or perhaps Claire had read one too many horror stories in her lifetime.

Claire and Byron would stay behind to continue their quest for true safety. The chopper could only transport six passengers at a time. As a last resort, they would fly in before the war erupted, if they weren't able to find the culprit. It had to be soon enough for them to alert the authorities and for government to put a stop to it. Either way, they would be safe, but Erica and millions of others wouldn't be so lucky.

They sat in the study, all three of their noses plastered to laptop screens, each of them assigned a different task. Byron's biggest concern, as he had explained, was the US's early detection satellites. They would respond within a minute or two and deflect it unless those detection satellites happened to be non-operational. All of their activities seemed rather mundane, designed to pass the time while they waited for another revelation from her. At the end of the day, her dreams were the only conclusive evidence they had.

"Maybe you should get drunk again," Byron called from his seat in the corner.

"Drunk?" Edward looked up, readjusting his square-shaped reading glasses.

"Byron thinks it helps my dreams if nothing clogs my brain."

"Does it?"

She and Byron looked to each other for the answer. She had had quite the revealing dream the previous time.

"Inconclusive," Byron said.

"Could you hand me those cards?" Edward asked. Claire bundled the pages she had already printed into a neat pile and handed it across the desk. If his astounded expression was anything to go by, he was intrigued and fascinated, even though he had already heard the entire story.

"Mmm."

"What?" she asked. Was that a good or bad 'Mmm'?

"Let's say, hypothetically, you never had the dream of the bomb. What would have happened?"

Where was this headed? "I don't know. Why do you ask?"

A clicking sound came from his cheek. "I'm wondering if the two of you were meant to meet differently, if you have somehow altered your natural timelines."

"Umm." *Natural timeline? What on earth? He's trying to psychoanalyze something that's a supernatural phenomenon.* "I don't think I would have met Byron if I hadn't pursued him.

He's kinda a lone wolf who works himself to death." And drank and smoked and stressed too much.

"We might have," Byron chimed in. "In Bend, where I met your friends."

"Nope, you wouldn't have met me there. I wouldn't have gone to a bar full of people with them."

"Maybe we could have met during another activity. You would have recognized me, right?"

"Maybe."

"And then?" Edward asked, as if they were putting on a play.

"Byron would have shooed me away when I approached him. The end."

"Probably," he snickered. "Maybe tried to seduce you and then shooed you away. Nah, you're too young and I was too preoccupied."

"Hmm..." Edward said again. *What did those noises mean?* "But you're together now, right? Perhaps you could've swayed him somehow."

The conjecture was making Claire anxious. They needed to focus. "I doubt it. The story of the bombs was the only way I got him to stick to me. He didn't believe me at first." She noticed Byron deep in thought, as if the game had provoked some question in need of an answer. She would ask about it later when they were alone.

They carried on searching. No results. She needed another dream.

After dinner, Claire took a too-long shower to sink the boat of torment that had pirated her soul. When she emerged from the bathroom, Byron was already in bed, laptop propped on his lap.

"Hey." He lifted the sheets for her to get in. "Everything okay? You were gone for quite some time."

"No." She had to get it out. "I'm not sure if we can trust your family. One of them sold us out. That person can do it again."

"Only my dad will see that letter. He'll understand the risks and do as he's told. They won't even know what's going on until they're inside the bunker."

"What did you say in the letter?"

"Bomb in the building. He already knows something is up. They won't ignore it."

"What if someone contacts the police?"

"Covered that, too." His shoulders sagged as if hopeless. "I know it's terrifying, but I have to keep them safe. Dan and the girls, at least."

She had no objection to that. She wanted them as far away from any bombs as possible. "Yeah, you're right. Listen, what were you thinking earlier when Edward asked all of those questions?"

He looked away. Guilty. "He has something to hide."

"You still don't trust people, huh?"

"I trust you."

"You sure?" she teased. "Because I recall that only a few days ago you had your doubts."

"Not my finest moment, I'll admit. Get some rest." He pulled her to his side and kissed the top of her head.

"Okay, you, too. Goodnight. I'm glad to have you back."

He grinned, satisfied. "Thanks for saving me."

"Yeah, you bet." She closed her eyes and settled herself into his chest. Alcohol wasn't the catalyst she needed; he was. Her dreams had always featured Byron Black. He was the concrete foundation. She rolled into the dream with nonchalant ease.

The laptop screen booted to life at a speed Claire had never witnessed. It had to be brand-new. The man clicked the Google Chrome icon and the search bar opened.

"You have internet?"

"Satellites are still in space," he murmured, half-heartedly. His fingers moved over the keyboard as he typed nuclear bombs into the search bar. Claire didn't know what he was looking for until the CNN video popped up on screen. 'US ballistic missiles hit North Korea'. And another: 'Does the nuclear attack on Russia mean nuclear war?'

He opened the first: A sturdy man with a thick mane of dark hair appeared on the screen. "The United States has launched an intercontinental ballistic missile at Pyongyang, North Korea. At this stage, it's unclear whether this was a warning attack gone wrong or if the US president was provoked to wage war." The small window in the top right swiveled to the center, showing the blast of the nuclear weapon.

The man paused the video. "The US is responsible. Does that answer your question?"

It did, but it changed nothing. "No." She looked around at the equipment. Interesting plumbing and electronics. The light in the room was too bright for her current mood. "What are you working on?" Claire didn't know why she asked. She didn't want to know. None of this could save Byron or anyone else. Now what? "Hey, is that a door?" Claire noticed a tiny gap as she stared at the wall.

"Yes, it's just another project."

"What kind of project?" Again, she wasn't interested in what he was doing. All she wanted to know was if the door led back upstairs.

"It's classified."

Claire woke to her heart pounding in her head. She slipped out of bed, snuck to the study, and typed the most obvious question into Google. 'Why would America start a nuclear war?' She scanned through the pages. Most of them explained how a nuclear war would start and what would happen if it started. Then, on the fourth page, she landed on an article describing how AI could start a nuclear war. Artificial Intelligence? That had never occurred to her. Surely that wasn't impossible.

The article explained how the president was the only person in the US with a nuclear button, except for the AI technology that could detect an attack and generate a reaction before the initial detonation. It was in the developmental phase, with no definite launch date planned as yet. Claire scrolled back up to check the date of the article: 4 November 2019. She had read once that computers would destroy the world. Bam! There it was, the most logical explanation. A bug in the coding.

45

Byron

Thursday, 30 June 2022, 5 am

Inaudible gabbles from Claire's mouth woke Byron. Her head pivoted restlessly from one side to the other. By now, he knew exactly what 'the dreams' looked like. Trying not to disturb her, he slid one leg out of bed, and then the next. At least she was a heavy sleeper something he still envied.

A faint glow of light came from the hall. Drew or Edward was already awake. He found both of them in the kitchen. Drew pulled an apron over his head. Edward sat at the island, a mug in one hand and a newspaper in the other.

"Morning." He glanced over his spectacles.

"Morning." Byron made for the coffee machine, like he was a regular tenant in the house.

"Claire still asleep?"

"Doubt we'll see her anytime soon. She sleeps in." He left out the part about the dream.

Edward shifted in place. *Uneasy. He's hiding something.* Byron couldn't put his finger on it. The man had saved him from jail. He was helping them bring everyone important to safety, but his body language told him he knew more than he revealed.

"Do you have any theories?" Byron asked.

"Too many variables at this stage. I'm not sure we'll be able to stop this unless Claire knows the source. Even then, this is too big."

He couldn't argue. Until now, their only mission had been to curb it in the cradle. Edward had provided them with an alternative, except for Erica and Penn. No, his battle wasn't over. With that, he traded the kitchen for an empty bedroom to exercise: Sit-ups and push-ups. Anything to lessen the worry lines.

Three sets in, a nervous knock came from the door. It pushed open. "There you are." Claire's voice sounded hoarse, as if she had just woken up.

"Go back to bed. I'll bring you some coffee."

She smiled thanks and nodded. He found a towel in the bathroom to wipe away the sweat, then filled a glass with iced water for himself before making Claire's coffee.

"Tell me about the dream," he said, placing the cup on the nightstand.

"Oh. It's not good news." She pulled the cup toward her, looking down at the contents. Her face was gloomy. "I know who started it and I don't think we can stop it."

Byron's heart came to life, prompted either by excitement or nerves. "Go on."

"It's us. America. We fired first."

All the blood in his body drained to his feet, leaving him woozy. "What? Who?"

"North Korea and Russia. I never saw the video about Russia, but the headline asked if the US was starting a war."

His head shook of its own accord. No. The president no matter how controversial would never deliberately start a war without cause. Unless he was influenced. As far as he knew, or what they wanted the public to know, their nuclear arsenal was strictly retaliatory. Apparently not.

Claire must have noticed his confusion when she pulled a laptop toward her and showed him an article.

Artificial Intelligent Detection

"I can see the steam coming out of your ears," Claire said. "You wanna stop this, but you don't know how, right?"

A knock on the door. Byron gave Claire a once-over to ensure she was decent. "Come in."

"I'm about to head out to collect the helicopter," Edward said. "Your father has received the letter. They'll be there." One less thing to worry about.

"Thank you," Byron said.

"Anything new?"

"Not yet," Byron answered before Claire could open her mouth.

Edward moved forward and handed him a phone. "I'll be in touch."

"Thanks again. For everything." Claire said on his behalf.

Later, as he reread the article, he heard the whirling chuff of the helicopter rotors outside. His glass and other objects on the desk vibrated when the landing stuck. He checked the time on the laptop: 7.53 am. The chopper was right on time. His family was about to make their way to shelter, all except for one one for whom he would gladly die.

"Hey," Claire approached through the door wearing a tight,

blue dress, of all things. "Anything else?"

"You look nice."

She ignored his comment. "Maybe Edward can help," Claire suggested with a shrug of her left shoulder. "He's an engineer, I'm sure he knows all about AI."

Of course, she would look to him. Byron didn't want him involved at all. "Maybe he even built it. In my dream he said he was working on something top secret." Her tone suggested she was joking.

He wasn't so sure. "What?"

"I don't know. He said it was top secret."

At once, bells started to ring all of them high-pitched alarm sounds. Edward was hiding something. He had believed Claire with no fuss, and he had a bomb shelter at the ready. In Claire's dream, he was in the safety of his lab when the bombs went off. He had pushed the limits to get Byron out of prison and to save everyone important to them.

He wanted to stow them away. They knew too much. If he was the developer, surely the bug was on purpose or... He said nothing to alarm Claire.

He half-bobbed his head in acknowledgment. It didn't matter if Edward was a damn encyclopedia, the way he stiffened when broaching certain subjects, and his change in speech suggested he was keeping things from them. The bunker was real, though. He had shown them work-in-progress pictures and profiles. He knew his family would be safe, at least.

"Come on, help me search for info on this computerized system," Byron distracted her.

Claire turned giddy at the prospect of being useful. She poured all of her energy into the research while Byron built a secret case against Edward Tomb. Too bad it was Edward's laptop and he couldn't explore the guy or save any profile document he created. A few hours later, the Skype icon popped up with the familiar ringtone.

"Who's that?" Claire asked.

"I think it's them." He answered. As expected, his whole family pushed into view. "Hi," he greeted with an awkward wave.

"Uncle By," Ellie said. "Mommy isn't with us. She's still in the hospital." His heart broke, shattered to pieces.

"I know Elle. I'm doing everything I can to make sure she'll be fine. Are you guys okay? I feared you wouldn't follow my instructions."

Doug snickered. "If someone sends you a bomb threat, you act, even if it's a hoax."

"I just needed to make sure you were safe."

Dan wore that same gruff expression. He was still furious.

"What does it look like down there?" Byron asked.

"Like a hotel," said Stacey. "But why are we here exactly?"

Next, his mom joined them, saving him from an explanation. They looked at each other, neither knowing what to say, it seemed.

"It's good to see you," she said, reaching out to touch the screen, then pulling her hand back.

"Yeah, you, too."

She had large purple bags under her eyes, her skin looked too big for her body, and the styled dark hair had to be a wig. She was terminal, no doubt.

"I'm glad you're with them." She wasn't a replacement for Erica, but at least the kids had time to meet their grandmother.

"Stay safe. I hope to see you all soon."

"I bet they're terribly confused," Claire said when they left, and Edward took over the screen.

"Everything okay?" Edward asked.

"Yes, everything's fine. There?"

"Everyone's settled in. A little scared and confused but... " Edward paused. "I think we might have a problem."

"What problem?"

"The FBI is still watching your father and Claire's parents. They'll be suspicious now that a helicopter has whisked off both of them. They might figure out I'm involved soon, and they'll show up at my apartment." Another pause followed by a deep sigh. "I won't risk going back. I'll work from here. I'll have a jet transport Drew and the rest of my people. The bus leaves tonight. I suggest you get on it."

Or he never planned to come back.

"But what about the people who helped us?" Claire stared him down.

"I'll send them the small airport's co-ordinates. They'll have to find their own way here. I'm sorry, Claire, I can't risk it."

"Edward," she went on, "do you know anything about an AI early detection system?"

The man's face turned to milk. He swallowed. "We'll talk when you get here." The screen clicked off.

A while later, Claire left to start packing and Byron used his chance.

"Drew," he called into the kitchen. Some enticing flavors wafted into his nose. "Can you help me with something?"

"Sure." The older man followed him to the study.

"I need your help." He scratched at his forehead. There was no easy way to ask. "I can't leave my sister behind and Claire will never get on that bus without me. We must knock her

339

out," he said in a hushed tone.

Slowly, Drew's head bobbed. He was used to following dubious orders. "I think we have some sleeping tablets."

"What's going on?" Claire glided inside.

"I lost connection to the internet. All sorted." Byron nodded in Drew's direction.

"Yes." Drew smiled. "Well, if you'll excuse me, I still have a lot to prepare."

He couldn't look at her anymore. Again he would betray her. Sometimes she was too hard-headed for her own damn good and he couldn't bear the thought of something happening to her. After they ate, he headed straight for the shower.

"Mind if I join you?" Claire slipped in behind him.

"Well, we would use less water."

"See, that's exactly what I thought."

They kissed and washed and kissed and dried. Then he walked her back to the bed and made love to her. Yes, he called it making love. Not because he was a sap, but it was different once you fell in love.

"Hey." He traced the perfect contours of her face. "You want something to drink?"

"Please? You are perfect, you know that?"

I bet you won't think so tomorrow.

Byron found the bottle of sleeping tablets behind the espresso machine where Drew had promised to leave it. He checked the dosage and slipped it into Claire's juice. *I'm so sorry.* Claire was proud of her independence and she wouldn't appreciate what he was about to do. As he watched as the orange liquid bob down her throat, he felt guiltier by the second.

"This tastes weird," she said but drank it anyway.

Not long after, her eyelids drooped, and her head fell into the pillow. Byron kissed her forehead. "I'm so sorry. Just know I love you."

A sleepy smile appeared. "Yeah, me too."

The moment her breathing evened out, he returned to the study and pulled the phone out of his pocket.

"Penn," she answered.

"Hi, it's me."

"Byron. How in the hell did you pull that magic trick?"

"I'll explain everything. Meet me in the basement of my father's building at 10 pm. Keep this between us for now." He hung up.

"You'll need this," came Drew's voice. Byron looked up at a small piece of paper in Drew's hands. "Best of luck."

"Wait!" Byron called after him. *What did he know?*

Drew didn't turn back or respond. He kept walking. Two codes were written on the notepaper.

A few hours later, Byron slipped a goodbye letter into a bag, then scooped Claire into his arms. Drew took their belongings while he carried the unconscious girl on to the bus. Inside, he gently laid her down on a double seat and placed the bag beside her. He kissed her one last time.

"Goodbye, Claire."

She opened her eyes. He shuffled backward, then bolted out of there and signaled for the driver to lock the door, but she didn't seem to follow him. He breathed as he re-entered the building, sidled down the steps into the basement. He knew she would hate him, but he could live with that. Being with her friends and family was what she had told him she wanted.

"Black," said Penn when he reached the bottom, "you'd better have a damn good excuse."

341

He removed the note from his pocket and flapped it, like it proved something. "Look around for steps." Their eyes searched the parking lot until they found the small drop into the ground. Byron entered the pin into the keypad and the door clicked open.

"What's this?" Penn asked, stepping into the lab.

"I'll explain." He did, with a lie or two to protect Claire's secret. He used the large whiteboard against the wall and wrote down his entire theory from beginning to end: How Edward was their source, feeding them info about the bombs. They left in search of him but started digging on their own. Byron explained that they stumbled on the article right before Claire mentioned that Edward was working on a top-secret mission. One and one equaled two. With the added suspicion of his bunker and inside info, he had the tail-end of a case. Sure, a lot of it was lies, but it brought the point across.

"Well, shit." Penn pulled at her lip. "Now, how do the girl's visions fit into all of this?"

He startled. "What?"

"I know, Byron. No need to deny it. I heard it from her mouth when she told her father on the phone." Penn shook her head, chuckling. "We were so desperate to find her because we believed her."

"Too damn late," he snapped. "She tried to warn you and you played it off as nothing."

Penn brushed him off. "Okay, we can't change the past, but we can change the future. Not without proof, though. We need to get into this guy's PC."

"We're not hackers, Taylor. It'll be password-protected."

"Don't worry, my new partner's a pro." Penn called her guy, and he showed up within half an hour. While he hacked, Byron told them the real version of the story. Their jaws literally dropped when he described Claire's visions.

"Hey, Black, I'm not sure if you know this, but Erica woke up yesterday," Penn said when he explained his reason for staying behind. "The doctors are running tests, but they're hopeful. She's still a little confused, so they're keeping her sedated."

"Thanks, that's good to hear. Listen, you're sure no one knows you're here?"

"Nope, Trevor thinks we're searching for the mole."

"And?"

"I'm gathering some proof. No one of significance just yet."

It took Agent Kaur hours to hack into the computer. Byron and Penn spent those hours searching the lab for other information that could prove useful, but when that led to a dead-end, they investigated Edward Tomb and all of his other projects. The guy was a genius. If he had planted that bug in the system on purpose, why?

Byron dipped his head to the ground, trying to think of something, anything, that they could have missed, when his eyes spotted a tiny gap at the bottom of the wall. He moved in for closer inspection. It was definitely a door. He pushed against it. Nothing. He felt around. Nothing.

"What's that?" Kaur asked.

"It has to be a door, but I don't know how it opens."

"It's controlled from the computer. I've seen the app. Didn't know what it was for."

Kaur opened the program and Byron entered the other passcode. The door clicked. This time when he pushed, it opened into a small room with a large, black box that looked like the servers one would find at NASA. It occupied almost the entire room.

"It must be a super or quantum computer," said Kaur. In the corner of the room stood two steel rings, more or less a foot apart; one at the top and one at the bottom, bound by six blue lasers.

"Wow, I feel like I've just stepped into the future," Penn said with a hint of awe in her voice.

"Not sure if this is the right time, but I managed to open the file labeled 'Top Secret'." Both Byron and Penn spun toward Kaur.

"Have you read it?" Byron asked.

"No, there are way too many files. I need help."

They fell straight into it, scanning everything remotely relevant. Byron tried to understand the contents, but it contained physics only the Stephen Hawking's of the world would understand. They weren't deterred. They kept looking for anything that could help them. For hours, they struggled through the files and videos.

"Uh, Black," Kaur called out in the early hours of the morning. "You said that this Tomb guy asked curious questions about Claire's dream, right?"

"Yeah, why?"

"I think you should look at this." He clicked on a folder named 'Reversing the Problem'.

Byron read it. He didn't understand the details, but he caught the purpose of the study: Edward was trying to turn back time to stop the bombs. The videos in the file were a step-by-step log of his progress, proving how he reversed objects through quantum computing. Each of them was an improvement on the previous one: From cubits to electrons, then molecules, then actual objects; milliseconds to seconds, to minutes to days. The last video, labeled "Conclusion", was recorded the day before Edward left for the bunker. It opened to a video of Edward's face.

"It worked," he said, removing his glasses. "I disproved the Second Law of Thermodynamics by creating negative mass/energy-matter, slowing down objects through traversable wormholes into imaginary dimensions until entropy decreased over time. "The girl received visions of her former life that she assumes are of the future, when in fact they are of the past. She must be the anchor I used, which is why she can remember and no one else can." A sigh followed.

"The desperation to save her boyfriend and family probably pushed her to risk her life for the minuscule chance that the project could return them to life. Pity she doesn't know the source. The experiment worked, but the outcome hasn't changed, except that she specified a date. At least with that detail I can get everyone safely to the bunker in time."

He shook his head. "Which I gather I couldn't do in the previous timeline, when I only managed to save myself and the girl. Her sacrifice just saved the rest of us."

No. Byron refused to believe it. No way. *No, no, no, no!* He slammed his fist on the table with all of his might. The two agents stared at him, their eyes as full of fear as his own. Claire couldn't see the future; she simply remembered the past. She had lived twice.

"Byron," Penn pulled at his arm. "I think you should sit down."

"I know this is all terribly shocking, but I think the more important thing here is that he wanted to stop the bombs.

345

Why?" Kaur intervened.

"I know," Byron agreed. "As I browsed the AI files, there seemed to be a sudden stop. When I moved on to the next in the sequence, it was a completely new project."

Suddenly, the door clicked open. Penn and Kaur both reached for their guns.

"He was removed from the project," came Trevor's thundering yet clipped voice. "This looks cozy. You want to tell me what's going on?"

"Sir," Penn spoke. "I will have to ask you to put your hands in the air."

Trevor chuckled. "I'm your superior."

"You asked me to search for a mole. I didn't want to believe it without proof, but this is all I need."

Kaur did nothing to back her up. The new revelation had left him spinning. Claire had been right all long. No one could be trusted.

"So, you've finally discovered that I am the mole." Trevor gave a slow clap. "I have to say Agent Penn, I didn't think you could do it." Trevor stepped aside, and a man moved into the room. He had one hand around Erica's neck and the other held a gun to her head.

"Your move Agent Penn. Are you going to kill her twice?"

Byron felt like he had been punched in the gut. His whole body was overcome by pins and needles. Erica's bewildered eyes pleaded for help as they bore into his. He looked down at her body: She was still in a hospital gown, bearing scrapes and bruises on her skin and a cast on her left leg.

"Let's all calm down," Trevor said, as if addressing a classroom of teenagers. "I thought Mr. Tomb had given up years ago. Apparently not." He looked around. "Impressive.

Sure is a shame we couldn't get him to join."

"Join what?" asked Penn, still aiming her gun at Trevor. "Talk."

"We call ourselves Genesis II." He wiped the case info from the whiteboard and wrote the words down. "Some say it's a cult, but that's such an ugly word, I prefer utilitarian group. We started out disposing of some of the worst criminals on which the FBI had given up, until we realized there were too many."

He turned toward them. "Most people despised Hitler, but he had the right idea. He didn't have the means nor the expertise to succeed. Look at the world: Gangs; drugs; rapists; corrupt politicians; overpopulation and poverty." He continued to list everything wrong with the world. "Where does it stop?"

None of them moved or made a sound.

"AI designed to deflect a nuclear attack will, in fact, start it. Mr. Tomb was the original lead on this project. We invited him to join, but he refused, so we got rid of him. He tried to expose us, but he didn't know who we were, nor did he have any proof."

The events played through Byron's mind. Trevor had been instantly interested in the sender of the letter, although he had played it off as nothing. According to Penn, he had allowed her to investigate him on no more than an inkling. He had been hell-bent on finding them since they knew more than they should and had even pretended that Claire was delusional. After pointing the government's intelligence in the wrong direction, he had taken over the case himself.

"Yes, Agent Black, let it sink in. That girl could have stopped us. I have to say, I was dying to meet her. She could have been such an asset.

You see, we only recruited society's most elite: The strong, smart, and healthy with no family history of violence or substance abuse... this list goes on. Which is why the two of you didn't make the cut." He said, pointing to Byron and Penn.

"You're not God," Byron roared.

"No, but I believe God gave Noah a similar instruction to build an ark."

"I'm pretty certain He would never allow someone to impersonate Him."

"Well, that's up for discussion. I'm trying to save the world, not destroy it. We'll be in the safety and luxury of a government bunker during the blasts and for the nuclear winter that follows. Then we'll start fresh."

Byron scanned his face. It seemed he sincerely believed he was doing a good thing. In principle, his theory had merit, although it was nothing short of genocide.

"You see," he looked at all four of them, "I don't want to kill you, so I'll give you one chance to join us. Before you decide, I have back-up outside that door."

Byron eyed Erica. He thought of the girls. They were outnumbered and outwitted. Out of desperation, he lunged forward, grabbed Kaur's gun from his hand, and shoved it into Trevor's face. "Let her go," he snarled through gritted teeth.

Despite having a gun between his eyes, the man sneered. "Impressive, but don't threaten me, Black. Your sister's health is still unclear, and our group has some of the best doctors imaginable."

Erica's face revealed the same confusion he felt inside. Perhaps if they pretended to join, they could still stop it. They were now grasping at straws. A whirlwind of emotions surged through him when Erica mouthed, "No."

They stared at each other, in silent communication. Erica jabbed her leg cast into her handler's groin, sending him into the wall behind them. A shot fired behind him and a bullet ripped into the flesh of the guard's heart. All other movements in the room jumbled together. *Penn, it had to be.*

Byron's finger made for the trigger when he felt the barrel against the back of his head. "Drop it," said Kaur's voice.

There was the faint sound of a gun loading. He jabbed Kaur in the stomach with his elbow and spun around. Guns fired as Kaur turned and sunk to the floor. Byron looked up to see Penn stagger back, clutching her side. Blood leaked from the wound as she fell to her knees. He threw himself forward, ripped off his shirt, and tore at the fabric. Without thought, he pushed it onto the wound.

"You're gonna be fine."

Her breaths were dim, barely there, and her eyes fluttering. "Be-hind... you."

He never heard the door opening, nor did he see that Kaur was unconscious with a similar bullet wound. Heavily-armed back-up streamed through the door. They had no chance of survival.

"Okay!" Erica yelled. "We'll do whatever you want, just don't shoot him!"

"Good choice." Trevor grinned, delighted. Hands tied, they were escorted to a car waiting outside like criminals.

"By," Erica whispered as the car started to move. "Dan and the kids?"

"They're safe. How are you feeling?"

"Like I'm stuck in a horrific nightmare."

46

Claire

Monday, 4 July 2022, 6 am

Drew showed Claire to her room. With the time it took them to get there, it was clear Edward hadn't been entirely truthful about the location nor the transportation. She kept her head down as she moped through the hallways that led to the living quarters. Now and then her eye glimpsed the extravagant furniture inside the building. It was not at all how she had expected a doomsday bunker to look. She muttered a quick "thank you" to him over her shoulder and stared at the bed.

She didn't even know if she had thanked Hoff, Leslie, and Jason for all of their help. She had, hadn't she?

Leanne jumped up from the bed on the other side of the room and threw her arms around Claire. She hugged her so tightly that Claire struggled to breathe.

"I'm so glad you're here," Leanne cried

"Mmm-hm." She had lost all enthusiasm. It's not that she wasn't happy to see her friend, but her soul was bathed in a level of depression she never knew possible. *How could he do this?*

"Clairy." Perfectly styled blonde hair appeared in the doorway. Her mother had a little more flesh than the last time she had seen her. "You do not understand how worried we were about you. You disappeared for days without as much as a text. Do you know what that does to a parent's heart? We had the police and the community involved. You could have told us. Then, Edward shows up. We almost didn't trust him. Lucky he brought Brent with him."

"I couldn't tell you, Mom. I'm sorry for putting you through that."

Her father's tall frame came in behind her, fiddling with his mustache. "I'm glad you're safe, sweetheart." His words were soon followed by those of Brent and Ted.

"So are we, hun," Brent agreed with a suffocating hug.

"We don't have time," said Claire. "Come on."

Claire searched the fluorescent-lit corridors and rooms with the trio steady on her heels. The completed parts of the place were incomprehensible, magnificent. As they dashed through the passageways of the maze, Claire brought everyone up to speed. None of the unfamiliar faces they passed had any info on Edward's hiding place, which was seemingly the most secluded spot the underground shelter had to offer.

They searched for over half an hour before Claire finally located the lab. The glass sliding doors required an access code, but no barrier would stand in her way. She pulled out Byron's gun and aimed it at the panel. "Edward," she bellowed, "You open this door right now, or I'll open it myself."

His desk chair wheeled around, eyes wide and unexpected. "Claire? What are you doing?"

"I don't have time for questions. Open the door!"

He walked to the entrance, scratching at his right eyebrow above the glasses. His left digit scanned the pad and the doors slid open. "Will you please lower the gun?"

"What do you know?"

"Not a lot more than you already do."

Brent flanked her. "And what's that?"

"This AI system was programmed for an apocalypse by a group of people who consider themselves to be saviors. I've been trying to destroy it forever, but they're hiding it."

"From whom?" Leanne spoke up from behind.

"Me," said Edward. "Initially, I was the lead on the project. When I refused to join their ridiculous cause, they got rid of me. That code won't be transferred to the Pentagon's server until the final moment they need it, and I don't know where else to look."

With tightly squared shoulders and new-found confidence, Claire aimed the gun at the Brit. "Then find it.".

Edward slumped down into his seat. "Believe me, I've tried everything. This bunker was my last resort."

Brent's head shook slightly with unsung words as he sat down next to Edward. "My family's still out there. We have to try, please?"

Edward hesitated, then nodded. "You have to know, breaking through the most secure firewalls you'll ever encounter is no picnic."

"Sounds like fun." Ted moved past her, rubbing his palms together with a mischievous glint in his eyes. He took a seat on the other side of Edward, who started to explain the procedure. Claire and Leanne didn't understand much, nor could they do much, other than watch the boys' fingers travel across the keyboard as code rapidly scrolled over the screen.

It was the most intense video game she had ever watched. All she heard were vigorous keys clicking and a string of profanities. A couple of times she asked what was going on and all she got was, "Firewall," weirdly in unison.

Claire sat down, grinding her teeth, pushing her fingernails deep into her skin. She felt the blood. A deep breath left her when they managed to bypass the first firewall, then the second. The third took hours. Leanne came in and out with food and distractions, but Claire was nailed to the chair. According to Edward, the fourth firewall was the most resilient, as it constantly altered.

"I wrote the preliminary part of the source code," Edward said. "It's meant to connect to missile defense units all over the country. If it's live, I'll find it immediately."

Minutes passed, then hours. Every so often her eyes closed, and she had to lift her drowsy head from her chest. She couldn't sleep, not until they had won.

"You all right?" Leanne lifted Claire's chin.

"No, not by a long shot."

Keys kept clacking in the background. It was a sound Claire now associated with desperation.

"I'm in," yelled Brent, dragging her back to the action. "I uploaded a poison pill through a security cam image, copied the maintenance engineer's private SSH keys, and installed it. We're in."

"People," Edward smiled, patting Brent on the back, "always the weakest links. Well done. Now, the next barrier: To find the code."

The men turned back to their screens and Claire watched as Brent easily logged into the server. Edward gave the instructions and Brent followed the path.

"It's live," said Edward, half-laughing, half-crying. "Okay, you need to upload the malicious code to destroy the AI. Security will be alerted if you try to access certain programs, so you have 20 seconds to destruct."

Brent did as he was told. The upload started. Seconds had never felt so long. One, two, three... 12, 13. And then she felt the first shudder. It rocked her back into Leanne. Again, she experienced a sense of déjà-vu. Small tremors, then bigger, then quakes until their surroundings started to fall apart.

It was too late; the bombs had already hit. Molly entered, followed by Kurt. No one in the room said a word. They simply stood together in a circle, clutching at each other for hope while everything shook around them. Tears ran down all of their faces as they realized their families hadn't made it.

They held on and Molly, her mother, began to pray when the surface above them shook with fury. It felt like the queen of all thunderstorms, only wilder and more brutal. But the quakes and falling apart never came. The building remained intact, even when the vibrations deepened. Claire wished it would; she wished it would whisk her away so that the pain could stop. Selfish, she knew.

Claire grabbed the bag she had thrown into a corner and ripped out the dumb letter he had given her. Like that was any consolation. She ran into an empty corner of the 'haven' and opened it. Tears gushed down her face as she stared at his scribbly handwriting.

Claire,

You probably hate me, I know, but I needed to say I'm sorry. There's no excuse, but I need you to look at it from my point of view. When you knew there was a chance I could die, you risked everything to save me. Claire, I love you too much to even consider the thought of you dying.

Edward's family and closest friends were on that bus. I knew you would be safe and reunited with your friends and family. That made it an easy choice. I've contacted Penn and we will try to stop it. If I succeed, I don't expect you to forgive me. If I fail, I hope you have a long and prosperous life beyond the bunker.

Thank you for showing me I was worth someone's love. You're one of the most amazing people I've ever met, weaved from sugar and kindness. I know you questioned why God granted you the ability, but I know. You're strong and brave and you care beyond measure. You saved all of those people, no one else. Always stay that way.

Byron

He had failed and so had she.

Claire looked up at the trembling roof. Their failure had led to his death. She had experienced that same inscrutable pain in her dream when that beam pierced his heart. It was so sharp and so visceral that no painkiller could ever counter it.

She couldn't save the world. She couldn't save him. But she did manage to save many people. Slowly, she pushed herself to her feet. It wouldn't be easy. They would have to weather the storm. They had survived. They had to make it count.

* * *

Fear not, the story will continue. Nothing makes me happier than to find a reader who enjoys my stories. If you did, I would appreciate it if you could leave a review to help others discover it. Also, if you need more of Claire Baxter right now, feel free to signup for my newsletter at https://nicoleputter.com/signup/ to receive a prequel novella absolutely free and news on upcoming books in the series.

Acknowledgments

Wow, this book has been quite a ride and I have so many people to thank. First and foremost, my mom, who has been my biggest cheerleader on this project. She read every chapter as I wrote it and kept me on my toes with critique and begging for updates. She's also the amazing graphic designer behind the cover and all of my website art.
Andrew Solomon, my mentor, who taught me all about drafts and structures, red herrings, and everything else that makes a novel. I don't think I would have finished this book without his guidance.

My wonderful editor, Michelle Bovey-Wood, thank you for making this shine with your input, valid concerns, and polished touch. All of my beta-readers who helped shape it from a rough draft into a sellable product. I have to single Lynette out because she has been in my corner since the opening lines. She sent daily email updates with her progress and the problems she spotted, but her praise for this story was highly inspiring.

My sister, Celine, who kept filling my coffee cup and babysat so that I could have a little time to write. Riana, who helped with the locations in the story due to all her travels. Lastly, my husband, who has been by my side every step of the way.

He gave me time off to write when I needed it, he allowed the funding and encouraged me to follow my dreams.

Then, to every reader, thank you for reading this, it fills my heart with immense joy.

About the Author

Nicole Putter is the author of the *Shattering Serie*s and several short stories. She studied creative writing and journalism as a hobby between a successful career in finance. When she's not writing fiction, she blogs about her passion for books and writing. She's also happily married, and a proud mom of one son and a Jack Russel Terrier named Striker.

You can connect with me on:
- https://nicoleputter.com
- https://twitter.com/NjpWriter
- https://www.facebook.com/nicoleputterbooks

Also by Nicole Putter

A Shattering Secret

https://nicoleputter.com/signup

At age five, Claire Baxter sees her mother bump a pot of boiling oil that causes the liquid to spill all over her. When Claire returns to reality, the pot is still on the stove and her mother's arms show no burn marks. It's odd but she's still too young to make sense of it. An hour later, she hears the scream and finds her father on the phone, exactly as the vision revealed. Can Claire see the future?

Fearing for her safety, Claire's parents raise her with the rule that she's not to share the secret with anyone. How will she manage a normal life when a single touch can lead to a vision? And what other mysteries and enigmatic dreams do this superpower hold?